Seducing Simon
Understood
Overheard
Undenied
Brazen
For her Pleasure
Stay With Me
Reckless
Love Me, Still
Into the Mist
Into the Lair
Golden Eyes
Amber Eyes
Be With Me
Songbird
The Billionaire's Contract Engagement
Pillow Talk (Fourplay Duology)
Soul Possession (Men out of Uniform Anthology)
Long Road Home
Exiled (Cherished Duology)

## Anetakis Trilogy
The Tycoon's Pregnant Mistress
The Tycoon's Rebel Bride
The Tycoon's Secret Affair

## Passion and Pregnancy Series
Enticed by His Forgotten Lover
Wanted by Her Lost Love
Tempted by Her Innocent Kiss
Undone by Her Tender Touch

## Sweet Series
Sweet Surrender
Sweet Persuasion
Sweet Seduction
Sweet Temptation
Sweet Possession
Sweet Addiction

## KGI Series
The Darkest Hour
No Place to Run
Hidden Away
Whispers in the Dark
Echoes at Dawn
Softly at Sunrise (novella available digitally or in print in the back of Shades of Gray)
Shades of Gray
Forged in Steele
After the Storm (December 2013)

## Scottish Historicals
In Bed with a Highlander (McCabe trilogy)
Seduction of a Highland Lass (McCabe trilogy)
Never Love a Highlander (McCabe trilogy)
Never Seduce a Scot (Montgomerys & Armstrongs)
Highlander Most Wanted (Montgomerys & Armstrongs)
Highland Ever After (Montgomerys & Armstrongs) TBA

## The Breathless Trilogy
RUSH
FEVER
BURN

Coming in 2014

# THE SURRENDER TRILOGY

Letting Go (Feb 2014)
Giving In (May 2014)
Taking it All (Aug 2014)

*For more information on Maya and her books, go to her website, connect with her on Facebook or follow her on twitter!*

**Website:** http://www.mayabanks.com
**Facebook:** http://www.facebook.com/authormayabanks
**Twitter:** http://twitter.com/maya_banks

# THEIRS TO KEEP

maya banks

All Rights Reserved © 2013 by Maya Bank
Published by Maya Banks

ISBN-13: 978-1492746621
ISBN-10: 1492746622

No part of this book may be reproduced or transmitted in any form or by any means, graphic, electronic, or mechanical, including photocopying, recording, taping, or by any information storage or retrieval system, without the written permission of the publisher.

This is a work of fiction. Names, characters, places, and incidents either are the product of the author's imagination or are used fictitiously, and any resemblance to actual persons, living or dead, business establishments, events, or locales is entirely coincidental. The publisher does not have any control over and does not assume any responsibility for author or third-party websites or their content.

Cover design by Kimberly Killion, http://thekilliongroupinc.com/
Interior text design by Elizabeth Parks

# acknowledgements

A special thank you to my readers for being so patient for the release of this book. It was supposed to have been released in the Fall of 2012, and it was with great reluctance that I delayed the release until I could be certain that I would be able to follow up with the subsequent books in this trilogy. I hope the wait has been worth it and that you'll enjoy it!

Special thanks to Megan House Burton for her help in naming the Tangled Hearts Trilogy!

And as always, I am deeply grateful to ALL of my readers for their amazing support. None of this would be possible without you!

# THEIRS TO
# KEEP

# chapter one

SHE CREPT ALONG THE DARK ALLEYWAY, wincing as her scraped, torn feet made contact with the cracked pavement. There wasn't a part of her that didn't hurt. She was so tired, she could barely keep herself upright, and hunger had long ago ceased. Now, all she felt was overwhelming emptiness. And fear.

There was a gaping hole in her mind. No memory. No past. Only the present. She had no money, no belongings, no place to rest and hide. She only knew that if she stopped, *he'd* find her.

And she didn't even know who *he* was, only that a shadowy figure haunted her mind. He'd hurt her. He'd wanted her dead. He'd left her to die in the river, but somehow she'd survived.

She stopped outside a building, shivering as a gust of wind blew down the alleyway. She may as well be wearing nothing for all the protection her torn clothing offered.

It was cold. So cold. She'd give anything for a warm place to sleep. Somewhere she could feel safe even if only for a few hours.

Drawing herself into the shallow alcove where the service entrance to the shop was, she huddled there numb and desolate. She glanced over at one of the windows. It would take nothing to break it. She could easily slide through if she could maneuver it upward. If only she could be warm and sleep for a few hours, she'd have the strength to keep moving. Maybe there would even be food within. She would leave again before daylight, and no one would be the wiser.

Desperation made her bold. It made her overlook the consequences of being discovered. She'd convinced herself that no one would know, that she would be able to hide.

Before she could change her mind and talk herself out of her foolishness, she got down on her hands and knees and scrounged through the dark alley for something she could use to break the glass.

Her hand fumbled over a rock, and she curled her fingers around it before pushing herself to her feet. She rose up on tiptoe, looking for the right spot to break. All she needed was access to the latches.

After deciding to break the upper panes, she reared back and smashed the rock against the glass, shattering it on impact. Pain sliced through her fingers, and numbly, she realized she'd cut herself. Warm blood slid over her hand, but she ignored it and smashed the rock against the glass a few feet over.

She reached in, fumbling with the latches. After she had them both unlocked, she pushed frantically at the window to raise it enough so she could gain access.

Relief was overwhelming when the window easily slid upward. She staggered and planted her palm against the brick wall to steady herself before she bent and stuck her leg through the opening.

Lowering herself so that her chest was flush against the sill, she eased her way inside and then shut the window after her. It seemed silly when the upper panes were smashed in to worry over closing the window, but it felt safer. An open window would draw more attention than a broken one, or at least that was the reasoning that filtered through her shattered mind.

She made her way through the darkness, unsure of what she'd find. It didn't matter. Already she was warmer. Finding a place to sleep for a while would be easy.

---

"Son of a bitch," Cade Walker swore as he rolled out of bed. He yanked on his pants, threw on a T-shirt then made a grab for his shoulder harness that held his nine-millimeter handgun.

He went to the computer monitor on his desk and punched in the codes to bring up the location of the alarm.

His bedroom door opened, letting in a flood of light. His friend and co-owner in his security and surveillance business, Merrick Sullivan, stood there, dressed, his gun holstered at his side.

Merrick was one mean-looking son of a bitch in daylight hours. Get him out in the middle of the night in some dark alley, and it was like looking at the grim reaper. But then he beat the shit out of people for a living as a mixed martial arts fighter and was even now training for a fight that would give him the title shot in the heavyweight division.

"You calling it in or we going to check it out?" Merrick asked.

"Fuck it, we'll go. Last time the alarm went off there, it turned out to be a damn cat. No sense getting the boys in blue out on a night like this. They'll be up to their ears in traffic accidents. People don't know how to damn drive when the roads are wet."

"Then let's go," Merrick said shortly. "I'll call Hank and let him know we're taking care of it."

Hank Stevens was the owner of the gun store and a client of Cade's and Merrick's. Cade ran a successful security consulting business, and Merrick helped out whenever he could. They installed systems and monitored them twenty-four hours a day. Which meant they could literally be called out any hour of the day, any day of the week.

The list of clients they provided personalized service to was small. Mostly they consulted, troubleshot and provided advice on a larger scale. But there were a few local businesses that they still felt loyal to. These were people that Cade and Merrick cared about and felt protective of. Hank had been a longtime friend dating back before Merrick began his career as a fighter and before Cade opened his own business. The two men looked out for Hank. Owning a gun shop wasn't always the safest business to be in, and they didn't want anything to happen to the older man.

It was colder than a witch's tit when Cade stepped from the front porch and hurried to the Hummer parked on the street. They had a garage, but it took too damn long to open and shut the garage door, and time was often valuable. Parking on the street gave them precious seconds that they weren't backing out of the driveway. Not to mention the Hummer didn't fit. Only Cade's smaller SUV did.

Merrick threw open the door to the driver's side and slid behind the wheel. Cade got in on the passenger side, and not even two seconds later, Merrick roared off down the street, heading toward downtown, where Hank's shop was located.

They made it in record time even with the streets being sloppy and a damn drizzle that made it hard to see. Merrick doused the headlights when they were a block away and pulled to a stop several businesses down.

He and Cade both got out and pulled their guns.

"According to the alarm monitor, it was the alley window that was compromised," Cade said in a low voice as the two men hurried down the sidewalk.

Merrick ducked down a side street so they could access the alleyway. When they reached the end, Cade flattened himself against the wall and inched his way toward Hank's store.

When he and Merrick were only a few feet away, Cade held up his hand and then put a finger to his lips. He concentrated intensely, straining to hear if any sounds were coming from inside.

He eased forward again when he heard nothing, and then he frowned when he saw the shattered glass on the rough, cobblestone street. Glancing up, he saw where the window was busted, but there was no light coming from within. No flashlights. Nothing. It was dark and silent as a ghost.

"Probably just some damn kids vandalizing," Merrick muttered.

Cade switched on his flashlight and shone it downward, skimming the immediate area. He stopped the beam on a large shard of the glass and then knelt to pick it up.

He held it up to Merrick, shining the light on the blood smeared on the edge. "Looks like our perp didn't get away unscathed."

"Let's check it out," Merrick said. "Dumbass could still be in there for all we know."

Walking into a gun store where a suspect may or may not be inside wasn't on Cade's list of favorite things to do, but neither did he want an entire squadron of patrol cars to converge and shoot up Hank's store.

Cade picked up his cell phone and punched the number and then the codes to deactivate the alarm system. Then he dug out the key to the back door and quietly inserted it into the lock.

He eased the door open and went in, gun up, flashlight in his other hand. Merrick hurried in after him, and the two flattened themselves against the wall and slid forward down the hall leading to the showroom.

When they got to the end, Merrick motioned toward the row of light switches above Cade's shoulder. Then he held up three fingers to signal on the count of three.

Cade switched off his flashlight, stuck it back in his pocket and then reached up with his arm so he could flip all the switches at the same time.

He took a deep breath and then counted out to Merrick. "One... two...three!"

He pushed his arm up, and suddenly the entire building was awash in light. Merrick gripped his gun and made a wide sweep of the showroom as Cade did the same, looking for any movement.

But there was none. Everything was quiet. No sudden sounds. No one startled by the light.

"Kids," Merrick muttered. "Just a bunch of damn kids with nothing better to do on a Saturday night."

Cade was about to agree when his gaze stopped on one of the large cabinets underneath the rifle display along the wall.

"Check it out," he murmured, gesturing toward the smear of blood right by the handle.

Merrick frowned and then circled around, separating himself from Cade. He dipped his head to the side to signal Cade to come in from the right while he closed in from the left.

Cade crept forward until they were directly in front of the cabinet. Cade bent and touched the drop of blood on the floor. It was still warm and fresh.

Surely... Well, he wasn't going to say surely anything, because he'd pretty much seen it all. If their intruder had heard Cade and Merrick, he very well could be hiding in the cabinet. It was large enough for a small person, and if Merrick was right about it being a teenager, then it was certainly possible.

Merrick took position, pointing his gun at the door, and Cade leaned away so he could open it and use the door as a shield. He hooked his fingers around the handle and then looked up at Merrick to make sure he was ready.

Merrick nodded and Cade yanked the door open.

Merrick's face went from pissed off to what the fuck in two seconds flat. His gun wavered, and then he slowly lowered it.

Cade lurched up and pushed around, wanting to know what the hell Merrick had seen.

To his utter shock, there was a small woman curled into a ball, cowering in the cabinet. She was staring at them both with wide, frightened eyes, and she was a complete mess.

"Holy shit," Merrick breathed. "Who are you lady, and what the hell are you doing in here?"

Her entire face crumbled, and tears simmered in her wide, blue eyes.

"I don't know," she whispered.

# chapter two

MERRICK STARED AT THE WOMAN huddled in the storage cabinet and immediately knew two things. One, she wasn't the average intruder out to steal money or merchandise, and two, she was scared out of her mind.

The blood covering her hands and other parts of her body worried him. It worried him a damn lot. She looked like someone had beat the hell out of her, and that enraged him.

He squatted down so that he was closer to her level, but she immediately shrank back, cowering farther against the wall of the cabinet.

And he couldn't blame her. He didn't exactly look like Captain America. He was a heavyweight fighter, and both arms were tattooed. His nose had been broken twice, and he knew he didn't look like the kind of man who posed no threat to a woman.

He was a big guy. Mean-looking. He scared normal women who didn't look like they'd already gone three rounds with some abusive asshole. He could only imagine how badly he terrified this one. And he *hated* that. The mere idea of hurting or even frightening a woman put a hole in his gut. Especially this woman who'd already been through so much.

"We're not going to hurt you," he said in as soothing a voice as he could manage. "Can you tell us what happened to you?"

Tears filled her eyes again, and she shook her head. At first he thought she was just being cagey, but there was a blankness to her expression that bothered him. It reminded him of fighters who got knocked out and had absolutely no recollection of the event. They woke up and lost the last seconds leading up to the K-O.

She looked…bewildered.

"I don't know," she whispered hoarsely. "Please, I'll leave. I just wanted somewhere warm to stay for the night. I'm so cold…and tired. I wasn't going to steal anything."

"I think that's pretty obvious," Cade said gently.

Merrick frowned. "What do you mean, you don't know what happened to you?"

She closed her eyes, turning her battered face away. She was a pretty thing, even with all the bruises, the bedraggled hair and the torn clothing. There was an air of vulnerability about her that immediately riled Merrick's protective instincts.

There weren't too many things that could get him all worked up in a short amount of time, but an abused woman would do the trick every single time.

"I can't remember," she said, her voice cracking in a low sob.

Merrick and Cade exchanged worried glances.

"Please, just let me go," she begged. "I won't cause you any trouble."

"Where the hell would you go?" Cade demanded.

Merrick sent him a silencing look. Then he turned back to the woman. Before he could say anything, panic filled her eyes.

"You're not going to have me arrested are you? Are you going to take me to jail?"

There was no faking the terror in her voice and in her eyes.

"Honey, listen to me," he said, pitching his voice purposely low so he wouldn't seem threatening. "Nobody's going to take you to jail. You're hurt. You're bleeding. You're cold, and you look like you've missed more than a few meals. Let us take you to the hospital to get you checked out, okay? Then we can call the police and nail whatever asshole did this to you."

Her pupils dilated, and she went stock-still until he wasn't even sure she was breathing anymore. She was already pale, but she went white as a sheet, and if possible, she made herself even smaller than before.

"No," she choked out. "No, no, *no*! I won't go. No hospital. No cops! He'll find me. He'll kill me. Oh God, he'll kill me."

She finished on a low moan, her hands protectively covering her head. Hands that were bloodied and cut and only made her look even more fragile.

Cade blew his breath out, but Merrick knew he was pissed, and it wasn't at the woman. Neither man had any tolerance for a guy who'd brutalize a woman, and it was obvious someone had done a number on this lady.

"Please, just let me go. I didn't steal anything, I swear it. I just wanted someplace warm to sleep. I just needed to rest someplace warm. Someplace he wouldn't find me."

Her voice was thick with tears, and the knot in Merrick's gut grew bigger. He just wanted to take her into his arms and swear to her that nothing would ever hurt her again.

Knowing how intimidating he'd look to a woman like her, he took a huge risk and touched her arm. She immediately flinched as if he'd burned her, and she shrank away, trembling violently.

Her pupils became even larger, and she stared at him like a cornered animal who had no way out.

Son of a bitch but someone had scared the shit out of her, and it was pissing him off more and more with every passing second. She should be in a hospital, warm and dry, eating a hot meal instead of skulking down a dark alley searching for a safe place to get warm.

He glanced at Cade, knew Cade wouldn't like what he was about to say, but at this point, he'd do damn near anything to get her out of Hank's store and someplace she could be taken care of.

Making damn sure his voice was soothing, he tried again. "All right. No cops. No hospital. I know a doctor who runs a clinic. He's a good friend of mine, and he can be trusted. Let us at least take you there so you can have those hands tended to and let him take a look at your other injuries. I swear to you that we won't do anything you don't want us to."

She stared back at him, her blue eyes huge in her thin face. She was scared out of her mind, but she was also desperate and at the very end of her rope. He could sense her need for shelter. Just something as simple as a place to lay her head for an hour or two. It only made him that much more determined to make sure he didn't leave without her.

"Y-y-you p-promise?"

Cade took over then, his expression one of utter gravity. "We only want to help you. You're hurt. You need medical attention. Let us help you."

She closed her eyes, and for a moment, Merrick thought she'd passed out. But then she opened them again, wide and troubled.

"Okay," she whispered. "My hands hurt."

Cade reached for one, being careful not to move too suddenly. He grimaced as he inspected the deep cuts. "I suppose they do." He gingerly pulled a sliver of glass from one of her fingers and flung the shard away.

She started to shift, but grimaced. It seemed her every movement caused her pain. Impatient and unwilling to watch her suffer, Merrick simply reached in, curled his arms underneath her and plucked her from the cabinet.

Her entire body went rigid, but he didn't give her an opportunity to protest. He started for the back door where he and Cade had come in.

"I'll call Hank's manager and have him come in and do cleanup so Hank won't have a mess in the morning," Cade said as he followed behind. "I'll make sure we have someone out to replace the broken glass."

Merrick carried his slight bundle to the Hummer and eased her into the back seat. He climbed in beside her and tossed the keys to Cade. He wasn't taking any chances she would get any crazy notions and bail out of a moving vehicle before they got to Dallas's clinic.

She wilted into the heated seat and sagged precariously to the side. The man sitting beside her caught her and eased her into his side so she could lean on him.

The two men scared the daylights out of her, and yet, at the same time, there was something about them that made her stupid. It was evident she'd lost all sense because she was blindly putting her trust into these two men. Two huge men who could easily snap her like a twig if they had a mind to.

And here she was alone in a vehicle with them. They could take her anywhere at all. No one would know differently. She didn't even know who she was, so how would anyone else know?

Despair filled her heart, aching and heavy. His grip tightened around her as they sped down the damp streets. The rain had stopped, but the cold was settling in for the long haul.

She began to shiver, not because she was too cold, but because she no longer had any control over her composure. She tried to stop shaking, but it seemed the harder she tried to make it stop, the harder she shook.

The man beside her cursed and then pulled her onto his lap. He wrapped a huge leather jacket around her body and put both his arms around her in an effort to keep her warm.

The jacket smelled heavenly. Warm. Spicy. So very masculine. It reminded her of something. She frowned. The fleeting remembrance was gone before she could place it. But it felt so very familiar to her. Comforting. It was a good memory that had been triggered, and those were so few and far between that she wanted to weep for losing it.

For just a moment, she forgot her paralyzing fear. Forgot that this man could harm her, that she shouldn't trust anyone. She felt…safe. Here in his arms, pressed to his massive chest.

She could feel the steady, reassuring beat of his heart. She absorbed his calm like an addict needing a fix.

None of it made sense. She was sitting on the lap of a guy who looked like he could be a drug dealer or, at the very least, a gang member.

He was a mountain of a man, solidly muscled, bulging arms and a massive chest. Both arms were tattooed, and his hair was long and unruly. Everything about him screamed dangerous, and yet his touch was gentle, his words were soothing, and he looked at her with kindness and compassion in his eyes.

"What's your name?" she found herself whispering.

He stiffened. In surprise? Then he touched a strand of her hair, trailing his finger downward.

"Merrick. What's yours?"

Pain flashed through her head. She raised a hand to press into her temple in an effort to alleviate the excruciating pressure.

"I don't know," she said in agitation. "I don't know!"

"Shhh," he soothed. "It'll come back. You're just scared and under an enormous amount of stress. You're cold and hungry and in shock. I'd be surprised if you did know your name at this point."

Relief took hold. He was right, of course. Everything would be better after she recovered. Once she got warm and had something to eat. Maybe even some sleep. Then she'd know who she was and who had done this to her.

# chapter three

DALLAS CARRINGTON STEPPED OUT OF the exam room, a grim expression on his face. Cade pushed off the wall where he and Merrick had been waiting. They'd put in the call to their friend, and he'd met them at his clinic in a matter of minutes.

Though Dallas ran a walk-in clinic in a poorer neighborhood, he also acted as Merrick's personal physician and often traveled to Merrick's fights. He'd monitored Merrick's recovery after his knee injury a year ago.

Cade, Merrick and Dallas had gone to high school together and had remained steadfast friends since their childhood.

"The son of a bitch who did this to her should be shot on sight," Dallas bit out in a pissed-off tone.

"Tell us," Merrick growled.

Dallas ran a hand through his hair and blew out his breath. "Hell, this is a mess. I probably shouldn't tell you anything, but this is hardly an official medical visit. The problem is, she doesn't have a clue who she is or what happened to her. She's deeply traumatized, and since she consented for you two to bring her in, I'm considering you the closest things she has to relatives."

"She really doesn't know who she is?" Cade asked skeptically.

Dallas nodded. "It's deeply upsetting to her, and it sets off another round of panic every time she tries to remember. Now, I don't know a lot about amnesia. It's mostly bullshit you find in fiction novels or movies. I've never actually seen a clinical case of it, though I've read a few case histories on the subject. I don't know if hers is because of a head injury or if it was trauma-induced and her mind has shut down in order to protect her from the horror of what happened to her."

"What exactly happened?" Merrick demanded.

Dallas held his hand up. "I'll get to that. If it's memory loss caused by an injury to the brain, then it could be permanent. Hard to say. If it's trauma-induced, it could be temporary. Hard as hell to say since there really isn't a medical diagnosis for not wanting to remember."

"It all sounds damn crazy," Cade muttered.

"Just get to the part where you tell us what happened to her and how badly she's injured," Merrick cut in impatiently.

"Someone beat the hell out of her," Dallas said bluntly. "That's the least of it."

Cade shot him an incredulous look. "What the fuck? That's the *least* of it?"

"Your girl has been through the ringer," Dallas said quietly. "This bastard beat the hell out of her. He raped her. And he shot her. *Twice*."

Merrick's jaw dropped, and then his eyes narrowed to menacing slits. "He shot her? I didn't see any sign of a gunshot, but then hell, she was a mess. It would have been hard to see over all the other blood."

"I had to sedate her to examine her," Dallas said. "She was hysterical the minute I touched her. Look, the law requires a rape kit and for me to report this. I mentioned that to her, and she went ballistic. I was afraid she was going to hurt herself. Oddly enough, she had less issue with me examining her than she did with me reporting this to the police. You even mention the cops and she goes batshit crazy."

"Yeah, we know," Cade said grimly. "It was the same when we told her we wanted to take her to the hospital and call the cops. She flipped out, said no hospital, no cops. We were barely able to convince her to let us take her here. I don't want to abuse her trust by throwing her under the bus."

Merrick's arms came over his chest. "Don't report this, Dallas. At least not yet. Did you find anything when you did the rape kit? Anything that could be used as evidence?"

Dallas slowly shook his head. "It wasn't recent as in the last day or even two days. And really, it could have been nothing more than rough sex, but given everything else going on with her, I highly doubt that was the case. There was vaginal bruising and tearing but no semen. He either wore a condom or it's been long enough that there's no viable semen sample. No DNA trace that I could find, and I was careful. I'd love to see the bastard who did this to her hang."

"You and me both," Cade ground out.

"And the gunshot wounds?" Merrick demanded. "What did he do, beat the hell out of her, rape her and then try to kill her?"

Dallas nodded. "That's my guess. And before you completely discount her fears of going to the police, there's something you should know. The bullet I dug out of her shoulder? Looks like a nine-millimeter hollow point. Now, it's not to say there aren't a lot of assholes floating around using that caliber, but it's a pretty standard police issue. Could explain her irrational terror anytime the word cop is mentioned."

"Holy shit," Cade breathed.

"Yeah," Merrick muttered. "Christ, what the fuck are we supposed to do with her?"

Dallas sighed. "Well, right now, what she needs is a place to rest and recover. She needs to feel safe. She's scared out of her mind. She's been traumatized and brutalized in the worst way a woman can be victimized. The other bullet only grazed her head. I gave her a few stitches, and that'll heal up good as new. The shoulder is another matter. She needs to be in bed. She needs hot food, and she needs someone to take care of her. Now I can call a shelter and see what arrangements I can make, but if they get wind of her injuries, they're going to turn it over to the police faster than you can blink."

Merrick scowled. "We'll take her home with us."

Cade whipped around to stare at his friend. "Are you out of your mind? Merrick, think about this. What the hell are we going to do with her? You have a fight to get ready for. If you win this, you're next in line for the title shot. You can't afford any distractions."

Merrick glared hard at Cade, his expression murderous. "Are you really going to leave her in some damn shelter to fend for herself? What if the asshole who did this to her comes looking for her when her body doesn't show up like it should? He left her for dead."

Cade didn't like it any better than Merrick did, but this spelled trouble with a capital T. The woman was jumpy as a frog. She wasn't going to like going home with two big-ass men who likely scared the shit out of her just by looking at her.

"Maybe you should go check in on her before you make your decision," Dallas suggested. "Let me know what you decide. But hurry, if you don't mind. I need to write some prescriptions for painkillers and antibiotics, and I'm also going to give her some sedatives so she can sleep. She's wound tighter than a spring, and when they're that wired up, you have to give them something to make them sleep."

Not waiting for Cade, Merrick barreled through the door to the exam room, leaving Cade to follow.

As soon as Cade laid eyes on her, he knew he was an absolute goner. All of his earlier bluster left in the blink of an eye. Looking at her now, he could well understand Merrick's fierceness when it came to her.

She was curled onto her side, her injured shoulder wrapped and her arm lying limply over her hip. Her knees were drawn protectively to her chest, and she was dressed in one of those skimpy hospital gowns that didn't cover much of anything.

Both hands were bandaged where she'd cut them breaking the glass.

He'd never seen a more vulnerable-looking female in his life, and it hit him right where he lived. It was damn hard to breathe when his thoughts were doubly occupied with murdering the son of a bitch who'd abused her so terribly and also the overwhelming compulsion to surround her with support, tenderness and whatever the hell else she needed to get back on her feet.

Merrick looked back at him challengingly as if to say, what now? Cade only sighed and nodded his agreement. There was nothing else to do for it. She was going home with them.

# chapter four

WHEN CADE PULLED TO a stop outside their house, Merrick gently took the woman in his arms and positioned his coat over her body to shield her from the cold rain. He ducked out of the back seat and made a dash for the front door. Cade had gone ahead and was holding it open.

"Take her into the living room," Cade directed. "I'll build a fire, turn up the heat, and I'll see about getting her something to eat. We have some soup somewhere."

Merrick took his precious bundle into the living room and eased her onto the couch. The sight of her, barefooted, in the soaked hospital gown and the bandages covering parts of her body, made his gut clench.

She was such a tiny, fragile-looking thing, and he couldn't imagine what would possess a man to hurt such a woman. *Any* woman, for that matter. It made him irrationally angry, and he had to control his expression because he didn't want to set her off again.

"I'm going to get you something to wear," Merrick said gruffly. "I'm also going to get you some blankets so you're warm. Are you hungry?"

She slowly nodded, the shadows deepening under her eyes.

"When was the last time you ate?" he asked in a more gentle tone.

Her eyes saddened. "I don't know. It feels like forever."

"Do you know how long ago you were…hurt? What's the last thing you remember?"

She looked down, staring at her bandaged hands. "Two…three days maybe. I woke up on a riverbank. I was cold. At first I didn't really hurt. I just felt numb. And everything was so blank. Can you possibly understand what it's like to wake up facedown in the mud and not remember who you are or how you got there?"

Merrick frowned, his gut tightening harder. "No, I can't."

"And fear. Most normal people would call for help. Go to the police. Try to do *something*. But all I knew was that I had to hide. It's the only thing I know. I may not know my name or what happened to me, but I know that I can't let anyone know about me."

Her tone was pleading, like she was begging him to agree with her, like she didn't want him exposing her to anyone else in any way.

He pushed himself upward, his gut tied in knots from all the clenching. Hell, he was ready to put his fist through a wall, but he had to be careful to be ultra sensitive and non-threatening. She was maintaining control by the thinnest of threads, and he didn't want to do anything to send her plummeting over the edge.

The problem was, he wasn't a sensitive guy. He used his fists and his body to make his living. How the hell was he going to know what to do with one tiny woman who needed care and understanding?

"I'll be right back," he muttered. "You need clothes and blankets. Cade's going to get you something to eat."

He went to Cade's bedroom since Cade was smaller in build than Merrick. He confiscated a warm sweatshirt that was bulky enough it shouldn't hurt her shoulder. He also snagged a pair of sweats with a drawstring waist so she could keep them on.

After rummaging in Cade's drawers, he went to his own room to get a pair of thick, warm socks she could wear on her feet.

When he returned to the living room, Cade came out of the kitchen wearing a frown.

"We don't have shit here that's suitable for her to eat. I need to go out and get the prescriptions filled anyway. Dallas wrote them in my name, so I'll get them filled and pick up something hot for her to eat. I'll only be gone half an hour provided the meds don't take too long. I'd hope at this hour there isn't a high demand."

Merrick nodded. "I'll get her changed and warmed up. But hurry. It's likely been three days since she's eaten."

Cade glanced at the woman and swore. He snagged his coat from the chair and stalked out of the living room. A moment later, the kitchen door banged, leaving Merrick to stand in silence with the woman staring nervously up at him.

Merrick sighed. "Look, there's no easy way to do this. I don't want to frighten you, but the chances of you being able to get into these clothes without my help are zero. I swear to you I won't hurt you. I'll try not to look. I'll be as quick as possible so it's over with and you can rest and be comfortable."

She curved her arms over her stomach, her hands gripping her arms. He could see the distress radiating from her. Her pupils widened. Her pulse rate kicked up, as did her breathing, and sweat beaded her forehead.

Hell, she was on the verge of a full-scale panic attack, and he had no idea how to offer her more reassurance than he already had.

"You can turn your back. I can untie the hospital gown from the back, and it will slip right over your arms, and then we'll try to get this zip-up sweatshirt on you without hurting you."

She licked her lips and swallowed hard, almost as if she was battling her fear and anxiety. That she was making such an effort not to melt down made Merrick respect her resiliency all the more.

She may be fragile-looking, seemingly helpless and in need of a lot of TLC, but a weaker woman would have likely already died. She certainly wouldn't have broken into a gun shop to try to find a place to sleep and hide for the night. Nor would she be holding her ground against someone as big and scary-looking as Merrick.

Slowly she sat up and then turned so her back was presented to Merrick. She let the blanket slide down and immediately began to shiver.

Cursing, he hurried forward and began to work the wet gown off her. But it was soaked through and sticking to her skin like glue. Hell, it was ruined anyway.

He pulled a pocketknife from his jeans, flipped it open and then cut through the tough knot at her neck. Once it loosened, he gently pushed the gown forward, baring her slender back.

The growl rumbled in his throat before he could call it back. There was a huge bruise covering her lower back, and damn if it wasn't in the shape of a shoe. A damn big shoe. Someone had kicked her.

Blanking his mind to his rage, he worked instead on getting the dry sweatshirt over her upper body. Then he got down on the floor at her feet and pulled the sweatpants up her legs, careful to keep his gaze averted.

When she was dressed, she immediately leaned back, pulling the blanket protectively over her body. She was still shivering, and Merrick turned with a frown toward the fire.

Deciding she was too far away and not wanting her to move, he got up and simply started sliding the couch forward until she was close enough to feel the warmth of the flames.

"Better?" he asked.

Only the tiniest curve to her mouth hinted at a smile. "Better."

He eased onto the couch beside her, careful not to touch her or get too close. Even though her expression didn't change, her eyes cut over to him, her gaze never leaving him.

The silence was awkward. He felt like a moron. He had no idea what to do in a situation like this. Females in distress weren't exactly something he came across a lot in his line of work. And frankly, if asked, he would have said they were something he would have avoided at all costs. They just seemed more trouble than they were worth.

But this one... There was something about her that had captured his entire attention from the moment he'd first laid eyes on her.

His protective instincts had been riled until they were a roar in his gut.

Nothing or no one was going to touch her. Not when she was with him. No one would ever hurt her again.

Even as he had the thought, he knew how ridiculous it sounded. It was as if he was making a permanent claim on her, like he'd always be there to protect her and watch over her. And hell, if he were honest, he knew it was more than that.

It shamed him. It disgusted him. But he wanted to hold her. Touch her. He wanted to shelter her from everything bad. He wanted to kiss her and show her how gentle he could be.

This was a woman who may never want to be touched by a man again. She'd been brutalized and violated. That knowledge sent his thoughts into a black rage.

He wanted to be someone she could turn to, who she could trust. No matter how ludicrous the thought was, given they'd only been acquainted a few hours.

"Is there nothing you remember?" he asked quietly.

Her brow furrowed, and her lips turned down into an unhappy grimace. He was immediately sorry for putting that look on her face.

"When I close my eyes and I concentrate, I can almost touch things. Does that make sense? It probably sounds stupid."

"No," he denied. "Not at all."

"It's like everything is cloaked in shadows, and I keep thinking if I could only get a little light there that I could see all I've forgotten. But it's scary because at the same time I know if I do shine light on the shadows that very bad things could be revealed."

Her lips drooped even farther.

"I'm scared."

She whispered the admission in a voice that ached with vulnerability.

No longer willing to keep the distance between them, he reached over and carefully pulled her into his arms. She stiffened at first and remained stock-still, almost as if she were battling her fear, but then she relaxed and melted into his embrace.

He shifted his body so he was closer to her, so she would benefit from his warmth, and he cradled her against his chest.

"I know it's scary," he said. "But I want you to know that you're safe with me and Cade. We aren't going to let anything bad happen to you. Everything that frightens you is currently in your mind and in your memories. Those things can't hurt you. Only real people can, and I'll kick anyone's ass who tries to get close to you."

She turned her face upward so their gazes connected. A small smile pulled at her lips. "Do you know I believe you? There's something in your voice. I don't understand it. It's probably stupid of me, but maybe I'm desperate to trust someone. I feel so..." Her voice choked off in a near sob. "I feel so alone."

Merrick brushed his lips across her brow. "You aren't alone. You have me and you have Cade. I promise you we aren't leaving you. We'll do whatever we have to in order to help you."

"Thank you," she whispered.

She laid her head over his chest, and he immediately put his hand to her bedraggled raven hair. Dark as midnight, a startling contrast to ocean-blue eyes. She was the sort of woman a man noticed in a crowd. Which meant he and Cade were going to have to be damn careful with her safety.

The door opened, and heavy footsteps sounded on the floor. The woman jerked upward, her eyes wide with fright, and she clutched at Merrick in an unconscious plea for protection.

"Shhh," he soothed. "It's just Cade. He's back with food and your medicine. It's going to be okay."

A moment later, Cade appeared with a takeout bag and a white pharmacy bag. He strode toward the coffee table and set down his purchases.

"What do you think you'd like to drink?" Cade asked. "I have water, tea and juices. I picked up orange and grape from the pharmacy."

"Water is fine," she murmured.

He pulled everything from the packaging and then opened a steaming bowl of chicken noodle soup. He opened a bottle of water and set it down beside the bowl and then motioned her forward.

"Can you sit up enough to eat, or should I feed you?"

Merrick saw the discomfort that crossed her face. She shook her head and then tried to push her way from Merrick's arms. He helped by holding her upright and not letting her move too fast.

When she was perched on the edge of the couch, Merrick draped the blanket over her shoulders, and Cade took her hands between his in a gesture that obviously surprised her.

He rubbed back and forth, infusing warmth into her fingers, and then he looked at her with tenderness in his eyes that Merrick understood all too well.

"As soon as you eat, I'll give you an antibiotic pill and something for pain as well. You'll sleep well after that."

She nodded her acceptance and reached for the spoon, fumbling clumsily as she tried to grip it with the bandages on her hand.

Finally Cade took the spoon and gently put her hands back into her lap.

"Let me," he said quietly.

## chapter five

CADE STARED INTO HER EYES and then lifted the bowl and the spoon before sliding onto the couch beside her. She was flanked by him and Merrick, and he wasn't sure how well she'd take that. More than one woman would feel threatened by having two hulking Neanderthals basically trapping her.

Cade wasn't as big as Merrick. He didn't sport the tattoos or the long hair. But he worked out with Merrick. He was his longtime training partner, and he adhered to the same strict regimen that Merrick did.

"I'm going to hold the bowl like a cup so you can sip from it," he said. "It might get messy if I try to feed it to you by spoon, not to mention, it'll take forever."

She offered a trembling half smile and allowed him to tip the bowl toward her mouth. Her bandaged hands came up to lay over his, and then she took an experimental sip.

She drew away, closed her eyes and sighed in seeming contentment.

"Good?" Cade asked.

She nodded.

He put the bowl back to her mouth, and she took a larger sip this time. She was slow, taking measured tastes as if waiting to see if her stomach rebelled.

Cade waited patiently until she finally sat back with a sigh and waved off any more.

"That was wonderful," she said.

He reached for a bottle of water and then fished out the medicine he'd gotten for her. After dumping an antibiotic pill and a pain pill into his palm, he put one to her lips and held the bottle up so she could swallow. After she downed the second pill, Cade stood to clean up the mess, but Merrick waved him off.

"I'll do it. You stay here with her."

Cade raised an eyebrow, but Merrick made a slight dip with his head, motioning toward the woman, and then looked pointedly at Cade. He wanted Cade to stay with her awhile so she'd grow more comfortable with him. It was obvious that Merrick had already done so judging by the fact she'd been solidly in his arms when Cade had returned with the food.

Cade had just returned his attention to the woman when her eyes went wide and she blurted out, "Elle!"

Cade frowned but leaned back so he was closer to her. "Who's Elle?"

The woman turned to him in wonder. "Me. I think. It's my name. Not all of it, but it's what I was called. I'm sure of it."

"That's good," Cade soothed. "See? That's a start. It'll all come back to you as soon as you feel safe. Elle is a pretty name. It suits you."

"Thank you," she said earnestly. "For being so kind. For understanding. And for helping me. I still don't know why you've done it. Most people would have washed their hands of me within minutes."

Cade scowled. "There was no way in hell Merrick and I were leaving you on your own. You need our help, and you're going to get it."

She reached clumsily with her bandaged hand and curled her fingers around his. "Thank you."

He felt that simple touch all the way to his heart. She was clearly terrified and uncertain, but it seemed she'd determined that she trusted him and Merrick both. Satisfaction ripped through his chest. He wanted her to trust him. Wanted her to have no qualms about depending on them.

Damn it, he wanted her to be his. He already thought of her as his. He doubted Merrick felt any different. The big man had been awfully growly and possessive when it came to her.

And it all caused a huge problem. They knew nothing about her or her past, and neither did she. She could already belong to someone. Hell, she could have a husband and a family somewhere. There could be people worried about her, and yet he and Merrick hadn't done what they should have. They hadn't taken her to the police or the hospital.

But her terror was very real when it came to mentioning police and hospitals, and Dallas had confirmed it. And Cade didn't think for one moment this woman had done anything wrong. She was clearly a victim, and he wasn't about to set her up for more brutalization by turning her over to the wrong people.

Until her memory came back and she could decide for herself, she was staying with him and Merrick, and fuck anyone who said differently.

## chapter six

"YOU MAY AS WELL SAY what's on your mind," Cade said, without looking up from the stove.

Merrick had walked into the kitchen five minutes ago, slid into one of the chairs by the bar but hadn't said a word.

Merrick wasn't much of a talker, at least on a deeper level. He could bullshit with the best. He also managed to get his point across with no problems. But Cade always knew when something was eating at him, because he always went all quiet and brooding.

He and Merrick went way back. They'd been friends since grade school. Dallas too. The three had been inseparable even when life had taken them in different directions after high school.

Cade had known he wanted to go into business for himself. Dallas had gone to medical school and after residency had opened his clinic. Though he was loyal to Merrick, Dallas had a calling to provide health care for disadvantaged families. But then they'd all grown up poor and knew what it was like to have little or nothing.

Merrick had gotten his MBA in order to help Cade with the business, but his heart had been with a career in mixed martial arts. After getting his degree, he'd devoted his efforts to training and working his way up the food chain.

He'd started in local gyms and on local fight tickets. He worked hard and would fight anyone willing to enter the ring. As a result, he'd been offered a contract with an international fighting association, and now he was one fight away from the possibility of a title bout with the current heavyweight champion.

Cade handled the bulk of the business, but Merrick helped when he wasn't training. When Merrick traveled for a fight, Cade and Dallas always accompanied him. In a lot of ways, Merrick was the glue that held the friendship together because Merrick was the common denominator. Without him, Cade would be busy with his business, and Dallas would be immersed in his clinic.

Cade's dad was involved in the business as well as Merrick's training. He was an invaluable source of support whether it was building Merrick up or helping Cade when Merrick wasn't available.

They owed a lot to his old man, and Cade knew that Merrick considered him a father every bit as much as Cade did. And to Charlie Walker, Cade, Merrick and Dallas were his boys. It didn't matter how old they got to be. He still threatened to tan their asses when they got out of line.

Cade would need to fill him in on Elle in short order. He was surprised the old man hadn't already popped in this morning to find out why the hell they weren't in the office.

He flipped another pancake then added it to the hot stack that had accumulated on the platter to the side, and then he turned to Merrick, who hadn't responded to Cade's statement.

Shaking his head, he turned the burner off and carried the platter over to the table, where he'd set three places. He wanted to let Elle sleep as long as she wanted, but he also didn't want her to be awake and afraid to come out. He'd put her in his room. He'd been quite adamant about it. He'd slept on the couch, but he'd wanted her in his space, and he couldn't exactly explain why he'd been so set on it.

He could always warm her pancakes back up. Right now he wanted to air out whatever was on Merrick's mind.

"You going to talk, or do I have to sit on you and pry it out of your tight ass?" Cade asked mildly.

Merrick scowled and forked three pancakes onto his plate. After drenching them in syrup, he cut into the stack, and for a moment, Cade thought he was going to ignore him. Then Merrick sighed and set his fork down.

"I don't even know how to say what all I'm thinking," Merrick said. "I feel like a complete dickhead for half of what I think, and for the other half, I think I've lost my goddamn mind."

Cade's lips twitched. "Okay, we'll start with why you're a dickhead."

Merrick made a rude noise. "It's all the same. I mean, what I think makes me a dickhead who's lost his mind."

"Do tell."

Merrick's shoulders heaved. "It's about Elle."

Cade rolled his eyes. "Yeah, I figured. What about her?"

"I want her," Merrick said bluntly. Then he grimaced. "Oh my God, that sounds so fucked up. Especially after what she's been through. Shit. It's not like I'm wanting to jump her bones. I'm not having stupid inappropriate thoughts. It's just that there is something there. A connection I don't even understand, but I know two things. I'm not going to let anything else hurt her, and I'm not going anywhere."

"Okay," Cade said slowly.

Merrick eyed his friend with a piercing stare. "Don't think I don't know that you feel the same damn way, which is why I didn't want to have this conversation. We have a woman in there who's been brutalized. She likely doesn't trust any man at all, and who could blame her? And she doesn't even know who she is or anything about her past. Hell, she could have a husband and kids somewhere for all we know."

Cade shook his head. "You tell me something. If she belonged to you, wouldn't you have turned this city upside down looking for her? She obviously doesn't belong to anyone because only a damn fool would just let her disappear."

"Maybe," Merrick said grudgingly. "That doesn't solve the issue between us, though. I'm not letting a woman come between us. We've never let it happen. We may as well be brothers. We're family. And I'm not ruining that. But…"

The corner of Cade's mouth lifted. "But you aren't backing down either, right?"

"Yeah," Merrick muttered. "I'm not backing down."

Cade remained silent a moment. He wasn't certain what to say. He understood Merrick's reaction. It was much the same as his own reaction to Elle. And no, he sure as hell didn't understand it either. His instincts screamed that she was his, and apparently so did Merrick's, which really muddied up the damn waters.

They were both jumping the gun in a serious way. Elle was fragile. They knew nothing of her past or present. They were taking a damn lot for granted.

But yeah, he was going to protect her just like he knew Merrick was, and neither of them was going to walk away from her, and they sure as hell weren't going to let her go without a fight.

Which was damn sure going to put them at odds in a way they'd never been pitted before.

"You going to sit there like you aren't having the same damn thoughts?" Merrick interjected. "You don't come to me demanding I start talking and then clam up when I tell you what I'm thinking."

Cade sighed. "What do you want me to say, Merrick? That I want her too? That I look at her and something just clicks and I know that I'm going to be front and center in her life from now on if I have any say? That I'm going to make damn sure nothing ever hurts her again? That I want her no matter how long I have to wait for her? And yeah, you're right. It makes us both out of our goddamn minds. We only just met the woman. This kind of shit just doesn't happen."

"Tell me about it," Merrick muttered.

"I'm going to go get Elle so she can eat," Cade said. "We understand each other. For now… For now, she's going to need us both to get her through her recovery and whatever else comes up. For now, we're going to have to put aside whatever crazy-ass thoughts we're having and focus on what's best for her."

Merrick nodded. "Yeah, in that we're agreed." But then his gaze met Cade's. "Don't let this fuck us up, man."

"Yeah," Cade said quietly. "I hear you."

# chapter seven

ELLE FLINCHED, AND A SMALL whimper emerged from her throat. Fear knotted her insides, and she strained to see her pursuer. She could feel him, could feel how powerful he was. Knew he was right there, waiting. But she couldn't pierce the thick cover of shadows to see his face.

She ran faster, even knowing it was inevitable that he would catch her. She felt the sweat that drenched her shirt, felt the heat enveloping her. The sun.

She tripped and fell face first in the dirt, her hands sprawling out to break her fall. And when she turned, he was there, looming over her, but the sun blinded her.

As he moved, the sun's rays caught on something clipped to his side. It was a *badge*. He reached for her, and she let out a scream, knowing it was her last chance to escape.

"Elle, Elle, wake up. You're safe. It's okay. Open your eyes, honey. You're safe."

Her eyelids fluttered, and confusion filled her. None of her surroundings were familiar. She had no idea where she was, and then her gaze found the owner of the voice.

A man was a mere foot away, and she was still so ensconced in the terror of her dream that she couldn't differentiate it from reality.

She rolled away with a cry of fright, ignoring the stabbing pain through her body. She fell off the bed on the other side, and she hastily scrambled upward, trying to gain her footing so she could flee.

But the man blocked her pathway.

He didn't make a move toward her, though. He just stood there, his expression calm, but his eyes were murderous. She shivered at the darkness in his gaze.

"Elle, take a deep breath and calm down, honey. Remember where you are. You were having a bad dream, but that's all it was. You're safe here. Remember last night? You're here with me and Merrick, and we're going to take care of you."

She stared back at him as the previous evening came back in bits and pieces. Cade. His name was Cade. He'd helped her. He and Merrick. They'd found her in the shop she'd broken into, and instead of turning her into the police, they'd taken her to a friend for medical help and then they'd brought her home.

"Cade," she croaked out.

"Yes, honey, that's me. Cade. I'm not going to hurt you. I came to see if you wanted breakfast. I made pancakes, and if you don't hurry, Merrick's going to eat them all."

She blinked at the lighthearted joke, and some of the shadows clinging to her mind melted away as she stared at the man standing a few feet away.

Where before he'd seemed so menacing, he now appeared gentle and kind. He was a big man. Tall, lean but very well muscled. He and Merrick were both dark-headed, but Cade had lighter brown hair where Merrick's was nearly black. Cade's eyes were blue, and she frowned as she tried to remember what color Merrick's eyes were.

Brown. Dark brown. Adding to his dark appearance. He had shoulder-length black hair, chocolate-brown eyes, and he was rugged and tanned. He was broader and taller than Cade, which said a lot because Cade was no small man.

Her rescuers should by all rights scare the holy hell out of her, but they'd been nothing but kind and gentle with her, and she desperately needed someone to trust.

Her past was a scary blank sheet that made her break into a cold sweat every time she tried to look back and remember. Someone had tried to kill her. According to Dallas, she'd been raped.

The mere thought of something so horrific happening to her and not being able to remember was a blessing and a curse all wrapped into one.

That she'd been violated made her stomach clench into a ball. Panic swamped her at the image of being so helpless while a man held her down and forced himself on her.

The other part of her was relieved she couldn't remember because she wasn't sure she could deal with the horror of a rape on top of everything else she'd endured.

"Elle, are you all right?"

She glanced back up and realized sweat had beaded her forehead and that her breaths were coming in rapid spurts.

"Dallas said I'd been raped," she blurted.

She recoiled in disbelief that she'd just put it out there that way, but her thoughts were a scattered mess, and that was the one thing prevalent on her mind. She'd been violated, couldn't remember it, but she knew it had happened.

Cade's eyes grew stormy again.

"I know, honey," he said in a soft voice. "He told us too. I'm sorry. I'd like to catch the son of a bitch who did this to you. I'd cut off his balls and shove them down his throat."

Whatever response she tried to formulate came out as a low sob, and then suddenly Cade was right in front of her, pulling her into his arms.

At first, she stiffened, but his strength and warmth bled into her, giving her comfort she desperately needed and wanted. She melted into his chest, closing her eyes as he held her. He rubbed a hand up and down her back and murmured softly into her ear.

"Is it wrong of me not to be sorry I can't remember?" she whispered.

Cade squeezed her and cupped the back of her head. "No. Your mind is protecting you. Right now, you're too fragile to cope with everything at once. When you're stronger, you'll remember, and Merrick and I will be with you to help you through it."

She carefully pulled away, staring back at him in complete befuddlement. How could he make a promise like that? How could he look so serious when making such a statement?

He looked as though he meant every word.

Before she could pursue it any further, he carefully took her arm and guided her toward the door. "Let's go have that breakfast, okay? Let's see if we can get some decent food into you, and then we'll give you your medicine again."

Numbly, she allowed him to lead her out of the bedroom and into the kitchen. As they reached the doorway, she self-consciously glanced down at her rumpled clothing. Cade's clothing.

As soon as they walked into the kitchen, Merrick stood from the table, his gaze intent on her. He stalked forward, and she pulled up, unsure of what to do or what he was doing.

Then he simply reached out and touched her cheek. "How are you feeling this morning?" he asked gruffly.

For some reason, the tenderness against such a rough-cut exterior made her teary-eyed.

"Ah hell," he said in a desperate sounding voice. "I didn't mean to make you cry."

Then she found herself enfolded in his beefy arms, surrounded by him. She soaked in the comfort just as she'd done when Cade had held her. It buoyed her flagging spirits and was a balm to her aching soul.

She rested her cheek against his chest and closed her eyes as he continued to hold her. She felt safe here, and that was saying a lot, because even her dreams were filled with fear and insecurity.

Somehow Cade's promise didn't seem so farfetched at this very moment. He and Merrick both had somehow managed to make her believe in the impossible.

Merrick's lips pressed to the top of her head, and then he carefully pulled her away so he could guide her to a chair.

"Are you hungry? Cade makes a mean pancake."

"Butter and lots of syrup," she said. Then she brightened, "I remember how I like to eat pancakes!"

Cade smiled at her and then reached for the plate of pancakes in the middle of the table.

"Let me give these a quick warming, and I'll bring back the butter. You want milk?"

She nodded and then settled more comfortably into her seat.

"You didn't answer my question," Merrick said as he sat back down. "How are you feeling? Still hurting?"

She touched her shoulder automatically and then glanced down at the bandages still covering her hands. "How am I supposed to eat?" she asked ruefully.

Merrick reached over and began to carefully unwind the gauze. "Dallas said we could remove some of the padding. He just wants to keep the cuts covered, and he gave us some ointment for when we change the bandaging. How about I take it off, let you eat, and then I'll reapply everything afterward."

Elle smiled up at him. "Thank you, and I am feeling a little better today. I feel...safer."

His hands went still, and then his fingers curled around hers. "I'm glad you feel safe, Elle. Cade and I are going to make sure you *are* safe. We aren't going anywhere. I need you to believe that."

She sucked in her breath. It was the second time such a promise had been made, and this time it was coming from Merrick.

He continued unwinding the gauze and then carefully pried off the bandages that were stuck to her skin by dried blood. He patted the cuts before tossing away the remnants of the dressings.

Cade returned and put a plate of pancakes stacked high in front of her. She flexed her fingers, checking for signs of discomfort, and then picked up a knife to spread the melting butter evenly across the surface of the pancakes.

"I remembered something," she said nervously. "I dreamed it, I mean. So I think I remember it. Or maybe it's just part of a really bad dream."

Cade sat down with his own plate on her other side, and he and Merrick looked intently at her.

"What was the dream about?" Merrick asked gently.

"Him," she croaked. "The man who...raped...me and tried to kill me. In my dream, I'm running and I *know* I can't escape. I saw a badge attached to his jeans, like at his pocket or belt loop or somehow at his side."

Cade and Merrick exchanged dark glances, their lips tightening.

Then something else occurred to her, and her eyes widened.

"It was hot," she blurted. "I mean, here it's cold. But in my dream, I was sweating, and the sun, it was bright."

"That's good," Cade soothed. "You'll get it back, Elle. Don't rush it, though, okay? Don't try to force yourself to remember before you're ready. Merrick and I will be here for you. I don't want you to be scared at any time, and you can tell us anything. We'll always be here to listen."

"You can't be planning for me to stay with you permanently," she said in bewilderment. "You know nothing about me. I broke into a building, for God's sake."

Merrick lifted an eyebrow. "Can't we? Where else are you going to go, Elle? Do you honestly think we'd let you just walk out of here knowing you have no memory, no money, no place to go?"

She stared back, having no idea what to say to that. Most people would just turn her over to the police and be done with her. But these two men knew of her terror, knew she didn't trust any cop, and they not only took her in and didn't push her to go to the police, but they made her a promise to be with her…long term.

"You guys aren't real," she whispered.

"The hell we aren't," Cade bit out. "I made you a promise, Elle. Merrick made you a promise. Neither one of us is going back on our word. We aren't letting you go, and we're damn sure going to protect you."

She closed her eyes, soaking in the firmness of his words, how determined they both sounded. A haven. Sanctuary. They were offering something she desperately needed. She'd be a fool to turn it down.

"Okay," she said in a shaky voice, taking the plunge.

If she couldn't trust them, who could she? There *was* no one else. She had no other options. Cade and Merrick were all she had.

She jumped when a loud bang exploded in the kitchen, and suddenly an older man appeared, staring over at Cade and Merrick.

"Where the hell have you two been? I've been at the office an hour waiting for your lazy asses. You pick today to sleep in?"

# chapter eight

"DAMN IT, DAD," CADE EXCLAIMED as he reached to keep Elle from bolting from the room.

Charles Walker glanced between the three, his eyes narrowing suspiciously, but then his gaze settled on Elle and he frowned.

"You blew off work for a one-night stand?"

Merrick groaned. "For God's sake, Charlie. Shut the fuck up for two seconds."

Elle was standing, her arm outstretched where Cade had caught her wrist to keep her from bolting. She was staring at Cade's dad like he was the antichrist. And, well, he couldn't exactly fault her suspicion. Damn old man had no filter whatsoever. He said what he liked when he liked and didn't much give a fuck what anyone thought.

"What the hell happened to her?" Charles demanded as he stared harder at her. It seemed to have finally sunk in that she was obviously injured and scared out of her mind.

Merrick stood and walked around the table to take Elle's hand. He glanced back at Cade. "You deal with him. I'll take Elle in the other room."

Cade sighed as Merrick herded Elle out of the kitchen, and then he turned to his dad.

"What did I say?" Charles asked, raising his hands, palms up.

"Oh for fuck's sake," Cade muttered. "What do you ever *not* say?"

Charles slid into Merrick's vacated chair. "What's the story on the woman?"

Cade leveled a stare at his dad. "I'm only telling you if you keep quiet, and I mean you don't say shit to *anyone*."

Charles shrugged. "Whatever you say."

"I'm serious, Dad. This is deep. I haven't said much to Merrick about this aspect of it, but we have to keep this quiet because he can't afford to fuck up his chance at a title shot. This could get twisted around and reflect badly on Merrick if we aren't careful."

His father's expression became serious. "What's the matter, son?"

Cade ran down the story from the time he and Merrick had responded to the breach in security to the present. By the time he was finished, Charles was wearing a scowl that rivaled Merrick's worst.

"Son of a bitch," Charles muttered.

"Yeah."

"So you're going to keep her?"

The incredulous tone to his dad's words rubbed Cade the wrong way.

"What do you want me to do, Dad? Toss her out? She's hurt. She's been raped and God only knows what else. The son of a bitch shot her twice. It's a miracle she's alive. And she's terrified of the police. So you tell me. What would you do with her?"

Charles sighed and rubbed a hand over his balding head.

"And you're a damn liar if you tell me you'd toss her out, so don't even try that shit with me, old man."

"Think you know me so damn well," Charles grumbled.

Cade cracked a grin. "I know you're a grumpy-ass huge marshmallow."

Charles flipped up his middle finger, and then he stared in the direction of the living room. "So seriously, Cade. What are you going to do with her? You and Merrick have enough on your plate between the business and his training and career. And the job doesn't run itself. You know I'll help in any way I can, but you've still got a huge problem on your hands."

"She's not a problem," Cade said quietly. "She needs to rest and recover physically, and she needs a place where she feels safe in order to do that. That's going to be with me and Merrick. When she's able, we'll take her into the office with us so she isn't alone. We'll figure it out."

"I'm reading a lot more than just a white knight in action here," his dad mused. "You're interested, Cade. I'd swear that you and Merrick are both sniffing around the same female."

Cade didn't answer.

Charles sighed. "That's never a good idea. This can't end well. You have to know that. You and Merrick go way too far back to let a woman come between you now."

"We'll deal with it," Cade said tightly. "Right now, all we're concerned with is getting her well and back on her feet. She has an entire past she remembers nothing of."

"That's a hell of a lot of baggage she's sporting, son."

"Nothing so heavy I can't help her carry it," Cade said in a quiet voice.

# chapter nine

ELLE SAT ON THE WORN, WOODEN bench and watched as Merrick sparred with Cade in the ring. Cade held a large punching bag, and Merrick ducked and feinted right and left before landing punches that pushed Cade back.

It had been three weeks since the night they'd found her. The bruises had faded. The gunshot wound was nearly healed. She looked and felt better, but her past was still a huge shadow in her mind, an impenetrable veil of darkness.

Part of her wondered if it was better that way. It made her a coward, but every time she tried to think, to focus her attention on the past, she broke into a cold sweat and dissolved into a panic attack.

If that wasn't a huge sign that she was better off not knowing, she didn't know what was.

After the first couple of days, the men had settled back into their routine and incorporated Elle into it. She went to Merrick's workouts with him. Then she'd ride into the office when Merrick joined Cade.

They'd been adamant about making sure she was never alone and that she felt safe at all times while she was recovering. Dallas had become a regular visitor to the men's home to check in on her progress.

Charlie stayed with her in the office if Cade and Merrick were out on a job. She was never without someone, and while some people would feel smothered by the constant company, it reassured her. She didn't *want* to be alone. Maybe she'd never want to be alone again.

It baffled her that four strangers had essentially gone so far out of their way for her. For a nobody. A woman with no past, a woman who, for all they knew, could be a criminal.

The thought made her shiver because she didn't *feel* like a criminal. Wouldn't she know? If she had been involved in crime, would she find the idea so repugnant now?

Cade and Merrick had dismissed her concerns without so much as a moment's consideration. They reminded her that she was the victim and that she'd done nothing wrong. Their faith gave her a much-needed boost in her own faltering beliefs.

They were simply too good to be true. And that worried her. If something seemed too good to be true, it usually was, and she was literally waiting to have the rug pulled from underneath her and for her to be cast adrift.

The thought scared her to death. Being alone frightened her. She had grown to depend on the two men way more than she'd like to admit.

And worse, she was developing feelings that weren't clear to her. They were more than gratitude. Couldn't be confused with psychological dependency. The whole falling for your savior thing. Besides, she had *two* rescuers. How could she explain her growing affection for both of them?

She winced as Merrick was taken down by one of his sparring partners. He trained with two younger fighters who were up-and-coming. She'd been around enough in the past weeks to know that Merrick was older. Not quite past his prime, but he'd started later than other fighters had. He was approaching an age where it was do-or-die time, and from what she'd gleaned from his conversations with Cade and Charlie, this was his last opportunity—or at least he perceived it was. If he didn't make a run for the title now, he'd never get another shot.

It took effort not to cheer when Merrick executed a triangle choke, and his partner quickly tapped. Merrick rolled away and then jumped to his feet. Cade tossed him a towel and a bottle of water, and Merrick sucked the water down as he scrubbed the sweat from his face.

The sparring session was early today so Cade could make it before going into the office. Twice a week, they got up before dawn and met at the gym before going into work. The other days, Merrick worked out with the other members of his training team, and Cade took care of the business.

Elle admired Cade's and Merrick's loyalty to each other. It was obvious they'd been friends for a long time and that their friendship was very important to them.

"How's he looking?" Dallas asked as he slid onto the bench next to Elle.

She turned and smiled. "He looks strong, but then I wouldn't even know if he didn't."

Dallas chuckled, and his gaze sought Merrick out. Merrick was talking to Dakota, his trainer, and Charlie and Cade in the corner of the ring.

Dallas was as common an observer at Merrick's training sessions as Elle herself was. He'd drop in on his way to his clinic in the mornings, and when Merrick trained late, he'd stop in after his clinic closed. On the mornings that Merrick ran early, Dallas joined him for the multi-mile run.

Elle marveled at the strong network of support that Merrick enjoyed. The loyalty of the people around him amazed her. He was surrounded by people who supported him unconditionally and were dedicated to seeing him succeed.

"Looks like they're wrapping up," Dallas said. "I'm going to go make sure he's feeling up to snuff, and then I'm going to head to the clinic. I'll see you later, sweetheart."

He tousled her hair affectionately as he rose and then left her to converse with Merrick and the others. A moment later, Dallas left and then the men walked in her direction.

"I'm going to grab a shower and then head in to the office," Merrick said.

His body glistened with sweat, and his hair was damp and clinging to his neck and shoulders.

"If you want to hang around, you can ride with me, or you can go now with Cade."

Elle swallowed and glanced up at Cade. She hated having to make decisions. She was forever worried that she was a burden and that they would grow tired of babying her.

Cade sighed as if he knew exactly what she was thinking. Then he simply slid his hand up her back and turned her in the direction of the door.

"She'll ride with me," Cade said. "I'll see you when you get in, Merrick."

※

"Young lady, you look like you're trying to solve global warming."

She blinked and looked up to see Charlie standing in the doorway of the office staring at her in amusement. Then she smiled.

"Nothing so serious. Was just enjoying my cup of coffee."

Charlie was a blunt, straightforward man who apologized to no one for speaking his mind. In the last few weeks, she'd grown to like him very much after a wary start. She'd been convinced that he was watching her and just waiting for her to do something wrong or to reveal she was a fraud taking advantage of the two men he considered his boys.

Instead he'd taken her under his wing and was every bit as protective of her as Cade and Merrick were. Between Cade and Merrick and Charlie and Dallas, she was surrounded by enough testosterone to float a battleship. Instead of annoying her, she found the shield they provided extremely comforting. They were her refuge.

Some of the best nights had been when Charlie and Dallas came over after Merrick's training sessions and Charlie cooked up something for the five of them and they sat around watching television and bullshitting. It made her feel almost like she had a normal existence and that she fit here in this world. With these men.

"Merrick was going to be delayed a little while, so Cade asked me to run over to keep you company while he's out on a job. Mind sharing some of that coffee?" Charlie asked.

She smiled. "Of course not. Help yourself. And he shouldn't have called you over. I can stay by myself for a few hours while they get their work done. I feel terrible. I can't even imagine how much they haven't gotten done because they've been more concerned with me."

Charlie went to the coffee maker, poured himself a cup of coffee and then settled behind Cade's desk.

"They know what they're doing," he said. "Nothing for you to fret over. Been kind of nice having you around the office anyway. Won't be the same if I stop in and you aren't here. I think they like having you here too."

"I just feel useless," she said with a grimace. "There has to be something I can do around here to help out. Paperwork. Phones. Something!"

Charlie rubbed his chin a minute and then pursed his lips. "You know, you're right. No reason you couldn't file, answer phone calls. Make calls to set up appointments. I don't know why they haven't thought of it. You have to be bored out of your mind."

She laughed. "They're too worried about overtaxing me. But I'd like to help. They've done so much for me. I'd like to return the favor."

"I think it's a great idea. In fact, if you want to come pull up a chair, I'll show you their filing system, such as it is. Between you and me, it sucks ass. If you have any organizational skills, you could have this office running like a dream in no time at all. I'd be happy to turn it over to you and run interference with the guys."

She rose eagerly, the thought of having something to do making her hands itch in anticipation. She put her coffee down on the desk and then dragged Merrick's chair over to Cade's desk so she could see what Charlie was doing with the paperwork.

"Most important are accounts receivable. We need a way to streamline the payment process. Make sure we stay on top of what is owed to us and that we're being paid in a timely manner and paid correctly. We also need to invoice as soon as a job is done. Sometimes those two knuckleheads don't send out a bill for weeks, and by then, the recipient has forgotten what the hell he's being billed for. They're also bad about updating the ledgers and making sure their bank deposits and statements and activity match up with what their entries are."

He turned to her, studying her intently. "Think you're up for all of that?"

She nodded vigorously, eager to get started.

He smiled. "Okay then. I'll go through the first few invoices so you'll know what you're dealing with. I'll show you how we mark it down in the ledger and then give you the bank log-ins so you'll know what's already been paid and what needs to be followed up on. If the phone rings, just wing it. No better way to learn than to dive in and pretend like you're the queen bee of the office. Before long, you'll have everyone saying yes ma'am and tiptoeing around you."

She grinned. "Thanks, Charlie. I really appreciate this. You've all been so kind to me."

He reached over and patted her hand. "We all need help getting back on our feet from time to time. You've bounced back amazingly well, and I know you'll continue to get stronger."

For the rest of the afternoon, Elle worked tirelessly on creating a filing system that actually made sense. She organized invoices, work orders and pending contracts, as well as a pile that needed to be followed up on.

She even managed to bullshit her way through several phone calls and was proud of the fact that she actually sounded like she knew what the hell she was talking about.

By the time Cade and Merrick walked into the office, Cade's desk was neat and tidy, and she could see the top in several places.

Cade and Merrick both stared at her with narrowed eyes, and then Merrick frowned.

"What the hell have you been doing? We don't expect you to come in and work your ass off all day."

She smiled. "I have singlehandedly made your lives easier. I've organized everything. Every single piece of paper, your contracts, invoices, checks, follow-ups. It's all filed in folders marked accordingly, and I set up an electronic calendar with reminders that will pop up on your cell phones as well as your email and your desktop computers."

"She's scary," Charlie piped up. "I hid in the corner."

Cade laughed. "Sounds like you cleaned up after our slobby asses."

Elle nodded. "I even answered the phones. I took messages and left them for each of you on your desks."

"Well, hell," Merrick muttered. "Looks like we owe you dinner at least."

Her mood brightened. "Like go out to eat?" Then her face fell. "But don't you have to go back to the gym tonight?" she asked Merrick.

Cade and Merrick exchanged surprised glances. She couldn't blame them. She hadn't ventured out of their home or their office in the three weeks she'd been with them. But today she felt freer and she felt safe. She couldn't spend the rest of her life hiding, and as long as she was with Cade and Merrick, she knew they wouldn't allow anything to hurt her.

So yeah, she wanted to go out to an actual restaurant and do something normal, like eat a good meal and discuss the day.

"You pick it, and we'll make it happen," Cade said, a smile broadening his features.

"I don't have to be anywhere but where I want tonight," Merrick said.

"Are you sure?" she asked hesitantly. The last thing she wanted was to interfere in Merrick's routine.

"Absolutely," Merrick said. "Now tell us what you'd like to eat."

She pursed her lips a moment and then pondered what sounded good to her.

"Do you have any good Thai places local? I don't know why, but right now I'd sell my soul for some really good Thai food."

"As a matter of fact, there's one three blocks from here," Merrick said. "Charlie, you in?"

Cade's dad shook his head. "You kids go on and have fun. This old man is going home to have a beer and some leftover pizza."

He bent over to kiss Elle's cheek, and then he waved at Cade and Merrick as he headed out of the office.

"You sure you feel up to going out?" Merrick asked.

She nodded. "Yeah, I want to. I need to. I can't go on hiding in your house and your office. Not to mention, I'll end up going stir-crazy. I know you won't let anything happen to me. I trust you, so I'm not afraid."

Cade reached over to touch her cheek. "That's good, Elle. Because it's absolutely true. Merrick and I aren't going to let anything happen to you again."

Merrick reached for her hand to pull her to her feet. "Let's go, sweetheart. I'm starving."

She walked out of the office and to the car solidly between the two men. And the hell of it was, it felt completely natural. Right there between them. Them flanking her protectively.

Just like she belonged to both of them.

And maybe she did. Maybe she already knew that.

But did they? And how would they react to such an absurd idea?

# chapter ten

ELLE'S STOMACH WAS FULL OF butterflies as she sat in the locker room where Merrick was preparing for his bout. Cade and Dallas were in the next room where Merrick was in the final leg of his routine when he mentally got set for the task ahead. Charlie sat next to her, along with a number of people Elle didn't know.

They were all involved with Merrick. His camp, as Charlie called them. Oh they'd been introduced, but their names and faces had all been a blur to her. Quite frankly, she was terrified to be away from the place she considered her refuge.

Las Vegas was a glittery city, the likes of which she'd never experienced. She had no way to know if it was true or not, but she fully believed she was a small-town girl at heart.

Cade and Merrick had insisted that she accompany them for Merrick's bout, and it wasn't that she truly wanted to remain behind by herself, but the idea of being so...public...scared the holy hell out of her.

It had been a concern for Merrick and Cade as well. With the media coverage of the event and all eyes on his fight to see whether he'd be granted a shot at the title, the very last thing they wanted was for her to show up on television or in a photo that circulated the Internet and media outlets.

They'd been extremely careful. She touched the ends of the blond wig she wore and wondered if it was truly enough to alter her appearance. She wore dark sunglasses, even inside the arena, and Dallas stuck to her like glue to give the impression that she was with him.

Cade and Merrick largely ignored Elle when anyone else was present, but she could feel their gazes on her. Knew they watched closely.

"Nervous?" Charlie asked in a low voice.

She glanced sideways and then quickly looked in the direction of the other occupants of the small room.

"A little," she admitted.

She'd watched Merrick train for a month. She'd even watched fights on television, but she'd never seen a live fight. She'd watched Merrick's opponent when the guys had watched footage from previous matches over and over to monitor strengths and weaknesses.

The guy Merrick was fighting was the other leading contender for the heavyweight belt, and she knew from listening to the others that his style was ground and pound, whatever that meant.

All Elle knew was that Merrick was willingly walking into a ring with a man who wanted nothing more than to kick his ass.

Charlie reached for her hand and squeezed. "Don't be. Merrick is ready for this. He's focused. He's confident. He's going to win."

"I just want him not to get hurt," she blurted.

Charlie smiled. "Now, I don't want you to get all freaked out over blood, cuts and bruises. That's what happens when two grown men go all out in the ring. Merrick's smart, though, and he's fast for such a big man."

Just then Merrick's trainer, Dakota Trayburn, walked over and touched Charlie on the shoulder.

"We're ready if you and Elle want to go on out. I'll have two men go with you. Dallas and Cade will be along in a minute. They're going to walk out with Merrick."

Adrenaline lurched through Elle's veins, and just as quickly, fear tracked close behind. She licked her lips and squared her shoulders, determined not to show these people that she was some kind of wimp.

Two broad-shouldered men with no necks and bulging biceps walked over to where she and Charlie sat.

"Ma'am," one said politely. "We'll escort you to your seats if you're ready."

Curling her fingers tightly around her bag, she stood. Charlie put his hand to her back in a reassuring manner, and they followed boulder number one out the door and into the arena.

The noise was deafening. The previous bout had finished, and the victor was circling the ring, pumping his fists into the air. All around them, people bumped and pushed. The two men escorting them positioned their bodies between her and Charlie and the crowd and pushed their way down the aisle, their arms out to keep everyone at bay.

There was a row of empty chairs ringside, and one of the men gestured for her and Charlie to take a seat on the end. As she eased down, she turned her head in all directions, taking in the enormous crowd crammed into the event center of the casino.

She jumped when the arena darkened. Camera flashes went wild, and ominous music began to play. On the opposite side, Merrick's opponent began to make his way to the ring. Elle watched in fascination as he worked the crowd and was introduced to a mixture of cheers and boos.

When it was Merrick's turn to enter the arena, her head turned automatically to search him out. It was like looking at a different person. Someone she didn't know. A celebrity who was going to walk right by her.

It hadn't registered with her, even during the weeks of training, that Merrick was this larger-than-life person. He just seemed so...normal. *Nice.* But the man making his way toward the ring looked anything but nice. He was someone who would scare the ever-loving shit out of her if she met him elsewhere.

The crowd roared, and she curiously looked around, seeing the approval of the fans. He was the favorite, judging by the crowd's response. It fascinated her that there were so many people rooting for him. These people knew who he was. They followed his career and his success. They were invested in him.

To her, he was just Merrick Sullivan. The man who made her feel... safe.

As Merrick and his entourage walked by, Merrick reached down and brushed his hand down her arm. It was brief. It could have been considered accidental. Only, she knew better. Even utterly focused, he'd sent her a message.

Dallas and Cade stepped up to the ring while Merrick was being introduced. Merrick stripped off his hoody and tossed it toward Cade.

Elle swallowed hard as she looked at the heavily muscled warrior in front of her.

All he wore was a pair of trunks and the gloves that were a great deal smaller than a boxer's. He danced in place, keeping loose and limber as his bare feet glided over the mat.

Dallas took a seat on the other side of Elle, but Cade remained ringside with two other members of Merrick's team.

"He's looking good," Dallas said in her ear. "He's focused and confident. He's going to win."

Dallas's words sent a thrill through her chest. She held her breath as she watched the two fighters face off as the referee outlined the rules.

She'd never seen Merrick so…fierce. She couldn't wrap her head around the difference in this man, the fighter, and the man who'd held her and comforted her so many times.

As the two men parted and the bell rang, signaling the start, Elle surged forward in her seat. Other than the light touch to her arm, Merrick hadn't acknowledged her in any way. She hadn't expected him to. He had to be focused. A distraction could cost him the match and could cause him serious injury.

Beside her, Dallas shot to his feet as Merrick and his opponent exchanged a flurry of punches. Dallas was yelling. Charlie was on his feet hollering something Elle couldn't decipher.

When Merrick took a shot to the head and stumbled back, Elle flew to her feet, her hand over her mouth.

"Don't look like that," Dallas yelled in her ear. "Suck it up. If he looks this way, the last thing he needs to see is you looking like you're going to puke."

His rebuke jarred her from her horror, and she schooled her features. But inside her chest, her heart was about to explode as she watched the flurry of action in the ring.

The first round lasted an eternity. The few minutes stretched into what seemed like an hour as the two men traded punches and wrestling holds. When the bell rang and Merrick returned to his corner, she stared hard, looking for any sign of injury.

He sat, looking calm and completely focused. At peace, which seemed ridiculous given he'd spent the last several minutes getting pounded by a man as big as he was.

But there was no blood, and his face looked untouched. The other guy hadn't been as fortunate. His eye was swollen, and a cut had opened up on his cheek.

"He won that one!" Charlie yelled over the crowd.

"Hell yeah he did," Dallas said.

"He won?" she asked in bewilderment. "It's over?"

"He won the round," Dallas said in a patient voice. "Points. If there isn't a knockout, the match is determined by points. Merrick won that round."

"Yes!" she hollered.

Charlie and Dallas both grinned at her, and Charlie pounded her on the back.

"That's the way to get into it, girl!"

She remained standing when the two fighters came out of their corners for the second round. Now that she knew Merrick had won the first round, it made sense to her why his opponent came out more aggressive.

"He's being careless!" Dallas said in a whoop. "Merrick will nail his ass to the wall. There isn't going to be another round. I guarantee it!"

Elle surged forward in the excitement, her fingers curled into tight balls as her nails dug into her palms. Her heart was pounding, and her gaze was glued to the two fighters.

Merrick's opponent lashed out with a high kick, but Merrick reared his head back, caught the guy's leg and then drove him to the mat.

"Damn it, I can't see!" Elle yelled in frustration.

Dallas turned, presenting his back to her. "Hop up."

She stared blankly at him, and he looked back over his shoulder.

"Come on, or you're going to miss it!"

She tossed her purse at Charlie and put her hands on Dallas's shoulders. As she jumped, he reached back, grasped the backs of her legs and hoisted her upward.

Elevated above Charlie and Dallas, she could now clearly see the action in the ring. Merrick was atop his opponent and was landing punches to his head. She winced but was grateful it wasn't Merrick getting his ass handed to him.

She knew from watching Merrick's training that just as much of the match was fought on the ground as it was standing upright and boxing. She'd read up on jiu-jitsu to familiarize herself with the holds and maneuvers so she wasn't completely ignorant of something that was obviously extremely important not only to Merrick but to Cade, Dallas and Charlie as well.

Merrick had an amazing support network, and now so did she. It hit her, standing right there in the middle of the crowded arena. She was a part of this. She had no explanation for how. Or why she was so fortunate to have ended up with men like Cade and Merrick and their extended group. Charlie, Dallas. Even Merrick's team.

She was a fixture at the gym and at the training sessions. They often had dinner together after training. She even rode in the back of the truck when Merrick went for his runs and his trainer timed him.

Staring in awe as the crowd roared, she scanned the flashing lights, the people thrusting their fists in the air, and then her gaze returned to the ring just in time to see Merrick execute a rear naked choke hold.

It was a submission move.

She strained upward, holding her breath as she watched Merrick lock it in. The wait seemed interminable. Adrenaline bolted through her body like a shock, and she found herself yelling until she was hoarse.

And then finally, Merrick's opponent tapped three times. The referee stepped in, waving his arms, and then he pushed in to separate the two fighters.

Merrick rose, arms held up, and then Cade was running into the ring to hoist him up. Charlie surged forward, climbing the steps to the ring. Dallas let her slide down his back, and then he threw his arms around her, hugging her until she couldn't breathe.

"He did it!" Dallas yelled. "He did it!"

He started for the ring as Charlie had, but then he hesitated, looking back at Elle as if he remembered he was supposed to watch out for her.

"Go," Elle mouthed.

Dallas shook his head.

"Go," she said again, loudly this time. "I'll be right here. There's nowhere to go. Merrick will want you there. You should be there."

Dallas grimaced. "He wants you there too."

"And I will be," she said. "Afterward. Go and be there for him. He'll want to share this moment with you."

Dallas put his hands out. "Don't move from this spot. I'll be back for you."

She shooed him away, and he bolted for the ring, joining in the mad celebration. She stood back, watching as the men she'd grown so close to whooped and yelled. In that moment, she felt incredibly alone and isolated. She wished she could be right up there with the others. But she had no idea of the possible evil lurking out there, and she couldn't take such a risk.

Two burly men stepped up beside her, boxing her in on both sides. One leaned in so she could hear.

"You're to come with us, ma'am. Mr. Sullivan wants you back in the dressing room to wait for him there."

Panic screeched through her veins. Dallas had told her to stay put. He hadn't said anything about someone else escorting her away.

She shook her head, trying not to freak out on the spot. She shrank back until her legs hit the chair she'd been sitting in.

Instead of pressing the issue, the two men simply stood there, hovering protectively as more of the crowd surged forward chanting Merrick's name.

In the ring, the announcer was making the official declaration of Merrick's victory. He held Merrick's arm up, and the crowd erupted once more.

And then Merrick looked directly at her. He smiled. It lit up the entire arena. He pointed at her and then balled his fist doing a pump in the air.

She grinned back and blew him a kiss.

Dallas squeezed in and cupped her elbow. "They're okay, Elle," he said, dipping his head toward the two men standing guard over her. "Merrick sent them to escort you back before things get too crazy. I'll go with you."

Relieved that Dallas was here, she allowed the two men to escort her and Dallas back to the dressing room. When they burst in, it was already chaotic with celebration, and Merrick hadn't even made it back yet.

Champagne bottles were being opened, and a glass was shoved into her hand. Just a few moments later, Merrick burst into the locker room flanked by Cade and Charlie. His trainer came in close behind him, and the other members of his team, as well as several other fighters who'd come to support Merrick, crowded around, fists in the air as they shouted their congratulations to Merrick.

It was hard for her not to go to him. But she was supposed to be here with Dallas. His girl.

Their gazes connected through the crowd. Both Cade and Merrick sought her out, their stares probing, the question clear in their eyes.

"I'm fine," she mouthed. "You did awesome," she said to Merrick.

He winked at her and then turned his attention to his well-wishers.

Elle retreated to a far corner so she could observe the festivities at a distance. It was on the edge of her mind to think how different her life was now, but how could she know that when she had no idea what her life had been before?

She'd been swept into a different world. But this wasn't her life. It was Cade and Merrick's life. And she had no idea how or *if* she fit into it.

# chapter eleven

"HEY, YOU GOING TO THE after party?" Dakota asked Merrick.

Merrick hesitated and then glanced across the room to where Elle was curled in a chair in the corner sound asleep.

"I don't think so, man. I'm tired. I could use a little peace and quiet right now."

Dakota followed Merrick's gaze to Elle. "Your fans are going to want to see you. This is an important lead-up to the championship fight. Did you see that Lash was at the fight? Second row. He left in a hurry after you submitted Carew."

Merrick shook his head. "I didn't see." And he didn't care. Lash was the champion, and Merrick wanted the belt. It didn't matter who it was. It wasn't personal.

"I think it's a good idea for you to at least make an appearance," Dakota persisted.

Merrick sighed and glanced over at Cade. In the past, he and Cade and Dallas would have gone to the after party and partied hard through the night. Now all he wanted to do was go back to his hotel room so he could spend some quiet time with Elle and find out what the hell she'd thought about all this.

"I'll send a car with two bodyguards with Elle back to the hotel," Dakota said, his tone persuasive. "They'll stand outside her room. No one will get near her. When you're done, you can head back. Spend an hour. I'll make sure no one bothers you after that."

Cade, who'd been listening in, looked torn as well. He glanced at Elle and then back at Merrick. Then finally he put his hand on Merrick's shoulder.

"This is your night, man. It's your call. I'll go with you to the party if you want to go. Dakota's probably right. It's probably a good idea for you to show up, at least for a little while. You had a ton of people come out for you tonight."

Dallas pushed in next to Cade. "You guys want me to go back to the hotel with Elle?"

"No," Merrick clipped out.

He trusted Dallas implicitly, but even the charade of Dallas being with Elle grated on him. He didn't want to see them leave together even if he knew the entire thing was a fabrication meant to make sure Elle wasn't thrust into the spotlight. It was utterly ridiculous, but jealousy was eating at him at the mere appearance that Elle was with another man.

He turned to his trainer, his lips tight. "You make damn sure she gets to the hotel safely and that the bodyguards don't leave her side until she's inside. I'll relieve them when I get back to the hotel. I'm holding you personally responsible for her safety."

Dakota nodded. "Get showered and changed, and I'll arrange transportation to the bar we've rented out for the night. While you're doing that, I'll have Catherine take care of Elle."

It took everything Merrick had to walk away from her and not go to her, leaving her sleeping in the chair. Goddamn but he hated this.

He shook his head and jabbed his finger at Dakota. "*You* take care of it personally. Catherine's a wonderful woman, but I'd rather you see to Elle's protection."

"Whatever you want, Merrick. Now go. I'll take care of things."

Elle was gently shaken awake by Catherine, Dakota's wife. Dakota was in his forties, and Catherine was likely in her late thirties, but she didn't look a day over twenty-five. And it wasn't because of artificial means. The woman was just beautiful and vibrant, and she had a smile that could light up an entire city block.

She was smart too. She was often involved in the business aspect of Merrick's career. Elle knew from just the short time she'd been associated with the guys that Dakota depended on Catherine a lot for advice and her opinions. She had the respect of all the men around her, and Elle admired her for that.

"Hey, you feeling okay?" Catherine asked.

Elle nodded and sat up quickly, embarrassed that she'd fallen asleep during Merrick's locker room celebration. A quick glance around told her that things were dying down and people were starting to clear out of the dressing room.

"This is what's going down for the night," Catherine said. "There's an after party. It's completely normal. Tradition, one might even say, for the winner to host a party for fans. It's important for Merrick to be there and have a presence. The organization is looking hard at him right now. They know he's a contender for the belt and he's likely going to get that offer soon. Public support is always a good thing to have on your side."

Elle held her hand up to stop the flow of words. "Catherine, I understand. Of course he should go. This is an important night for him. I just wish…"

Catherine's face wrinkled in sympathy. "What do you wish?"

"That I could be there too," Elle said wistfully.

Catherine put her hand over Elle's. "I know you do. I can only imagine."

Catherine and Dakota both knew of Elle's situation. Merrick could hardly keep it a secret from them since he needed their cooperation in keeping Elle out of the public eye. Most of Merrick's camp knew. And Dakota and Catherine had both been wonderful to her.

But what they didn't or couldn't know was the extent of her relationship with either Cade or Merrick. How could they when even Elle didn't know?

As far as they were concerned, Elle was a woman in trouble, and Cade and Merrick were lending her a helping hand and support until she got her memory back.

Elle knew in her gut that she wanted more. But damn if she could even put a finger on exactly what she wanted from the two men. Or maybe she knew, and she was too afraid to admit it even to herself.

"Dakota has a car to take you back to the hotel. If you don't mind, I'm going to catch a ride back with you," Catherine said. "I'm beat, and as thrilled as I am for Merrick, I don't have it in me to pull a late nighter tonight."

"Of course I don't mind. I'd love the company," Elle said honestly.

"Dakota is sending two bodyguards with us, and they'll remain outside your suite until Merrick and Cade return."

Elle nodded, not bothering to say it was unnecessary. How could she say that with any certainty? She had no idea who'd tried to kill her or where he was now. All she knew was that the only time she felt safe was when she was with Cade and Merrick.

Dallas walked over and bent down to press a perfunctory kiss to Elle's forehead. It could easily be interpreted as an affectionate kiss from a man to his lover, and Elle knew Dallas did view her affectionately, but it was a pretense.

"You going to be okay with Cathy?" Dallas asked. "I'll go back to the hotel with you if you want."

Elle shook her head. "Go and have fun. Enjoy the moment, and make sure Merrick does too. And please don't let them worry about me. Catherine has been nice enough to ride back to the hotel with me, and I'm going to curl up and get some sleep. I'll be fine."

Dallas smiled and then ruffled her hair. "Okay, will do. You two be careful."

"See ya, Dallas," Catherine said.

Dakota walked over then with the two mountains who'd escorted her to her seat earlier.

"Elle, this is Carl and Steven, and they'll be escorting you back to the hotel."

"I'm going to ride with her, babe," Catherine spoke up.

Dakota's brow furrowed. "You sure?"

"Yeah, I'm tired. You guys go and celebrate."

Dakota pulled her into his arms and kissed her. It was clear the couple cared a lot for each other, and Dakota wasn't hesitant at all about demonstrating that love for his wife regardless of who was watching.

"See you later then," he said. Then he nodded at Elle. "They'll take you out now."

Elle followed behind Carl while Steven fell in behind her and Catherine. As they walked toward the door, Merrick came out of the shower, his hair still damp. Elle stopped a moment to absorb the image of him standing in the dressing room wearing a T-shirt advertising his training facilities and a pair of jeans that hugged his body in all the right places.

Cade walked over to where she stood, his stance casual. Merrick came up behind him until both men were mere inches away.

"You okay?" Cade asked softly.

She nodded and smiled. "Yep. Congratulations, Merrick. It was an awesome fight."

The corner of Merrick's mouth lifted. "You watched? Or did you hide your eyes the entire time?"

She huffed indignantly. "You submitted him with a rear naked choke hold."

Both men laughed. Cade started to put his hand out to touch her but pulled it back at the last minute.

"We'll see you later, okay? If you need anything at all, call my cell. I'll be checking it."

Elle nodded, and after one last lingering glance, she turned and walked away with the two bodyguards.

# chapter twelve

ELLE WAS IN A VERY modest pair of pajamas when she heard the slide of a keycard in the door. A moment later, it opened, admitting Cade and Merrick into the suite.

She glanced up from her perch on the couch as they trudged inside.

The room was dark, with only a corner lamp burning. She'd been sitting by the window staring at the Las Vegas strip and the dazzling array of lights that cascaded up and down the boulevard.

"Hey," Cade said softly. "Why are you still awake?"

"I wanted to wait up for you guys," she said. "I didn't get to talk to you earlier. It was frustrating."

Merrick scowled and then plopped onto the couch beside her, extolling a weary sigh that worried her.

"It was damn frustrating," he agreed in a low growl. "I didn't want to go to a fucking party. I just wanted to come back to the room where it was quiet, pop a few pain pills and…see you."

She got a giddy thrill from the admission, but she latched onto the pain in his voice and the comment about pain medication.

"What's wrong?" she asked sharply.

She turned, hovering over him on her knees, examining him for some sign of injury.

Cade went to the bar and pulled out a bottle of water. Then he went to the pack on the countertop, pulled out a bottle of pills and shook out two. He carried them and the water over to Merrick and handed them to him.

"What's wrong with him?" Elle asked anxiously.

Cade settled on her other side, his hand sliding soothingly down her back.

"Fighting's rough, honey. Just because he isn't bleeding or cut open doesn't mean he isn't sore as hell. His ribs took a beating, and he got clocked a few times in the head."

"Do you need to go to the hospital?" Elle demanded, her hands automatically going to Merrick's body.

"Dallas has already had a look at me," Merrick mumbled. "I'll take it easy for the next few days, heal up, and then I'll start all over again."

Elle gasped. "So soon?"

"The title fight will be in a few months," Cade said. "They'll give him time to train, make sure Lash is healthy, and then they'll set a date. Then they'll start promoting. Things will get a little crazier for this. This is the big time, Elle. This is what Merrick's been working for."

Was it a warning to her that she would be in the way? Would she be a hindrance to Merrick and his concentration? She hated the uncertainty of her position. That she wasn't in any position of equality. She had...nothing. She *was* nothing.

She lowered her head, not looking at either man.

"Elle?"

Merrick's soft inquiry reached her ears, but she didn't look up.

He reached for her then, cautiously touching the side of her arm. He and Cade were both careful like that. As if they feared startling her.

"Elle, he wasn't saying that for any other reason than he wanted you to know what you were in for."

"I'll be in the way," she said quietly.

A string of colorful curses burst from Cade. In an instant, she found herself turned and pulled onto Cade's lap. The shock of his touch and the intimacy of their positions sent a jolt of awareness through her body.

He cupped her chin and forced her gaze upward until she met his intense stare.

"Listen to me," he said succinctly. "You are *not* in the way. I didn't say those things to make you think you aren't welcome. I want you to be prepared for what's to come. For someone who's never experienced this sort of thing, it's going to be overwhelming. Especially to someone who's already fragile."

"I don't want to be a burden," she said earnestly. "I want Merrick to *win*. I don't want to be a distraction."

Merrick reached for her hand and threaded his fingers through hers.

"How about you let me worry about what is or isn't a distraction? I want you here for this, Elle. We both do. We're going to worry about you, and there's nothing you can do about that, so deal with it, okay?"

She nodded, relief making her light-headed.

"Now, what do you say we go home tomorrow and get back into our routine?" Merrick said.

It seemed so odd coming from this man. A man she'd seen in a whole different light tonight. He was a public figure. He had masses of adoring fans. He was a complete badass in the ring.

But to her?

He was her savior. A gentle giant with a heart of gold.

For all the damage he could inflict on an opponent, he'd never touched her with anything but exquisite gentleness. It seemed impossible that the man who'd rescued her and who lived in a quiet neighborhood in the small town of Grand Junction was quite possibly the next IMMAO heavyweight champion.

"Just like that?" she asked softly.

Merrick looked at her in question.

"You can turn it off just like that? Go back home to the quiet routine and shake off the hoopla surrounding the fight and your career?"

He smiled, and it was a tired smile that showed the lines of fatigue and strain on his face.

"Yeah, I can do that."

She leaned over him, worried and anxious. "Are you okay? Are you hurting still?"

He opened his eyes and focused his stare on her, and then he smiled, easing some of the lines from his eyes.

"Yeah, I hurt. I'm going to hurt for the next few days, but Dallas will take good care of me, and Cade always pulls his mother hen act after a fight. I'll be fine, baby."

The soft endearment sent a shiver of pleasure coursing through her veins.

"Then let's go home," she said softly.

"Hell yeah," Cade echoed.

# chapter thirteen

"HAVE YOU MADE A MOVE yet?" Merrick asked quietly.

Cade jerked his head around to stare at his friend. There was fire in his eyes. Anger. Surprise. And the beginnings of something that looked like fear.

They were sitting in the kitchen of their house, both in tense, irritable moods because Elle had talked them into letting her go out to the grocery store by herself.

After six months of them never letting her out of their sight and six months she'd spent recovering and gaining confidence, she'd wanted to venture out on her own, and it was making the two men nuts.

She was always with either him or Cade. Whether it was her attending his training sessions or her going into the office with Cade. She spent every waking minute with at least one of them.

Merrick worried that she would eventually get bored, but she seemed to soak up every aspect of his career as well as learn every part of his and Cade's business.

She studied the language and terms of mixed martial arts. She learned the holds, the positions, and studied his training regimen. She poked and nagged at him when he ate something he shouldn't. She hovered when he seemed tired after a workout. And she studied his diet, memorizing the ins and outs and how much protein he needed to take in.

In short, she'd fit in perfectly into his and Cade's lives, and it was hard to remember what they'd ever done without her. It wasn't something he wanted to contemplate—being without her.

Which was why today made him antsy. Maybe it felt too much like she was chafing under the constraints she was placed under. Maybe he feared she was ready to move on.

Merrick didn't understand what she felt she needed to prove. He didn't want her out of his sight. He knew Cade didn't either. They both felt better when she was with them.

Elle had come a long way from the terrified, wary, broken woman they'd found in the cabinet of a gun store. She'd gained much-needed weight. The dullness and fear had receded from her eyes. She smiled spontaneously, and she was affectionate with him and Cade.

And it was driving him crazy. He wanted her. Wanted more than the role of protector. But he also knew Cade wanted the same, and it was time to address the elephant in the room.

"Of course I haven't made a move," Cade snapped. "Have you?"

Merrick shook his head. "You know I wouldn't without talking to you about it and until I was comfortable that she was ready. I mean, I'm not talking sex here. I just want to take things to the next level."

Cade let out a raspy breath that sounded like a snarl. Then he dragged a hand over the top of his head before slapping it back down on the table.

"I've known this was coming. That it was inevitable. Maybe I was in denial and wanted to keep on pretending that it wouldn't come to this. I think we both know we have a problem."

"Yeah," Merrick agreed. "What are we going to do about it?"

Cade looked uneasy. He opened his mouth then closed it again, a sure sign he had something he wanted to say but for some reason was hesitating. Which wasn't usual for him. He typically never had a problem stating his mind. It was one reason he and Merrick got along so well. They were both blunt people, and there was little room for misunderstandings when you had two friends who always said what was on their mind.

"Cade?"

Cade bit out a curse. "You're going to think I'm nuts. Hell, maybe I am. This would probably never work."

Merrick leaned forward, his brow furrowed as he frowned. "What the hell are you talking about?"

"I've been doing a lot of thinking. About our situation. The way things have been so far and the fact that you and I both have a strong interest in Elle."

"Go on."

Cade met his gaze, his lips pursed, and then he blew out his breath, puffing out his cheeks as he expelled it all.

"What if we left things as they are now? I mean with the three of us. Only we'd take things up a notch. But the three of us would remain together. She'd be with...*both* of us."

Merrick reared back, leaning against the back of his chair as he let Cade's words sink in. Holy shit, but this hadn't been what he'd expected at all.

He cupped a hand over his nape and rubbed hard as he struggled to make sense of the situation and, hell, just to imagine it.

"That's assuming she'd even ever agree to such a thing," Cade said evenly. "She still has a lot of issues to work out. All we know is that we want to be with her for the long haul. It wouldn't be easy with just one of us. But if both of us are involved? It's going to be ten times as hard."

"No shit," Merrick muttered.

"Is that all you've got to say?" Cade asked in frustration. "I've put it all out on the line. Me, us, her, our friendship."

"This is heavy shit, man. I mean, I can't wrap my head around it. I know such relationships exist. Hell, there was a damn documentary on one of the cable networks a few months ago."

"Think about what it solves," Cade said quietly. "I don't want this to ruin our friendship. Our partnership. Your career. We'd have to be extremely careful to keep this private. The thing is, Elle trusts us both. I think she feels something for both of us. Maybe I'm reaching here, or maybe it's wishful thinking. But I think we could make this work, as bizarre as it may sound. You and I already trust each other. We're as close as brothers. I'm not going to screw you over, and I know you won't screw me over. If we were, we wouldn't be having this conversation and trying to salvage a very sticky situation."

He took a deep breath and plunged ahead.

"Trust is key in a relationship like I'm proposing. We can't be stupid, jealous bastards. We have to know going in that we're basically a family unit and that we have to work together, not at opposites. We have a common goal. We both care for Elle, and we both want to see her happy, safe and protected."

Merrick nodded. The more Cade talked, the more this craziness was starting to make twisted sense. Or maybe he was just scared shitless that he'd lose in a showdown, and this was his chance to hedge his bets.

"I don't know what to say," Merrick admitted. "I wasn't expecting something like this."

"You were expecting worse," Cade said grimly.

Merrick nodded again. "Yeah. I've been dreading it. If it were any other girl, I'd back off, you know? I'd say no woman was worth a lifelong friendship, a partnership and a vested business interest."

"But she isn't just any girl," Cade finished.

"Yeah, exactly. She's…" Merrick broke off even as the firm realization took hold. "She's the one." And he knew as he said it that it was the irrevocable truth. Somehow speaking it aloud gave it more strength. It solidified what he'd been grappling with for months now. It was a relief to get it out, to say the words, for Cade to know where Merrick stood.

His pulse was pounding in his head and chest like a freight train roaring down the tracks. He stared back at Cade as the enormity of their discussion hit him like said freight train.

"Now you know why I've been doing so much thinking about this," Cade said in a grim voice. "Because I feel the same way, and I know you do too. One of us has to lose, and I don't want that. I don't think Elle wants it, even if she doesn't know exactly *what* it is she wants."

"You're telling me you would be okay with…sharing…her with me?" Merrick asked in disbelief.

"What I'm asking is whether you'd be okay with sharing her with *me*," Cade said. "I know what I'm okay with. I don't know what you are. I've had several months to make peace with this. I don't see an alternative. At least not one that offers us all a chance at happiness."

He was right. It was insanity, but Cade was right, and Merrick couldn't even wrap his brain around it. Didn't know how to respond. What to say. How to even agree to such a bizarre proposition.

"We don't know if she'll ever go for this," Merrick muttered.

"Of course we don't. But how stupid would it be for me or you to even mention it to her if we weren't in agreement ourselves? If we do this, we have to present a united front, and we have to be damn convincing. She's not going to want to cause trouble between us. I think she'd up and disappear on us if she even thought this would strain our relationship."

"Christ."

"Yeah, exactly. We have to be careful, man. I don't want to lose her. She's been through enough. I want her to be happy. I want to make her happy. Hell, I want *us* to make her happy."

"And what about her past?" Merrick asked, putting into words the thought that had haunted him the last six months. What happened when she remembered everything? What if she had a life she wanted to return to?

"We cross that bridge when we get to it," Cade said quietly. "What else can we do? Look, no one has been looking for her. We've had feelers out. Dad has been monitoring missing persons through his friend at the station. From everything we know, I'd say whoever was in her life was the one who tried to kill her. There's nothing for her to go back to."

"That's my feeling too, but my gut is screaming that this could backfire on us in a big way. We get emotionally invested, and then she gets yanked away from us."

"Merrick, we're *already* emotionally invested."

Merrick was quiet for a long moment. "You got me there. I am. That's not going to change."

"So let's do something about it," Cade urged. "We talk to Elle. Find out how she's feeling. I don't want to rush her. I'll wait for damn ever if that's what it takes. I don't want to push her into a physical relationship. I just want and need her to know what's going on here…and what we want."

Merrick swallowed hard. This may well be the most fucked up, insane thing he'd ever agreed to in his life. It also might be the most rewarding. He closed his eyes and sucked in a deep breath. When he reopened them, Cade was staring back, determination etched in every one of his features.

"Okay," Merrick said quietly. "Okay. We'll try it."

# chapter fourteen

ELLE PULLED INTO THE PARKING lot of the local grocery store, a goofy grin attacking her face. She'd done it! She'd left the sanctuary of Merrick and Cade's house—on her own—and had driven to the grocery store…by herself!

Her triumph didn't temper her caution, though, and she glanced carefully around the parking lot before she got out and hurried for the entrance. Despite her upbeat mood, there was still lingering insecurity over the fact that, for the first time since Cade and Merrick had found her in the gun shop, she was striking out on her own. The first time she'd been without at least one of them since the very beginning.

She grabbed one of the carts and pulled out her list, checking to make sure Merrick's debit card was still securely in her pocket. Then with a deep breath, she began her shopping trip.

It was all absurdly normal, and she got an equally absurd thrill that she was doing something so mundane as grocery shop. Something everyone else likely considered a humdrum necessity and not the veritable mountain of an obstacle Elle considered it.

It took her half an hour to check off everything from her list. She'd been careful to ensure she bought things that Merrick could eat—and should eat—with his strict training regimen. But she'd also incorporated a few treats. It wouldn't hurt for him to indulge every once in a while, and she wanted to pamper him and Cade every bit as much as they'd pampered her.

It may not seem like much, but she was determined to give something back to them.

Elle piled her groceries onto the checkout conveyor and then hurried to stand in front of the cashier. Her hand slid into her pocket for the debit card Merrick had given her, and she froze and then stared at all the items she'd chosen.

Her heart began to race, and dismay crowded her mind. She swallowed hard and then glanced nervously at the woman who was rapidly scanning the groceries.

No. Not now. Damn it. She couldn't freak out and melt down now. Not when she was so close to victory. She could taste it. She was a few short moments away from driving back home, a huge hurdle in her recovery overcome.

She closed her eyes as despair swamped her. Despite her best efforts to push through the panic and fear, she utterly failed.

For just a moment, she'd allowed herself to believe she was a normal woman going to the grocery store to buy the fixings for all the yummy things she wanted to make Cade and Merrick. As a thank you. Just to do something more to pull her weight.

But she had no money. She didn't even have identification if she was asked for it. Merrick had given her the pin number, stressing there wouldn't be an issue as long as she didn't use the credit option.

None of this was hers. She had no right to Merrick's credit card. Or his money. Or to be here like she belonged.

Despair weighed down on her. And panic. What if she never remembered? She couldn't depend on Cade and Merrick forever. Couldn't expect them to support her and for her to continue on in her helpless frustration.

Her mouth had gone completely dry, and she withdrew her hand from her pocket just as the cashier scanned the last item.

"I'm really sorry," Elle said in a low voice. "I've forgotten my wallet."

She began backing away from the register as she spoke. A look of annoyance creased the cashier's face. Then the cashier surveyed the groceries that the bagger was steadily working on.

"They'll be in the cart if you want to run home and get it," the cashier said. "We can't wait long, or the refrigerated goods will go bad."

Elle nodded and turned and all but ran from the store, hoping she hadn't drawn too much attention to herself. She felt like the worst sort of idiot. It had seemed like such a good idea, a fun idea, to go out on her own. Take the plunge. Be *brave*.

The last months had been so wonderful. She'd made friends. She had a circle of people—Merrick's and Cade's people—who accepted her and she hung out with. But she'd still remained solidly dependent on Cade and Merrick, never going anywhere without one of them.

She'd wanted to do something normal, something brave and independent. Only she *wasn't* normal. She had no way to pay for the items, and it felt wrong to pull out Merrick's credit card and blithely pay for her whims.

The grocery store was close enough to walk and that had been her plan to walk the three blocks, but Cade and Merrick had flipped out over the suggestion.

They hadn't wanted her to go alone at all, but they'd put their foot down when she'd mentioned walking. The mere idea of her being so exposed without their protection had broken both men out into a sweat, so she'd backed down quickly.

Cade insisted she use his SUV, and she'd balked at the idea of driving without a license or identification. Both men had said they'd rather chance her driving the three blocks than walking. Now she was glad they had because she just wanted to be back in the sanctuary of their house.

She liked being close to them. Today had been more of a test of herself than it was the idea that she was actually facing her fears and venturing out on her own. That's the way she'd presented it to the men, but she'd known the truth. She'd been terrified but determined to force herself out of her comfort zone. Out of the isolation she'd existed in for the last six months.

Yes, she associated with the people in Cade and Merrick's circle. Good people. But she still led a very isolated existence, and she knew it. She did nothing outside of Cade's and Merrick's interests. Nothing for herself. Nothing on her own.

The truth was, and she realized it more than ever, that she didn't want to go anywhere without them. Cade and Merrick had not just become parts of her life. They'd become the most important aspect of her existence.

She depended on them for everything. Even if it was just a comforting smile and the assurance that she'd always have a place with them.

That part always baffled her, but they were absolutely sincere. In fact, they'd settled into a comfortable existence that she took for granted more with each passing day.

It had been an alarming realization just the day before that she found herself hoping that she didn't have to deal with her past and any possible issues it could present. She was happy and content with Cade and Merrick. In the present. Today. Now.

She was hopelessly in denial, but she didn't *want* to correct the problem. She found refuge in denial. If she didn't think about it, it didn't exist, and it couldn't hurt her.

She had to temper the urge to put her foot down on the accelerator. Instead she eased out of the parking lot, being supremely cautious. Sweat rolled down her neck when a patrol car passed in front of her and turned right at the next street.

Her hands grew clammy, and panic rose sharply. She tried to keep her breathing measured and then accelerated past the side street and focused on getting home.

Home.

It was what she considered Cade and Merrick's house.

Her home.

She didn't want to be anywhere else.

No matter where she traveled to with Cade and Merrick for Merrick's fights or training, she considered their little house in their quiet little subdivision home, and it was where she felt the safest.

A few minutes later, she pulled into the driveway and hurriedly got out of the SUV. She rushed for the front door, so happy to be back where she felt secure that she was nearly giddy with relief.

When she entered through the kitchen, both men turned around from where they were sitting at the table. Their gazes found her instantly, and then they both frowned.

"What's wrong?" Merrick asked sharply.

"Where are the groceries?" Cade asked. "Do you need us to bring them in?"

She shook her head mutely, and the crush of her stupidity hit her full on. She was embarrassed over her panic attack. Now that she was back in her sanctuary, all the fear faded, and calm descended.

Merrick rose and walked toward her, concern burning in his eyes. "Elle, baby, what happened?"

She pulled out his card and thrust it in his direction.

"I'm an idiot. I was fine. I picked out all these goodies and meats and had plans to make certain meals. It was something I wanted to do for the both of you. And then when I got to the checkout, I realized that I had no right to spend all that money. Money that isn't mine. I don't even know who I am. I have no ID. And I'm there using your card like I have the right, and I just felt so ashamed."

A curse blew past Merrick's lips. He closed his hand over hers but didn't take the card. In the background, Cade rose and walked over to where Elle and Merrick stood. His expression wasn't any happier than Merrick's.

"You have *every* right," Merrick bit out. "Elle, you belong to us. It's our job to take care of you and your needs. We took that on willingly. We don't regret that for a minute. Part of seeing to your needs is providing you the means to buy whatever it is you need. Like clothing. Food. Whatever makes you *happy*."

"You were happy when you left here," Cade interjected quietly. "You were *excited* and looking forward to going out on your own. What happened?"

She threw up her hands in frustration. "I freaked out. I just started thinking that none of this is mine. I have no money. No identity. I'm a complete burden to both of you. And then when I was driving home, I saw a cop, and I had a panic attack right then and there. I mean, when does it end? I can't go on like this. How can you even stand to be around me? I'm a hot mess. A complete head case."

Merrick reached out, put his arm around her neck and pulled her against his chest until her face rested over his heartbeat. He kissed the top of her head, but then what he did next completely shocked her.

As he pulled her away, he leaned down, palmed the back of her head and pressed his lips to hers in a hot, hungry kiss. He didn't try to overpower her. In fact, he was extremely gentle. But she *was* overpowered from the first moment their lips met.

Her knees went weak, and heat pooled in her belly, rushing rapidly through her veins.

This time when he pulled away, his eyes were flush with desire, and he stared at her like…like she was something *special*. Someone he cherished. She stared back, mystified, and then her gaze skirted to Cade because she found herself suddenly dreading *his* reaction. She didn't like the feeling that she had just in some way betrayed Cade. It was a stupid thought because they were nothing to her, and she was nothing to them. Was she? But then why had Merrick kissed her? Why had he looked at her with warm possessiveness that made her shiver in delight?

What came next was even more baffling because Cade stepped forward, circled her wrist with gentle fingers, and then he pulled her to him. He cupped one cheek in his palm, gently caressing her as he lowered his mouth to hers in a sensual, passionate kiss.

She was too stunned to react. She went rigid, wondering what kind of mess she'd gotten herself into. They'd both kissed her. One after the other.

She pulled abruptly away from Cade and glanced nervously back at Merrick to gauge his reaction. But there was no anger in his expression. There was nothing at all to denote he wasn't happy with Cade kissing her.

When she looked back at Cade, she saw the same calmness in his eyes, and her head started to spin.

This was crazy. The pieces just wouldn't come together.

They'd made it clear she belonged to them, but she'd never really given it any deep thought. She just considered them two knights in shining armor who'd gone above and beyond for a woman they didn't know.

That was it. Eventually she was sure they'd want to move her out or that they were just waiting for her memory to return so they could push her on her merry way back to whatever life she'd lived before.

But then there were all the comments about them being with her for the long term. About being there to help her even once her memory returned.

What did it all mean?

"I think we need to talk," she said faintly.

"What happened with the groceries?" Cade asked.

She blinked in surprise at the abrupt change in topic. For a moment, she couldn't remember what she'd done with the groceries. They were the very last thing on her mind. The minute the two men had kissed her, thoughts of anything else had fled.

"I, uh, left them at the store. The cashier said they'd keep them there in the cart if I wanted to go back for them, but they wouldn't hold them for long because they didn't want anything to spoil. I'm sure she thought I was a complete moron. They've probably already put everything back."

Cade reached for the keys she held in her other hand. "Okay, I'm going to go see about the groceries, and when I get back, we'll have that talk. You're right. It's time. There are some things we need to get out in the open."

She swallowed nervously, but then Cade leaned in, kissed her hard and then was gone in the next second.

# chapter fifteen

ELLE TOOK REFUGE IN THE bathroom as soon as Cade left. She stared at herself in the mirror and thought she looked scared and off balance.

She frowned. Damn but she was tired of being afraid. She wanted her life back but not in the sense that she wanted whatever she'd come from before. She wanted a normal life *now*. Right where she was. She wanted the reassurance of knowing who she was and that she had a place in this world. But she didn't want that knowledge to change a single thing about her life now. She just wanted…peace. And to be able to offer Cade and Merrick something more than a helpless, dependent freak who didn't even remember her past.

Her biggest fear was that when her memory came back it would destroy her present, which was laughable given she didn't have a present.

She had nothing.

She was surrounded by people who gave her the hope of having *this* life, and yet she was living a farce. This wasn't hers. But she *wanted* it to be. She wanted to go with Merrick to his title fight. Wanted to be there when he won and to join in the celebration. She wanted to have a role in Cade's business, be instrumental in his work on a daily basis.

Was she asking too much? And was she not trying *hard* enough to remember her old life? Was she subconsciously sabotaging her efforts by suppressing her memories?

In the beginning, Cade and Merrick had wanted to launch their own investigation. Get with a few of their friends on the police force. Search missing persons records. Even put her picture on local news broadcasts then go wide on the Internet.

The mere thought had sent such irrational panic and fear through her that she still couldn't bear to think of it. She didn't know much about her past, but she knew that if she didn't stay hidden, *he* would find her. And she didn't even know who *he* was.

*Stupid bitch. I'm going to kill you, but first I'm going to have what he's been having.*

The words popped into her head like they'd been read off a cue card. Only, the voice wasn't hers. It was a man's. It struck ice in her veins, and she *knew* without question she was remembering what had happened right before he raped her.

She leaned over and pressed her forehead to the counter, sucking in deep, steadying breaths.

What did it mean?

She shook her head, not wanting to remember. She wanted his voice out of her head. She never wanted to hear it again. Never wanted that prickle at her nape or the instant tightening in her belly. It was the closest she'd come to having any memory at all of her violation or the events after.

She didn't want it to come back!

If she never remembered what had been forced upon her, it would be just fine with her. She didn't need that part of her past. Forgetting was the kindest thing that could have happened to her even if she sacrificed her identity in the process.

"Elle, are you all right in there?"

Merrick's voice through the door startled her, but at the same time, she was so relieved that she yanked open the bathroom door, and before he could say anything, she flew into his arms.

Her pulse was beating a rapid staccato, and her chest felt like it was going to explode. She clung to him, wrapped around him so tightly that he couldn't have pried her away with a crowbar.

"Elle, what the hell is going on?" Merrick demanded as he tried to maneuver down the hallway toward the living room.

But she didn't want him to move. She wanted him to stand right where he was so she could hold on. She buried her face in his chest and squeezed her eyes shut so the words would go away. So *he* would go away.

"Baby, you're shaking like a leaf."

She found herself lifted, hoisted in the air, and she made a grab for his neck, afraid that he'd let her go.

"Please," she croaked. "Just hold me a minute."

He took her into his bedroom across the hall and sat on the edge of the bed. "Of course I will. As long as you want. What's scared you so bad, Elle? Talk to me."

The urgency in his voice stirred her. She loosened her hold on his neck and then carefully eased away, but she wouldn't meet his gaze.

She was cold. On the inside. Her fingers were numb. Even her lips felt cold.

"I heard him," she said falteringly.

"Who did you hear?"

She closed her eyes and leaned forward until her forehead met his lips. "Him. The man who r-raped me. The one who tried to kill me."

Merrick went completely stiff. He wrapped his arms around her, surrounding her and enveloping her in his embrace. She loved the sensation of being surrounded by him. Nothing could hurt her when he held her. He was invincible.

"What do you mean you heard him? Today? At the store? Did you see something that made you remember?"

She shook her head. "In the bathroom. I remembered…"

He hugged her to him for a long moment as if to allow her time to gather her composure. Then he gently pulled away so he could look into her eyes.

"What did you remember?" he asked in a low voice.

She sucked in a deep breath. "Just words. His voice. He s-said that I was a stupid bitch and he was going to kill me, but first he was going to have what he's been having."

Merrick frowned. "Is that all? Nothing else? Could you picture his face or his features?"

She closed her eyes and shook her head almost irrationally. No, she didn't want to remember. She *welcomed* the blankness.

"I don't even understand. The man said, 'I'm going to have what he's been having.' But who was he talking about? Who is the *he* the man mentioned?"

Merrick touched her cheek until finally she opened her eyes and trained her gaze on him.

"Elle, baby," he said in a tender voice. "He can't hurt you anymore. Cade and I *will* protect you. He *can't hurt you*."

Tears swam in her eyes. "I don't want to remember, Merrick. I don't. I'm…happy…here. With you," she blurted. "And Cade."

He leaned down and carefully kissed away her tears. His lips were warm and electric on her face and skin. And oh so very tender.

"You do know that you aren't going anywhere, don't you?" he said as he drew away. "We aren't going to toss you out. We aren't going to get tired of you. We aren't going to do anything at all but take care of you and protect and cherish you."

"B-both of you?"

She hated the hope his words instilled, because what she was asking was impossible.

"How about we have this conversation when Cade returns," Merrick said gently. "This is important to him—to us. To *me*. Some things just need to be said. Worked out. I don't want there to be *any* misunderstanding over this."

Slowly she nodded and then sagged into his chest. "I'm still afraid, and I *hate* it," she whispered. "I hate being so damn helpless and powerless. I hate being a coward who doesn't *want* to remember, who prefers a blank slate to remembering the person I was."

He stroked his hand over her hair. "You went through a horrific ordeal. It's only natural that you're scared. Don't beat yourself up over it. Just know that Cade and I are here, and if you're ever scared, all you have to do is come to one of us. As for the rest, it will come in time. Don't be so hard on yourself. When you're ready and able to hold up under whatever it is that's hiding in your past, you'll remember."

His words bolstered her flagging spirit. They slid soul deep, offering her comfort in the darkest places of her mind and spirit.

She sighed and melted into his embrace, allowing his touch to warm and soothe her shattered senses.

In the distance, she heard Cade call that he needed help with the groceries, and she popped her head up.

She scrambled off Merrick's lap but then hesitated, standing between his knees. Then she leaned down and kissed him softly on the lips.

"Thank you. I don't know what happened to send you and Cade to me, but I thank God for you both every day."

Merrick smiled. "Ever consider that we thank him for giving us you?"

Her eyes widened, because no, she hadn't ever considered such a thing. Frankly it seemed ludicrous to her that the two of them would thank anyone for having such a burden dumped on their lap.

Merrick rose and took her hand. "Come on. Let's go help Cade with the groceries, and then you can figure out what you want to make for dinner. That was what you said, right? You picked out lots of yummy stuff to make for us?"

The hopeful note in his voice made her smile. "Yeah, I did. I was careful to get stuff you can eat. You know, high protein. Low carbs. I didn't want to mess up your training."

The look in Merrick's eyes made her stomach coil into a tight knot. Warmth brimmed in those dark eyes, and he pulled her to him, his hand cupping her cheek.

"That was sweet of you," he said in a husky voice.

She thought he might kiss her again, but instead he kept hold of her hand, squeezing lightly as he headed in Cade's direction.

They entered the kitchen as Cade was bringing in an armful of sacks.

"There more?" Merrick asked.

"Just two," Cade said.

"I'll grab them. You and Elle start putting up."

Elle turned to open one of the sacks, but Cade put his hand out to her. His expression was troubled and inquiring as he stared at her.

"You okay? You look upset."

She offered a smile. "I was, but I'm okay now. Really."

He tugged her into his arms and kissed her, warm, sweet and lingeringly. And then he slowly pulled away, his eyes sparking with heat. She stood there, a little befuddled, while he began putting the milk and eggs in the refrigerator.

"Hey, no slacking," Merrick said as he came through the door.

She blinked and then looked down at the still-full sack in front of her. Things had changed. Big-time changed. After six months of treating her with the utmost care and patience, suddenly they were being... She wasn't even sure what it was they were being. They were still certainly careful and patient. So very gentle and loving. But now it was *different*. It was almost as if they were testing her...readiness?

Her ability to handle intimacy?

It was an insane thought, but she swore that was precisely what they were doing. And if so, *was* she ready? Or was she traumatized by something she couldn't even remember?

More importantly, and what was making her head spin right off her shoulders, was that *both* men had expressed interest. Those kisses hadn't been the kiss of a friend or acquaintance or even some affection for a woman they felt sorry for.

There may be a lot of things she couldn't remember, but passion definitely wasn't one of them. The heat that emanated from those kisses had nearly set her on fire.

But both of them?

It had occupied her thoughts enough, but she'd never breathed a single word aloud. She'd never even hinted that she'd had such a ridiculous thought.

She'd kept her ache secret and buried so deep that only she knew what had weighed so heavily on her mind.

She knew she had feelings for both men. Complex feelings. Some of which she didn't even understand. All she knew was that it wasn't something so simple as gratitude or attachment to the men who'd saved her. Nor was she latched onto them solely because she felt safe with them.

She *wanted* to be with them. *Both* of them. But never, ever had she imagined such a thing possible. She would have never brought it up, so afraid was she that it would ruin everything.

But now it seemed that they were bringing it up in their own way. Was it possible that they'd had the same thoughts she had?

She'd written it off as crazy. Something that happened with other people. People you saw on television shows or daytime corny talk shows.

She was so scared and hopeful at the same time she wanted to burst. The more she thought about it and weighed it in her mind, the more she considered that they wouldn't both be saying the things they were saying and wouldn't be both kissing her if they didn't have some sort of plan of both being a part of her life. Her future.

Cade's hand came down on her shoulder, and then his other hand slipped underneath her chin, and he tilted it upward until she met his very worried gaze.

"Elle, you sound like you're about to hyperventilate, and you've been staring into space for several minutes. What's going on?"

Some of the haze cleared, and she stared back and then beyond him to where Merrick stood, a frown marring his face. He looked as worried as Cade did.

But the one thing she saw in both faces, in both their eyes, was something she wanted so desperately that she was afraid to even breathe for fear of losing it.

She saw something more than simple affection or worry. She saw something deeper. Something very much like...*love*.

# chapter sixteen

ELLE STARED AT THE TWO men whose gazes rested so fiercely on her, and she felt light-headed over what she was about to do.

"C-can I ask you something?" she asked, the words tumbling awkwardly from her lips.

Cade reached out and palmed the side of her face, rubbing lightly in a sweet caress.

"You can ask us anything," he said, his tone utterly serious. "There's nothing you can't say to us, Elle."

Merrick reached for her hand, tugging her forward.

"Let's go into the living room so you'll be more comfortable."

She followed Merrick, her hand still held tightly in his while Cade followed behind her, his hand to her back.

Merrick sat on the couch and pulled her down so that she'd be positioned between him and Cade. But she couldn't sit this way, having to look back and forth. She didn't want to miss a single reaction. Facial expression. This was too important. She was putting far too much on the line.

She was terrified.

She pushed herself up from the couch, despite protests from the men. For a long moment, she stood with her back turned to them as she gathered her courage and wrapped herself in its protective embrace.

Then she slowly turned back around to face her...future? It was scary and exhilarating all at the same time. She was taking a proactive step to regaining her life. Taking it back. Living it instead of *enduring* it.

"I have to know if the two of you feel, or rather reciprocate, any of what I feel for you," she said in a rush. "I know it sounds absurd. Ridiculous. I'm absolutely crazy, right?"

Before she could say anything further or continue to babble her fool head off, Cade came off the couch. He moved so quickly and was standing in front of her before she could blink.

He grasped her chin with his fingers, his mouth hovering over hers.

"You're *not* crazy," he growled.

And then he kissed her, his mouth devouring hers in a forceful, possessive manner that left her breathless.

His tongue brushed over hers, testing and tasting. He explored her lips, licking over every inch and then inward to dance over her tongue playfully and then more strongly.

Everything about the way he kissed her screamed...*mine*. Like he was putting his stamp on her and wanted her to know she belonged to him.

When he finally pulled away, she was dazed and off kilter. She stumbled back, but he caught her arm and righted her as she stared fuzzily at him and then at Merrick.

Before she knew it, he'd sat back on the couch and pulled her down onto his lap so she was facing Merrick but she was nestled firmly against Cade's chest.

Merrick's brown eyes were serious and focused as he stared back at her. Everything about Cade's posture signaled that he was every bit as serious.

"Elle, we've actually wanted to talk to you about this very subject. We just haven't known how to bring it up. The truth is..."

Merrick sucked in a deep breath, and it was then she realized that he was just as nervous as she was. Just as unsure. It baffled her, but there it was. This big, fierce man was worried over how she'd react to whatever it was they wanted to say to her.

Automatically her hand flew to his. She wanted to offer him comfort and reassurance. She curled her fingers around his and kept them laced tightly together.

"The truth is, we both care a great deal about you. You've become very important to us. You have been since the day we found you in the gun shop."

Her eyes widened, and her heart started beating faster. Could it be true that they were feeling everything she was? That they both returned her…attraction?

She was afraid to hope, but what else could he be saying? They weren't cruel men. They weren't the type to pull off some sick, twisted joke.

Cade's hand stroked down her back as he broke in.

"What Merrick is trying to say is that we want you to stay with us. Not just in the capacity as a guest or someone we're helping. We want to go beyond that. And the thing is, we both want a relationship with you. We want to see where this leads and where it takes us. Which means that the three of us would be involved. Together. You'd be with the *both* of us."

Merrick cleared his throat and plowed forward, picking up where Cade left off, almost as if they were both afraid that if they didn't state their case immediately and get it all out, she'd freak out and run screaming from the house.

If they only knew how often she'd dreamed of them saying these exact words.

"Obviously you'd be making a commitment to more than one man," Merrick said in a hesitant tone. "But we'd both be making *one* commitment. To you. And even though you would in essence be with two men, we'd absolutely be faithful to you. You would be the only woman for the both of us, and we would be the only men in your life. Are we making sense?"

There was so much worry in his voice that her heart melted. She pulled up his hand that was still tightly entwined with hers, and she kissed the rough palm. Then she turned to Cade and met his lips softly with hers.

"I understand perfectly."

"And what do you think of the idea?" Cade asked.

"I think it's something I want more than I can possibly describe," she whispered.

There was such relief in both their eyes that it weighed down on her, crushing in its intensity. Cade wrapped his arms around her, holding her so tightly against him, his lips pressed to her temple, that she could scarcely breathe.

He vibrated against her, so much nervous tension leaving him in waves that she shook with it.

She waited until he loosened his hold before drawing away so she could capture them both in her view. What she had to say next made her just as nervous, perhaps more so simply because she ventured into the unknown. Into the black hole of her past, a giant, yawning abyss that frightened her just thinking about it.

"What's wrong, baby?" Merrick asked gently. "What are you thinking?"

She inhaled sharply through her nose. "I don't know what I can give you…physically. You both know what happened to me. I know what happened to me. And yet I can't remember it. I'd like to say that since I can't remember it, it can't hurt me, but I'm nervous and a little scared. Not of you," she rushed to say. "Never of you. But my mind is already obviously protecting me. Who's to say what else might happen if those barriers are breached?"

Cade pressed another kiss to her temple and then carefully smoothed her hair behind her ear with coaxing gestures.

"We aren't in a hurry, honey. We've got all the time in the world. What do you say we take it one day at a time. See what each day brings and face it together."

She relaxed, breathing in a huge sigh of bone-melting relief. "I say that's a wonderful idea."

Merrick leaned forward to touch his lips to hers. "Cade's right, baby. We've got nothing but time. We'll get there. But for now, all we want is you with us. No guilt for taking anything we give you. No hang-ups over letting us take care of you. We're working as a unit. Together. Just the three of us."

She smiled and nodded her acceptance. "You'll let me continue helping out in the office and come to the workouts?"

"Hell yeah," Cade was quick to say. "I like having you there with us. I sure as hell don't want you going to work for someone else."

At the very mention, Merrick scowled, his face going dark. "Of course I want you with me. You're part of this. Part of us, Elle. I like having you there when I finish. I like seeing you sitting there outside the ring. But I want you there as mine. Not pretending to be with Dallas. I want you to be mine. Which means, hell no, as Cade said, we don't want you working anywhere else. Call us selfish, but we want you with us, with one of us, at all times."

She laughed, her heart soaring. "I have no intention of working for anyone else. How could I anyway? I have no driver's license. No birth certificate. No Social Security number. I officially don't exist."

Cade sobered. "Eventually we're going to have to conduct a thorough investigation into your past, honey. You need to know that. Sooner or later, we're going to have to find out who you are."

She went silent but nodded slowly. "I know," she finally said. "Maybe one day I'll be ready. For now, I just want to be…happy…and not worry about what lies in my past or what scary thing lurks around the corner."

"I think we can arrange that," Merrick said, his lips easing into a smile. "Now what about that yummy dinner you promised us?"

She laughed. "Is that all you ever think about? Food?"

He pretended to give it careful consideration. Then he grinned. "Yeah, pretty much. Sex and food. That's it for most guys, baby."

Her heart lightened. Cade relaxed against her. The awkwardness was over, and perhaps now the hard part began. Making it work. Pushing it from the realm of fantasy and fiction into real life.

Could they make such a relationship work in reality?

There was only one way to find out.

# chapter seventeen

WHEN ELLE WALKED INTO THE kitchen the next morning, she felt self-conscious, and it was automatic to be shy and reserved instead of finding that comfortable routine they'd settled into over the last several months.

But things had changed. Yesterday, they'd taken a giant leap. She couldn't say whether it was forward or not. Who knew what the future held? In order to effectively have a future, one had to embrace and come to terms with one's past.

It would be so easy to shut her eyes, shake her head and refuse to allow any part of the past in. A huge part of her didn't want to remember. She wanted to start over. In so many ways, her life had begun the day Cade and Merrick found her.

And it wasn't to say that she had nothing or was nothing without the two men. But in those awful few days between the time whatever horrible thing had happened to her and when Cade and Merrick had found her, she'd been desolate and hopeless.

They'd given her strength. And faith that she wasn't consigned to that fate forever.

She never wanted to feel the utter devastation that she'd endured when she'd awakened on the riverbank, cold and shivering, her mind a blank and filled with only one thing.

Terror.

"Mornin'," Cade called out.

Merrick paused at the blender, where he was concocting his high-protein breakfast shake that he always drank before his morning workout at his gym. He stared at her, those eyes brooding but unerringly able to ferret out the slightest shift in her mood.

"What's wrong?" Merrick asked bluntly.

Cade arched a brow, but he too was staring at her like he knew something was off.

She gave a slight grimace and trudged toward the table where she could sit and see both men.

"Nothing's wrong. I'm just a little..." She pursed her lips and then frowned. "I'm not sure what I am, to be honest. But let's face it. Yesterday was pretty heavy. I guess I'm not sure what it is I'm supposed to do now."

"Just because we laid out how we feel about you doesn't mean that things change," Cade said mildly.

She glanced over, and he'd turned to the side from the stove, his hip cocked against the edge as he held a spatula in his left hand.

"Logically, I know that. Or at least I think I do. I'm just afraid. Of so many things. Right now, I'm freaked out by my own shadow. It's hardly a time to be contemplating a serious relationship. I don't know why the both of you aren't running like hell in the other direction. What could you possibly see in me?"

Merrick's expression immediately grew stormy. Cade's brow furrowed in a clear what-the-fuck manner, and she held up her hand to stop the inevitable blowup.

"I'm not being all woe is me here, guys. I'm not even saying it to garner sympathy or to build up my ego. I'm not even spouting a bunch of crap of how I'm not worthy, and you're too good, blah blah blah. I'm being brutally honest here. I'm a complete and utter hot mess. I'm so twisted up that it could take years to untie all the knots. Why on earth would you put yourselves through this? I'm genuinely baffled."

Merrick's face softened. He dumped the now-empty blender into the sink and then walked to where she sat, taking the chair next to her. He reached for her hand, twining their fingers together.

"How do you explain why the sun rises every morning? How do you explain the stars in the sky? How do you understand why no two snowflakes are alike? Some things just are, baby. And this is one of them. I can't give you pretty, dressed-up answers that are so polished they don't even sound sincere. I can only tell you that for me, it's you. It's always going to be you and nobody else. Fuck explaining it. I don't *need* an explanation. I just need *you*."

"Not that I can do near the job he just did with that oh-so-eloquent speech," Cade said dryly. "But I'd like to put my two cents in at least."

Her chest was so tight that she wasn't certain she could take any more like what Merrick had just stunned her with. She was speechless. And her heart fluttered so wildly that she felt light-headed and dizzy. Drunk on sensation.

The hope that had sprung in the last little while had started as a slow trickle that she kept a very tight rein on. She'd feared getting ahead of herself.

But now it was all out there. It was impossible to misunderstand their intentions. They wanted her. Both of them. And God, she wanted them too.

Cade touched a finger to her cheek and tenderly traced the lines of her face, landing on the fullness of her lips, until it was all she could do not to swipe her tongue over the tip.

"A lot of what Merrick said is exactly how I feel. Maybe I fought it more than he did in the beginning because I couldn't wrap my head around how we could possibly make it work. It's not going to be easy. It's going to take the ultimate commitment from all three of us, and we'll have to work three times as hard as a couple in a traditional relationship.

"But with that said, once I stopped fighting it and allowed myself to say…what if? It was freeing. I began to think of the possibilities. I thought of how happy that I *know* we can make you. If you'll just give us that chance," he ended softly.

"But will I make *you* happy?"

"You already make us happy," Merrick said.

Cade leaned down and kissed her forehead. "I understand why you feel the way you do, honey. I get it. I really do. I know we didn't meet under the best circumstances. I know you have a lot of fears and insecurities over not knowing what's in your past, and I know you worry that you're a burden to me and Merrick and that somehow we've got it all screwed up in our heads, that we're suffering some kind of savior complex, and that's why we're so into you."

She blinked, unable to even respond to that.

"I'm right, aren't I?"

Slowly she nodded. "That's about it in a nutshell."

"Put it out of your mind," Cade said, as blunt as Merrick had been just moments earlier. "It's not remotely true. You're here with us because we want you here. There are a number of agencies we could have turned you over to. Hell, we could have just called the police and washed our hands of you months ago. But we didn't do any of that because we want you here with us, and we'll do damn near anything to persuade you that it's where you need to be."

She smiled then and reached up to take his hand, squeezing for all she was worth. "I don't know if it's where I need to be, but it's where I *want* to be."

"Good enough for me," Merrick said. "Now, I vote we stop rehashing this so we stop making ourselves crazy, and we go out and do something fun today. The weather is beautiful. It's warm, and the sun is shining."

"Oh, that sounds great," she said in a wistful tone. "But what about your workout? Shouldn't you be leaving?"

The sun wasn't even up yet. It was routine for them all to rise early so Merrick could run and be at the gym by sun up. He put in several hours on the mat, and then he'd go into the office to help Cade. In the evenings, he ran again and worked on conditioning.

Merrick leaned forward to kiss her, his lips cold from the shake he was drinking.

"Tell you what. Let me get my morning workout over with, and then we'll go do something together. Just the three of us."

"The local park is beautiful. Has a great lake where ducks gather to be fed. I could pack us a picnic lunch, and we can hang out in the sun. Bring a jacket, though. There's still a nip to the air," Cade advised.

Spring was slowly struggling to make its presence known in Grand Junction. Autumn chill had come quickly in October, as she'd well known because it had been when she'd dragged herself from the Colorado River to collapse on the bank.

It was plenty cold here, and she knew enough about the new Elle to know she wasn't used to the colder, drier climate in Western Colorado. Wherever she had come from, the temperatures were much warmer. The question was, how had she ended up here. And why?

She shook off the lingering worry and fear, determined to move forward, out of the shadows.

"That sounds great," she said, injecting the proper amount of enthusiasm into her voice.

And it *was* perfect. She'd get to spend the day with Cade and Merrick. She'd become fiercely dependent on the comfort and support they offered. They were her security blanket. As much as she hated to admit it to herself, she knew she wouldn't be where she was right now emotionally if not for the two men who'd taken her in and helped put her back together.

"Here, eat your breakfast," Cade said, handing her a plate with scrambled eggs, a blueberry muffin and bacon. "When we're done eating, we'll head down to take in Merrick's workout and then we'll come back so he can get showered and changed. I'll work on getting us something packed for lunch."

She relaxed, enjoying the simple routine they'd fallen into. Breakfast together in the mornings. Merrick's workouts in the gym. The office during the week and then evenings together with Merrick and his conditioning team and workout partners.

No, she hadn't ventured out much on her own. Yet. But she'd get there. She had every confidence that with Cade and Merrick's support, she'd regain her confidence and her certainty of her place in the world.

In a perfect world, she'd be able to do all of that on her own. She wouldn't need anyone to assert her independence. But everyone needed someone at some point, right?

She had no knowledge of the person she'd been before. The person she couldn't remember. She'd like to think that she hadn't always been this needy, insecure, clingy person she was now, and it was her hope that she could somehow find the old Elle and shed the hesitancy with which she approached everything now.

At other times, she acknowledged that she was being too hard on herself, and that given what she'd endured and God only knew what else she didn't know about, it was no surprise she wasn't ready to light the world on fire and seize the day.

"Time," she whispered. "I just need time."

"What's that, baby?" Merrick asked.

She blinked and looked up at him and then smiled at the concern brimming in his dark eyes. "Nothing. Nothing at all. Just something I needed to remind myself of."

Cade settled down on her other side, his plate piled high with food.

"Whatever it is you were worrying yourself over, let it go," he said matter-of-factly.

"I'm trying," she returned softly. "I really am."

"Good," Merrick said in his gruff voice. "Let's just enjoy the day, and tomorrow will take care of itself."

# chapter eighteen

THE BREEZE BLOWING OFF THE small lake had just enough nip to make Elle shiver, but she burrowed into the warm, fleece-lined jacket and shoved her hands into the pockets as they searched for just the right spot to set up.

It was an absolutely spectacular day. There wasn't a cloud in the sky, and deep blue spread out for as far as the eye could see. The trees had begun budding out, and green was popping through the brown of winter.

The first buds of flowers had slowly begun to unfurl, and the air was sweetly scented with the fragrance from a multitude of flowering plants and bushes.

Merrick had cut his training session short that morning, and she only felt a little guilty that she was taking him away from his regimen.

Things had been so fast and furious since his win in Las Vegas. The call had come in and the contracts signed for the title bout scheduled for late spring in Los Angeles.

His training had intensified, but along with adding sparring partners and beefing up his conditioning, promotion had taken up a huge chunk of his time.

He traveled more than he had previously, and he granted interviews and had media coverage of his training camp. And through it all, he and

Cade had tried their best to keep Elle out of the public eye.

Catherine had been invaluable, taking over a lot of the publicity for Merrick. Merrick hadn't wanted to bring in a publicist, even though most fighters in his position had an entire media team. But Merrick wanted only people he trusted around him, and so he'd kept his entourage small, and he'd continued to train quietly, drawing as little attention to himself as possible.

The people in his circle were good people. They'd made Elle feel welcome into Merrick's inner sanctum. Catherine and Dakota were just like family, and Elle knew Merrick considered them such. Other fighters in the organization had moved to Grand Junction to train with Merrick and help him prepare for the championship match. There was a lot of loyalty surrounding Merrick, and Elle liked her place among the people who'd allied themselves with the gruff warrior.

She breathed in another deep breath, enjoying the sweet-scented air.

"Oh, look, that's perfect," she said, yanking her hand out to point at a rock that jutted over the water's edge.

The huge boulder was flat on top and afforded a great place to sit and enjoy the view. She eagerly moved forward, leaving the two men behind so she could claim her spot.

She clambered up and stood, gazing over the water and to the opposite bank where mothers pushed baby strollers, there was a dad trying to get a kite up for his son, and there were a few joggers making a circle around the small lake on the worn walking path.

When she glanced back for Cade and Merrick, they were standing just below her, indulgent smiles on their faces as they watched her. She hopped down from the rock to help them spread the blanket on the bank. When the wind kicked up, curling up one of the corners, she plunked the picnic basket down to hold the blanket in place.

"What did you bring to eat?" she asked eagerly.

Merrick chuckled. "You look like a kid in a candy store, baby."

She grinned, her enthusiasm not at all dampened by his gentle teasing.

Cade drew her in to kiss her forehead and then reached to open the basket.

"I made some kick-ass sandwiches. I brought some chips and sodas, but the pièce de résistance? Fudge brownies."

"Oh my God. Gimme!"

Both men laughed, and Cade snatched the basket up before she could attack.

"Be a good girl and eat your lunch first," Cade admonished. "No dessert until you've cleaned your plate."

She elbowed him in the ribs and sat down cross-legged, a disgruntled twist to her lips.

Cade chuckled again. "Whoever says pouting doesn't work clearly hasn't seen you pout. I'd damn near give you anything with that bottom lip stuck out so prettily."

Her cheeks warmed, and then she eyed him devilishly. "Does that mean I get to eat dessert first?"

"Dive in," Cade said.

Merrick shook his head. "What a wuss. You didn't hold out five seconds against her."

Elle turned her pout on Merrick and gave him her best impression of doe eyes.

"Ahh, hell, give her the damn brownie," Merrick grumbled.

Cade burst into laughter, and then Elle followed suit. Merrick grinned good-naturedly and made a grab for one of the sandwiches.

Elle devoured the brownie first, groaning in pleasure the entire time. As she licked the last of the crumbs from her fingers, Cade held out a sandwich to her.

After eating her fill, she eyed another brownie and sighed wistfully.

"I want it, but I'm so stuffed I can't possibly eat it."

Then she yawned so broadly that she nearly cracked her jaw.

Cade smiled and patted his leg. "Lie down for a while. Take a nap in the sun. You can eat the brownie when you wake up."

She reclined between him and Merrick, resting her head on Cade's thigh and propping her feet over Merrick's lap. Cade ran his fingers through her hair, smoothing the strands in a soothing rhythm.

Contentment eased through her veins, warming her from the inside out. A lazy, lethargic sensation took hold, a gentle lullaby that had her eyelids fluttering with the effort to stay awake.

Cade's palm descended over her forehead, and he traced lines from her temple over the curve of her cheek. She lost the battle and closed her eyes, sinking further into the darkness that awaited.

She dreamed of a beach. Warm sand beneath her feet. Waves lapping at her toes. And she was happy. Laughing and smiling.

Firm hands gripped her waist and then went to her arms, sliding down their length until they captured her hands.

There was power in his hold. And it was a man. Someone she knew intimately. She could see the muscles ripple in his chest and forearms. How broad his shoulders were.

And then he kissed her. Hard, deep. Like he knew everything there was to know about her and how she loved to be touched. His hands roamed freely over her body, possessive and demanding.

She wasn't afraid. She welcomed his touch. She wanted more.

She looked up, straining to make out his features. To put a face to this nameless man who knew her so intimately. She squinted against the sun, blinking as he pushed in close to once again claim her mouth.

*I love you.*

She came awake, gasping as the words echoed through her mind. She'd been thinking them. That she loved this man. Someone who was no more than a stranger to her. Or was he? Was he someone from her past?

"Elle? Elle? Are you all right?"

Cade's voice broke through the haze of confusion surrounding her. She pushed herself upward, warding off his and Merrick's hands and instead wrapping her arms protectively around her waist, hugging herself tight.

She climbed onto the rock, seeking the warmth of the stone surface as she huddled, knees drawn to her chest, staring out over the water.

What had the dream meant? Had it even been real? Was it a memory tucked away in the dark recesses of her mind, or was it just a dream and nothing more?

She touched her forehead to her knees and closed her eyes, trying to recapture the images from the dream. If she only knew what he looked like. What his name was.

"Elle, baby, talk to us, please," Merrick said just beside her. "Tell us what's going on. Did you have a bad dream? Did you remember something?"

How could she say no, it wasn't a bad dream. It was a *good* dream. She'd been happy. Full of joy and love.

"I don't know," she whispered. "I don't know if it was real."

"Tell us what it is so we can help you sort it out," Cade said.

"I wasn't afraid," she choked out. "I don't know if it was a memory or just a random dream."

"Then why did it upset you so much?" Merrick persisted. "Elle, can you look at us, baby?"

She kept her head down, hot tears sliding down her cheeks. She was a complete head case. Why would such a happy dream cause her so much distress? Shouldn't she be relieved that someone out there had cared about her? That she'd cared about someone else?

But if she'd been so damn happy, and this man in her dream had cared about her and knew her so intimately, then why had she blocked him out, and why wasn't he looking for her?

She wiped at her cheeks, not wanting them to see her crying. The muttered curses that echoed so close to her told her she hadn't been successful.

Strong arms surrounded her, pulling her in close. Merrick tucked her head underneath his chin and rubbed his hand in a small circle over her back.

Disgusted with herself, she muttered, "I ruined the whole day."

"No you didn't," Merrick said quietly. "We still have the day. You slept an hour. Not long at all. We can do whatever you want. If you want to go home, just say the word."

She shook her head. "I want to stay here with you and Cade. It's a beautiful day. I don't want it ruined because I'm a basket case."

"Shhh," he admonished. "Just sit here a while until you get your bearings."

Slowly she raised her head up and gazed over to where Cade stood just beside the rock she and Merrick were sitting on. He was holding a brownie.

Staring at the offering, she teared up all over again. She had the two most wonderful men in the world, and it shouldn't matter to her who she'd dreamed about.

That was her past. These men were her present. And her future. They were who mattered. Not some faceless, nameless ghost in her past. Someone who could have been the person who'd raped and tried to kill her.

"Don't cry," Cade said in a low voice. "You're going to kill me, sweetheart."

She took the brownie and sent him a watery smile. "Thank you. I love the brownies."

"And I love you," Cade said simply.

Her eyes widened, and she stared agape at his blunt declaration.

Taking advantage of her lapse in speech, he leaned in and kissed her lips.

How it must look to others, her snuggled firmly into Merrick's embrace while Cade kissed her.

She didn't care.

All she cared about was those three little words. Words so sweet that they echoed through her mind.

"Do you mean it?" she whispered, pulling away so they were just a breath apart.

He touched her face and then ran his thumb across her swollen bottom lip. "I don't make a habit of saying shit I don't mean."

She kissed him again. This time she was the aggressor, going in to claim his mouth. She tasted the chocolate on his tongue, absorbed the heat of his lips. Deeper and deeper until she was drowning in…desire.

It hit her with speed that surprised her. After so much fear, so much hesitation. So much worry that she'd never be able to be intimate with him and Merrick.

She'd responded to them both emotionally. But physically? She enjoyed their kisses. Soaked up their touch like a parched desert desperate for rain. But she hadn't felt the razor-sharp edge of desire, the yearning so deep in her body that it was nearly painful and yet so wonderfully good all at the same time.

Her nipples tightened. Her breasts ached. A pulse began between her legs that had her squirming to alleviate the tension.

When Cade drew away, he was breathing hard, and his eyes were glazed with the same passion she was experiencing. And still, there was a heavy layer of tension between them. The thick, pulsing arc of electricity that vibrated through the air.

Merrick's hand coaxed up her back eliciting a bone-deep shiver. She was hyper aware. It was as if her body had left its latent stage and shed every ounce of fear and reluctance. She recognized, in Cade and Merrick, men she could trust. And did trust. Her mind knew it, but her body had been slower to respond.

"I'd like to go home now," she said, her voice laced with the hum of arousal they couldn't possibly miss.

Cade held out his hand. "Come on then. Let's go home."

# chapter ninteen

ELLE SLID HER HAND INTO Merrick's as they walked back toward the SUV while Cade carried the picnic basket and walked on her other side.

Cade popped the back of the SUV and tossed the basket in, just as Elle caught a glimpse of a uniformed police officer walking in their direction.

She froze, her heart speeding up until it was pounding like a jackhammer. Her hands grew clammy, and sweat popped out on her forehead until it was slick, and she got an overwhelming feeling of sickness in her belly.

Merrick looked at her, brows furrowed, and he was about to say something when the police officer called out to them.

"Cade! Merrick! Hey, how are you guys?"

Merrick and Cade both swiveled in the direction of the cop and offered welcoming smiles.

"Hey, Greg, how's it going?" Cade offered as he extended his hand to shake the other man's.

Panic scuttled up Elle's spine until she was literally shaking. Her knees threatened to buckle, and she stood, stock-still, praying to be taken away from the situation.

Merrick shoved forward to shake the cop's hand but inserted his body between her and Greg so she was hidden from view.

Cold crept over her, leaving her numb and so scared that she couldn't process the simplest thought. The three men conversed. Exchanged pleasantries. Greg enthusiastically offered his opinion that Merrick was going to kick Lash's ass. It went on and on until the world spun in a crazy circle around her.

*Stupid, interfering bitch. You just had to stick your nose where it didn't belong. He can't save you this time. You're a dead woman. But first I'm going to have you so that the last face you see is mine while I fuck you like the whore you are.*

Her stomach heaved, and she locked her jaw so she didn't fall apart right here in the middle of the parking lot.

She wasn't going to be able to hold it together for much longer. She yanked her head around, desperately searching for a place she could be sick in private. Everything she'd eaten at lunch had bunched into a tight ball and weighed a ton in her stomach.

Saliva pooled in her mouth, and when she swallowed it back, it made her even more nauseated.

No longer able to maintain any semblance of normalcy, she broke and made a run for the public bathrooms that were about fifty yards away.

She burst inside, uncaring of who was there or if anyone could see her. She yanked open a stall and barely made it to the toilet before she was violently ill.

Her stomach convulsed and heaved. She shuddered over and over, the retching still continuing even when she'd emptied her stomach of its contents.

The door flew open, and Merrick pushed inside the bathroom, his hands immediately going to her hair as he pulled it away from her face.

He didn't say anything. Thank God. He just stood there, his hand on her back, rubbing a soothing pattern until finally she stopped the horrible gagging and her stomach unknotted.

Her knees buckled, and she would have hit the floor, but Merrick caught her, anchoring her to his side as he helped her from the stall. He guided her toward the sink, where he wet several paper towels and applied them to her face.

Then he handed her a bottle of water and said, "Here. Rinse your mouth out."

She did as he instructed, numb to everything else. She performed robotically, like she was a programmable thing. Then she folded her arms over the sink and lowered her head to her wrists, resting there as she took in huge gulps of air.

"What the fuck is going on, Elle?"

Cade's low voice cut through the horrific buzzing in her head.

"Sorry," she croaked. "Just want to go home. Is he gone?"

She picked her head up long enough to see Merrick and Cade exchange quick glances.

"Baby, Greg is a friend. He doesn't know a thing about you, and he won't. You have our word on that. He just wanted to shoot the shit a minute," Merrick offered.

Frustration was sharp and consuming. "Logically I know that. I *do*. I told you I'm a mess. I tried to warn you about what you're getting into."

"Stop. Just stop," Cade said sharply.

She went silent, her eyes widening at the look on his face.

"Now take a deep breath for me and relax."

She inhaled deeply through her nose and let it out her mouth in a noisy rush.

"That's better. Now, let us worry about what we're getting into," he said in a calm tone. "Merrick and I are big boys. We know what we're doing. Stop worrying about what we think or feel and concentrate on what's scaring the hell out of you so bad. Can you remember anything at all? Anything that we can use to help you?"

She shook her head, despair creeping over her shoulders, slumping them downward with its weight. "Just him. Again. And words. What he said to me. Oh God. He hated me. He wanted to punish me. He told me he'd kill me but first he was going to fuck me like the whore I was so that the last face I saw was his as he raped me."

"Son of a bitch," Cade swore, fury laced in every word.

"Can you picture him?" Merrick asked gently. "Can you remember anything that would help us identify him?"

Panic slammed into her, nearly knocking her to her knees. She shook her head violently, refusing to remember, not wanting to remember. God, if she put a face to the monster, then she'd never rid herself of that image. Of him over her, hurting her, violating her and hating her with every breath.

"It'll come," Merrick said quietly. "When you're ready, it'll come."

She nodded slowly, taking in the words and holding them like a talisman. Even as a voice whispered in the back of her mind that she didn't want it to come. She never wanted it to come. What would it solve? And who would believe her if she could remember him? If she sought justice for what he'd done, if she could actually put a face and a name to her attacker, who would take the word of an amnesiac who had a tenuous hold on her sanity?

Damned if she did. Damned if she didn't. All she wanted was to forget. Or rather not remember, since she had nothing to forget except those words. Such hate-filled words. Was it someone she knew? Had someone she'd trusted betrayed her? Or had it been a random act of violence?

No. It couldn't be random. The man knew her. He'd said he wanted what *he* was having. Some other man. Her lover? Boyfriend? Husband?

Oh God, the idea of having a husband filled her with panic all over again. How could she commit to Cade and Merrick when she didn't even know if she was already legally committed to another man?

Cade pulled her into his arms and hugged her tightly. It was purely comforting. There was nothing sexual about his hold. It told her more than words that he was there and that he wasn't going anywhere and that she could get through anything with his and Merrick's help.

She grabbed on to that silent promise.

"Let's go home now," he said gently. "I think you've had enough excitement for one day."

She nodded her agreement. Just the idea of being back in the place she felt so safe bolstered her spirits.

Single file, her lodged between Cade and Merrick, she walked out of the bathroom. Once outside, they adjusted so they flanked her on either side as they strode toward the truck.

Merrick opened the door for her, and she slid into the front seat, next to Cade. Merrick climbed in back, and Cade wasted no time pulling out of the parking lot.

She sighed in relief and rested her head against the window, closing her eyes as they drove away from the beauty of the lake. Some things were more beautiful for what they offered. The modest home that Cade and Merrick shared was the most beautiful spot in the world to her. It stood for all the things she needed most.

Comfort. Security. Protection.

Love.

Her sanctuary. Her place to just be. No questions. No demands. No intrusion from the outside world.

Cade reached for her hand, but she didn't react. He curled his fingers tightly around hers and squeezed. A simple reminder that he had her back. She squeezed back, sending him the silent thank you.

He loved her.

It was almost too much to comprehend. How could he love her? He didn't even know the real her. What if he didn't like the real Elle? What if the old Elle was someone nothing like the new Elle?

What if she remembered everything tomorrow and discovered she was a terrible person?

She couldn't lose Cade and Merrick. No matter what or who she was in the past, it was never too late to be someone else. Was it?

Bone deep weariness assailed her. She felt as wrung out as an old dishrag. There was nothing more she wanted than to stumble into bed and stay there. She wanted to forget today ever happened. Wanted to wipe the dream from her mind and memory and to erase the horrible panic she'd endured when the police officer had walked her way.

Even now, a curl of nausea twisted her stomach into knots all over again.

When they rolled up in the driveway, she opened her door, desperate to be out and to go inside, close the door and shut herself off from the rest of the world.

She knew she was in huge denial of her situation. She knew that this wasn't a long-term solution to her problem. But she wasn't equipped to deal with her past right now. Maybe down the road. But not now.

"I want to go lie down," she murmured as Cade and Merrick followed her inside.

Merrick touched her clammy face, frowning as he drew his hand away. But he didn't say anything. Just simply nodded and then leaned forward to press a kiss to her forehead.

"I'll check in on you later," he said.

She nodded and walked down the hall to the small bedroom she occupied. Not even bothering to undress, she crawled beneath the covers and curled her knees to her chest so she was in a protective ball. She pulled the covers to her chin and closed her eyes, praying she wouldn't dream.

# chapter twenty

MERRICK SAT IN THE DARKNESS, brooding silently as he listened to the rain patter against the roof. A weather system had moved in—a cold front—in the latter portion of the afternoon while Elle was sleeping.

Today he'd done something he'd never done. He'd cancelled a training session. Dakota had called, worried. And then Catherine had called on her husband's heels. He'd known, though, that he ran the risk of being injured if he sparred because his concentration was shot to hell. He was focused on the woman curled up in the bed in the next room.

He'd checked in on her twice, worried that she'd remained sequestered in her room. But each time, she'd been deeply asleep. She hadn't so much as moved from the spot she'd curled up in.

He didn't know what to do or if there was anything *to* be done. He was tired of the patience route. He wasn't one to sit around and spout psychological bullshit. Elle was on the verge of cracking, and he was helpless to do anything but sit and watch.

Maybe he and Cade were wrong to discount her fears of her past. It was easy to say her past didn't matter and that they were her future. But the truth was, until they knew exactly what was in her past, they had no idea what they were dealing with.

And if she'd been in trouble with the police, they could have a clusterfuck on their hands.

A noise in the hallway alerted him, and he turned his head to look over his shoulder to see Elle shuffling toward the kitchen.

"Finally awake, sleepyhead?" he called out in a teasing voice that he hoped covered his relief at seeing her.

She ignored him and continued on, disappearing from view. There was something off about her. The way she walked. She never even reacted to his voice, and if she hadn't been aware of his presence, he should have startled her.

Frowning, he pushed himself up from the armchair and started toward the kitchen only to hear the door slam shut.

What the hell?

He charged into the kitchen only to find Elle gone. He glanced toward the door and saw the silhouette of her body heading through the garage.

"What the ever-loving fuck," he muttered.

He yanked open the door just in time to see Elle walk from the confines of the garage straight out into the rain.

"Elle! Elle!" he yelled.

He sprinted out of the garage, flinching when the cold rain pelted his face. Elle had stopped at the end of the walkway and stared sightlessly into the street. God, what if he hadn't been up to see her walk out of the house? She could have been killed!

He grasped her shoulders and steered her back toward the house. She blinked in surprise and then seemed to come back to reality.

She stared up at him, rain sluicing down her face. Her hair was bedraggled and soaked through.

"Merrick?" she asked in confusion. "Why are we standing in the rain?"

She looked down, holding her arms out as her clothing dripped water, and then back up at him in bewilderment.

"Come on, let's get you back inside," he said in a grim voice.

He herded her back through the garage and into the kitchen.

"Stay right where you are. Let me grab a towel."

He ducked into the small laundry room and pulled a towel from the dryer. When he returned to Elle, she was shivering, partly from cold, but she seemed to be in shock.

He wrapped the towel around her and rubbed vigorously.

"We need to get you out of these clothes and into a hot shower."

She allowed him to lead her toward the bathroom. Her expression was still mostly blank, as if she had no idea what had just transpired. He sat her down on the closed toilet seat and then turned on the shower.

"What happened, Elle?" he asked as he started removing her shirt.

He hoped if he could get her talking that she wouldn't focus on the fact that he was stripping her down to nothing. He didn't want her to freak out, and it was entirely possible given her current emotional state.

"I don't know," she said blankly. "The last thing I remember is going to bed and then suddenly I was standing in the rain with you in front of me."

Merrick cursed. "Never known anyone who sleepwalked, but it sure as hell sounds like that's what happened."

"Why on earth would I walk out of the house?"

Her voice shook, and he could see how freaked out she was over the idea of just walking out without realizing it.

"That I don't know, baby. You scared the hell out of me. God only knows what could have happened if I hadn't been up and seen you walk out the door."

Reaction set in on him about the same time it hit her. His hands shook as he pulled her up to peel down her wet pants. He and Cade would have woken up and found her gone, and they may never have found her again.

Or she could have been killed or seriously injured.

Or she could have simply walked away and kept on walking.

"Slip out of your panties," he said in a gentle voice. "We need to get you in the shower and warmed up. You need help, or can you make it on your own?"

She glanced down and remained still for a long moment. "I can do it," she finally murmured.

"Okay, but I'm staying right here. I'll get another dry towel and a change of clothes for you, but then I'll be back."

She nodded and stepped into the shower, flinching when the hot water hit her cold skin.

When he was certain she wasn't going to take a header in the shower, he quickly left the bathroom to get the towel and something for her to wear. He hesitated outside of Cade's bedroom a moment, pondering whether to wake his friend.

It wasn't that he couldn't handle the situation with Elle, but if they were going to be in this together, Cade needed to know. Merrick would be pissed as hell if this had happened while he'd been sleeping and Cade hadn't woke him up.

And there was the fact that Cade could brew a pot of hot coffee while Elle was in the shower. Then maybe they could sit down together and hash this out.

He knocked on Cade's door and then stuck his head in. Cade stirred and stuck his head up, his eyes blurry with sleep.

"What's up?" Cade asked.

"I'll explain more later, but I need you to put on some coffee so we can warm Elle up. She was sleepwalking in the rain. I have her in the shower now."

Cade was up in an instant. "What the fuck?"

"Yeah, that was my reaction," Merrick muttered.

Cade dragged on a pair of sweats and was throwing on a T-shirt when Merrick ducked back out of the bedroom.

He entered the bathroom to see Elle standing under the spray, her head down, eyes closed. Her face was contorted as if whatever she was thinking was causing her pain.

He hated the helplessness of the situation. His helplessness. He'd do anything in the world to help her, and yet there was no way for him to take away whatever private hell she was enduring.

His worst fear was of losing her. And hell, he didn't even really have her yet. Not fully. And it had nothing to do with the fact that he hadn't touched her sexually or made love to her. Fuck all that. He didn't need a physical relationship with her to feel like what they had was real.

He didn't have her fully yet because her past still had a firm hold on her mind. Though he didn't doubt one bit her desire to commit to him and Cade, he knew she couldn't fully do so until she'd resolved what had happened to her.

And he wanted her. More than he'd ever wanted another woman.

Realizing that it was likely she'd stand there in the shower in whatever daze she was currently in all night, he reached in to turn off the water.

When his hand closed over her shoulder, her skin was hot and flushed. Her eyes flew open, and she gave him a startled look before relaxing when she realized it was him.

"Come on, baby," he said in as gentle a voice as he could manage. "Let me dry you off."

He helped her over the edge of the tub and made sure her feet hit the bath rug so she wouldn't slip. Then he briskly rubbed her down with the towel before wrapping her dripping hair in it and arranging it atop her head.

"I got you something to wear. Can you manage on your own?"

She nodded, nearly toppling the towel from her head. He righted it and motioned to the pair of sweats and the T-shirt on the counter.

"Cade and I will be in the living room. He made fresh coffee. Come on out when you're dressed, and we'll talk."

She grimaced but nodded. Her arms had crept up to her waist, and she wrapped them protectively around herself as she stood naked and vulnerable to his gaze.

Not wanting to make her any more uncomfortable, he averted his eyes and then backed from the bathroom, though the image of her standing in the shower, water running down her sleek body, was still firmly imprinted in his mind.

Cade was pacing the living room floor when Merrick appeared. When Cade saw Merrick, he pulled up abruptly, his face a cloud of concern.

"What the hell is going on? You said she was sleepwalking. In the fucking *rain*?"

Merrick blew out his breath. "I was up. Couldn't sleep. Guess I was worried about her. I checked in on her twice, but each time, she was sleeping soundly. I was sitting in the chair over there and heard her come down the hall. I called out to her but she kept walking. Next thing I know she's out the kitchen door, through the garage and standing out by the street. I don't even want to know what could have happened if I hadn't been up."

Cade let a vehement string of curses fly. "Maybe I should call Dallas."

"That might be a good idea," Merrick said grimly. "This is beyond my scope. I don't know how to help her, Cade."

Cade went quiet, his gaze moving beyond Merrick. Merrick turned to see Elle walk into the living room, her feet bare, and she was shivering.

Merrick was at her side instantaneously, his arm going around her. "Come sit on the couch and get warm."

Cade was there with a blanket as Elle settled against the cushions. She tucked her feet underneath her, and Cade arranged the throw securely around her body. Then Cade perched on the couch next to her, worry creasing his brow.

"What happened, Elle?" Cade asked.

She closed her eyes for a moment, and when she opened them, they were swamped with confusion and fear.

"I don't know," she said helplessly. "I don't remember anything except waking up outside in the rain when Merrick shook me."

"Were you having a bad dream?" Merrick asked. "Think about it. Try to remember."

She frowned, her lips pursing in concentration. "I remember a badge. And bright sunlight. It glinted in the sun."

She broke off abruptly, her hand going to her forehead. Her fingers shook badly as she rubbed over her eye.

"Elle?" Cade asked gently. "What is it? What do you remember?"

Her hand slowly dropped, delving below the blanket to touch her hip through the sweats she was wearing.

"I remember the badge digging into my hip while he…"

Her voice broke off in a sob, and her hands flew to her face to stifle the escaping sound.

She hated the feeling of helplessness that assaulted her the moment she thought back on that awful dream—the awful *memory*. It wasn't a dream. It had really happened. To her. She'd been violated. Held down, helpless, while a man forced himself on her. Had hated her. Had every intention of killing her. He'd tried to kill her. He'd shot her.

What could she have done to inspire such animosity? She couldn't fathom that kind of hatred. Couldn't imagine having done anything to deserve something that awful. But what woman did? No one deserved to be raped. It wasn't a woman's fault. There was no excuse for a man to violate a woman, no matter how angry he was. No matter what the perceived sin of the woman.

Logically she knew that, and yet she still couldn't wrap her mind around it all. There had to be a reason, didn't there? But no. Women were raped all the time for no other reason than a man wanted to exert his power, that he wanted to degrade and punish her.

The fault wasn't with her. She knew that. And yet she couldn't get past the idea that she'd done something to warrant a man raping and trying to kill her.

Cade slid his hand around her nape and pulled her head to his chest. She shook violently against him, and she heard the low curses from both Cade and Merrick. She heard the worry in their voices, and the anger. Not at her. But at what had happened to her and the grip her past still had on her even though she couldn't remember it.

"It's okay, honey. You're with us. It's okay to remember. He can't hurt you now. Talk it out if you want. We're here. We'll listen."

"I don't *want* to remember," she said, her voice muffled by Cade's shirt.

Merrick sighed, his heart softening at the vulnerability in her voice. He ran his finger up her bare arm and rubbed his knuckle back down in a soothing manner.

"I don't claim to understand what you've been through, baby. I won't insult you by saying I do. But I *do* understand why you don't want to remember. I get that. But I also know that this is like a festering wound, and it's not going to go away. At some point, we have to face it. Together. And you need to know that Cade and I are going to be here to help you in any way we can."

She picked up her head and met his gaze, her eyes burning with emotion.

"I think..." She licked her lips nervously and glanced back at Cade before returning once more to Merrick. She seemed to be waging a horrific war with herself, not just over the dreams and memories that tormented her, but over the here and now and about what she was about to say. "That is, I'm pretty sure I love you both. And I've battled with myself until I'm exhausted over it. I keep thinking that I *can't* love you. That I can't love *two* people. That the very *last* thing I can offer someone in my current emotional state is love. I keep questioning whether my feelings are real or whether they're the result of you saving me and taking me in. But they feel real. I *want* them to be real."

Merrick was momentarily struck speechless. Cade was no less affected by the sudden declaration.

She looked distressed as she continued on. Not at all like a woman should look when she'd just confessed her love for a man. She was clearly nervous and unsettled and seemingly anxious to get her point across before they could respond.

The words tumbled out of her mouth, so fast he could barely keep up.

"And I know you're wondering what that has to do with what happened tonight or, well, anything, but it has *everything* to do with it, because I don't want to remember my past because I'm terrified that it could come between me and the two of you. It's a fear I live with *every single day*."

When she would have continued on, Cade took her hand, engulfing it in his much larger grasp. "Elle, I don't give a shit about your past other than the fact that it's a source of pain and emotional stress for you."

Merrick was still reeling from the powerful words she'd uttered. He couldn't seem to get his mouth to work, and he couldn't afford to screw this up. He *had* to get this *right*.

"Elle."

Her name came out barely a whisper, and he had to clear his throat so he didn't croak the rest of the words.

The weight of emotion in her gaze took his breath away. She looked... scared. As if she'd taken the biggest risk of her life by blurting out those words.

Viewed from her eyes, it had to be terrifying to lay so much on the line when she had no past, nowhere to go, no one but him and Cade to rely on.

In the end, there was no deep, drawn-out explanation. There was nothing to say to her but the utter truth in all its simplicity.

"Ahh, baby, I love you too," he said hoarsely.

He framed her face in his hands, rubbing the pads of his thumbs over her cheekbones. The relief was crushing in her eyes. Her entire body sagged, and then she turned her mouth into his hand to press a kiss to his palm.

"Do you mean it?" she whispered.

He could barely form the words. He was too shaken by the emotion welling in his chest. When had he ever felt so much for another person? It was a completely new experience for him. Nothing had prepared him for this. It *undid* him. He was tough. Strong. A mixed martial arts fighter. He could take apart a man in the ring without remorse. He could lock his emotions away until they were encased in stone. But this slip of a woman unraveled him as no other person had ever even come close to.

"I love you," he said more firmly, knowing he owed her conviction. "I think I fell hard on my ass for you the very first time I laid eyes on you."

She glanced nervously at Cade, her teeth sinking into her bottom lip as she took in his reaction to the scene unfolding.

Cade stroked her hair with one hand. Then his gaze met Merrick's, and there was determination there.

"We're okay with this, Elle," Cade said in a firm but gentle voice. "This isn't something we've approached lightly. I don't want you to ever think we did. You're important to us both. You mean everything to us. You don't have to walk on eggshells around us for fear of pissing one of us off because you think you left one of us out."

She reached for Cade's hand, pulling it to her mouth to kiss the inside as she'd done to Merrick.

"I love you."

Cade's eyes softened. He seemed to melt right there on the couch. He cupped her face and leaned in, angling his mouth over hers to apply gentle pressure with his lips.

"I love you too, sweetheart. We're going to get through this. I promise."

Her eyes glittered with unshed tears, and Merrick could tell she was battling for control.

"I don't know what to do," she choked out. "I don't know how to fix me. I wish I did."

"Shhh," Cade said as he kissed her again. "I'm going to call Dallas and see what he has to say. He may can offer insight or at least address the sleep issue."

She hesitated, opened her mouth as if to say something and then closed it again.

"What is it?" Merrick asked.

"Maybe... Maybe it would be better if one of you slept with me. In case it happens again."

"I think that's a very good idea," Cade said.

He glanced up at Merrick as he said the next words, as if he were checking Merrick's reaction.

"I think it would be best if you slept between us. No way for you to slip out of bed if you have to crawl over one of us."

Merrick nodded immediately. Elle looked relieved. She rubbed her hands up and down her legs, pressing tightly against the sweats.

"Call Dallas," she said in a quiet voice. "I want to fix this, no matter what I have to do. I want to be able to move forward."

# chapter twenty-one

ELLE HAD A RELAXED RELATIONSHIP with Dallas. He checked in on her regularly, even calling the guys for frequent updates. Since having a regular doctor was out of the question when she didn't even know who she was, Dallas had taken over her care as well as Merrick's.

If she had an ailment or needed an exam, Cade and Merrick brought her in after work hours and Dallas would see her in his clinic.

Tonight, he was making a house call.

Merrick had called him, concern vibrating in his voice as he'd asked Dallas to come over. It was no wonder Dallas showed as quickly as he did after hearing the way Merrick sounded.

Dallas listened first to Merrick's account of how Elle had walked out of the house in her sleep. Then he talked to Elle, and she told him of the dreams and of hearing her attacker's voice. The badge and how it had dug into her skin. She didn't even realize she rubbed her hip the entire time she was recounting the story.

Dallas put his hand over hers. "As you heal, you can likely expect more of your memory to return. And by heal, I mean emotionally. Sometimes the mind takes much longer to recover than the body, and I certainly believe that to be the case in your situation."

She nodded because she agreed with him there. There were days she didn't feel like she'd ever truly get beyond the barriers to her past.

"Don't fight it. Let it happen naturally. But don't push yourself to remember either," he advised. "Be patient. You'll remember when you're ready."

"And what can I do about the sleepwalking?" she asked. "Do you think it's just a freak occurrence? To my knowledge, it's never happened before."

"I'll write you a prescription for something to help you sleep. Sometimes the mind doesn't shut off just because the rest of you does. Cade and Merrick will be watching you a lot more closely from now on, so I have confidence that I won't have to worry about you walking into the streets," he said with a smile.

"Thank you," she said sincerely. "You're a good friend, Dallas."

His features softened. "I don't want you to be too hard on yourself, Elle. You've been through a lot, and you can't expect to just bounce right back from that. Cut yourself some slack, and lean on Cade and Merrick."

She smiled for the first time since the guys had taken her on the picnic. "I plan to. I promise. They're pretty good boulders to prop on."

"Boulders?" Cade asked. He glanced at Merrick. "Were we just insulted?"

The two men stood in the background, silently observing Dallas as he spoke with Elle. Until now. They moved forward as Dallas completed his discussion with Elle.

"What do you think, Dallas?" Merrick asked in a serious tone.

Dallas sighed. "This isn't my area of expertise. I'd like to be able to do a CT scan just to check for any damage to her brain, but for obvious reasons, that's not possible. In all likelihood, it's a simple matter of her mind protecting her from the horror she endured at her attacker's hands. Will she ever remember? I can't say. It's probably dependent on her *desire* to remember."

Her cheeks flushed, and she ducked her head. They all knew she didn't want to remember. She'd been brutally honest about that fact.

"So I'm standing in the way of my own recovery," she said quietly.

Dallas shook his head. "I stand by my assertion that you'll remember when you're ready. It's only been seven months, Elle. That's not very long. It takes many women years to come to terms with being raped. We don't even know what else you went through."

She blew out her breath and nodded her understanding.

He pulled out a prescription pad and scribbled down an order for medication. But then he took another blank sheet, flipped it over and scrawled something over the paper.

"I'm giving you the name of a therapist. She's a friend of mine, and I'll only contact her if you give me permission. I trust her, and she'd be someone good for you to talk to. Maybe she can help you more than I can."

"Thanks," she said softly. "I'll consider it."

Dallas touched her cheek and then rose. "Time for me to head home. I'm due at work in just a few hours."

"Thanks for coming by, Dallas," Merrick said. "We appreciate it."

"Not a problem," Dallas returned. "I'll see you all later. Call me if anything pops up or if you have any concerns."

"Will do," Cade promised.

Elle watched as Merrick walked Dallas out to his car, and then she sagged back onto the couch, closing her eyes.

She was a complete clusterfuck—to borrow one of the guys' favorite expressions. It was certainly an appropriate term for her life and her situation.

It made her head hurt to think of all the ways she wasn't able to give Cade and Merrick what they deserved. But she needed what they gave to *her*. It was the only thing keeping her together. If it weren't for them, she would have shattered a long time ago.

"What do you say we try to grab a few hours of sleep before we have to get up for Merrick's training and work?" Cade asked as they waited for Merrick to return.

She nodded, too tired to even voice the words.

He extended his hand down to Elle's.

"Come on, sweetheart. It's been one hell of a day. Let's get you into bed and between me and Merrick, which is just where you belong."

# chapter twenty-two

ELLE STARED DUBIOUSLY AT THE medicine bottle that Cade had picked up from the pharmacy and then quietly shoved it into the bathroom drawer. In the few days since the sleepwalking episode, she'd been leery of taking medication. So far, there hadn't been a reoccurrence of the event, and unless there was, she wanted to stay away from drug-induced sleeps.

The guys had moved her into Cade's room, though she still kept her clothes in the spare bedroom. Even the toiletries she'd kept in the hall bathroom had now been moved to the ensuite bathroom in Cade's bedroom.

After checking her appearance, she straightened the camisole pajama top and then smoothed her hands down the soft, cotton bottoms.

Most people thought in terms of forever. She was on a day-to-day basis, afraid to look further than the present for fear of what the future held.

It was disconcerting to have no past or future and not to know what more than a few hours would bring.

There was a soft knock on the bathroom door.

"Elle? Honey, everything okay in there?"

She opened the door to Cade, who loomed just outside, and offered him a smile.

"Just fine. Was brushing my teeth."

He swept his mouth over hers, tasting the mint from the toothpaste. "Ready for bed?"

She let him lead her to the king-size bed, and she crawled up, positioning herself in the middle.

"Where's Merrick?" she asked, not seeing him.

"He's showering in the other bathroom."

Cade slid in next to her and held out his arm. Accepting the silent invitation, she snuggled into his embrace, seeking the warmth and comfort of his chest.

"Take your medicine?" he asked.

She hesitated. "No. I didn't want it."

Cade sighed. "There's nothing wrong with taking the pills. If they help you sleep better and keep you from sleepwalking or putting yourself in a dangerous situation, you should take them."

"We'll see how it goes," she said. "If... If I need them, I'll take them."

He kissed her temple. "Fair enough."

Merrick walked into the bedroom toweling his hair dry. He was wearing boxers and no shirt, and she stared, mesmerized by the beauty of his physique.

He tossed aside the towel, ran his hand over his head and then turned back for the light switch.

"Ready for lights-out?" Merrick asked.

"Yeah," Cade replied.

Merrick hit the switch, dousing the room in darkness, and then the bed dipped beside Elle as Merrick climbed in next to her.

It was instinctive to move from Cade's embrace to Merrick's. She molded her body against the hard contours of Merrick's chest and nestled her head underneath his chin.

She loved the feeling of being securely between the two men. She'd slept better the last few nights than she had since she'd come here.

She turned over, pressing her back to Merrick's chest. He put his hand over her belly and anchored her firmly against him, pulling her behind into his groin.

In the dark, she reached for Cade, her hand sliding up his arm until she was touching both men. Cade took her hand, pulled it up to his mouth and pressed his lips warmly to her fingers.

"I love you," she whispered.

"Love you too, sweetheart," Cade said, his breath blowing over her forehead.

She'd very nearly drifted off when the peal of a cell phone startled her fully awake. Behind her, Merrick let out a curse and sat up, turning the lamp on.

"Goddamn it. Not tonight."

Cade's phone went off, and he reached to pick it up.

"Alarm's gone off at Bo's dealership. We better get down there to check it out. Might want to call this one in ahead of time."

Elle shook the sleep fuzz from her head and pushed herself up into a cross-legged position.

"I don't think we should leave Elle alone," Merrick said bluntly. "I'll go. You stay with her."

Cade held up his hand. "You aren't going alone. Call it in and let the police deal with it."

"The alarms will still have to be reset."

Cade blew out his breath and glanced at Elle.

"I'll be fine," Elle protested.

Over the last seven months, the guys had gotten called out several times in the middle of the night. It wasn't uncommon.

She could see her assertion hadn't inspired confidence in the two men.

"I'm not leaving you here alone," Merrick said firmly. "I don't think you understand what seeing you walk out of this house, completely unaware of the potential danger, did to me the other night."

"I won't go to sleep," she said. "You know I never do when you're gone anyway. All the other times you've been called out, I've waited up for you. You're wasting time, and you need to get out of here."

"She's right, Merrick. We don't go out alone. That's the deal. You know it," Cade argued.

"Christ. I don't like this," Merrick said even as he got out of bed to pull on his jeans.

Cade grabbed Elle's cell phone from the nightstand and tossed it to her. "Keep that close, honey. Call us if you need anything at all. We'll keep you posted on how long we'll be out."

Then he leaned in to kiss her before pushing back and hurrying to dress.

"You two worry too much," she admonished. "I'll be fine. Go on and get done so you can come back to me."

Merrick turned, tucking his shirt in. "You can count on that, baby."

"Did you call it in?" Merrick asked as they neared Bo Cameron's used car lot.

The building was new, and Cade and Merrick had advised Bo against having a brand new showroom built in a neighborhood that was as questionable as the one he'd chosen to open his business in.

The area was run-down and high in crime. Vandalism was common, but add in the lure of the automobiles on the lot, and it was a recipe for theft.

"I asked for a squad car to meet us there."

"I don't like this," Merrick muttered.

"The situation or leaving Elle?"

"Neither."

Cade went silent as they pulled up to the lot.

"Look, Cade! Over there."

Merrick pointed as Cade slammed on the brakes. The door of one of Bo's vehicles was open, and it was obvious someone was trying to hotwire the car.

Cade and Merrick jumped from the SUV and sprinted toward the gate. They hurdled it just as two hooded figures popped up from the vehicle and started running in the opposite direction.

Merrick pointed right to send Cade after one while Merrick broke off in pursuit of the other intruder.

Son of a bitch but this wasn't part of the job description.

In the distance, a siren sounded. It spooked the guy in front of Merrick enough that he hesitated, trying to decide which way to run. It was enough time for Merrick to flatten him with a flying tackle.

The two men hit the ground with enough force to jar Merrick's teeth. He had no idea if the intruder was armed, and he wasn't taking any chances. He quickly disabled the struggling would-be thief and cuffed him.

He sat on top of him for a long moment while he caught his breath. Then he yelled across the distance for Cade.

Moments later, an officer ran up, gun drawn. Merrick quickly identified himself and held his hands up so the cop would know he wasn't a threat.

Cade came over shoving the other hooded figure in front of him.

The two immediately started mouthing off, swearing that Cade and Merrick had attacked them. That they were innocent and that they'd been set up. Merrick rolled his eyes and got off the squealing perp and dragged him up to push him toward the police officer.

The officer called for backup, and the three men started for the patrol car, the two thieves cuffed and stumbling along in front of them.

"You have no idea who you're dealing with," one of the lowlifes yelled back.

"Yeah, yeah," Cade growled. "Save it for someone who gives a shit."

When they approached the squad car, another sped up, lights flashing. The car pulled in just ahead of the first patrol car on the scene, and the officer hurried out to assist.

Of the two thieves, one was a scrawny, scruffy guy about five foot six. But the other was a damn brick wall. As one cop took the smaller man to stuff him into the back of the patrol car, Cade and Merrick assisted the officer in getting the gorilla into the back of the other car.

As soon as they got close to the patrol car, the bigger man started resisting. The officer pulled pepper spray just as Cade and Merrick slammed the guy into the side of the car, bending him over the trunk.

"Don't add resisting and assault to the charges you're already facing, dumbass," Merrick bit out.

The hood fell away, revealing a bald, heavily tattooed skull. The thief bared his teeth, the gold glinting in the lights from the dealership.

"You'll regret this shit," the perp hissed. "No one messes with me and gets away with it."

"Guess what? We just did," Cade said.

The officer shoved the guy into the back seat with help from Cade and Merrick. The guy snarled and spewed threats and expletives until spit frothed around his lips. The officer slammed the door, effectively silencing the tirade.

"I'll need you to come down and give your statements," the officer said.

Merrick sighed, knowing the drill. "We'll follow you back. I'd like to make this as quick as possible. Have someone waiting at home."

"Don't we all," the officer said.

Merrick pulled out his cell as he and Cade headed back to the SUV.

"You calling Elle to let her know what's up?" Cade asked as he slid into the driver's seat.

"Yeah. I don't want her to worry. And I want to make sure she's awake."

# chapter twenty-three

ELLE SMOTHERED ANOTHER YAWN AT her desk and winced when her jaw popped. It was a struggle to get through the afternoon when she'd gotten little sleep the night before.

By the time the guys had gotten home from the police station, it had been time for Merrick to go into the training camp, so they'd stayed up, had coffee and had hit the gym a little early.

And at first, it had been fine, but as the day had grown longer, she'd fizzled. Merrick had joined her and Cade for lunch, and afterward they'd dropped her by the office while they headed out to a client meeting. She was struggling to keep herself upright. She couldn't imagine how Merrick must feel after no sleep and an intense workout.

Her cell rang, and she glanced down to see Cade's number pop up. Smiling, she picked up the phone and hit receive.

"Hey," she said. "How's it going?"

"Hey, sweetheart. Fine here. What about there? Has Dad made it in yet?"

She rolled her eyes. "No. Did you make him come in because you guys had stuff to do?"

"Damn right," Cade said. "He should be there shortly. I talked to him on our way out, and he said he'd be right over."

"I'll be sure to put on some fresh coffee then," she said in amusement.

An explosion sounded, startling her into a scream. Glass shattered, spraying her with tiny shards. It registered quickly that it was gunshots she was hearing and that bullets were peppering the walls of the office. Cade's roar echoed through the phone as he yelled her name.

She dove under her desk, the phone flying from her hand.

More breaking glass and the sound of impact. It was different than the gunshots. And then she smelled...smoke?

Not daring to raise her head, she lowered herself so she could peer out from underneath the desk. To her horror, she saw another Molotov cocktail hurled through the now-open window.

It hit the floor close to where the other had landed, and flames spread rapidly. They were already climbing the curtains and the walls and were dangerously close to her desk.

If she moved, she might be shot. If she didn't move, she'd be burned alive.

※

Cade listened in shock as Elle's scream echoed through the phone. Then he heard a crash and the unmistakable sound of breaking glass.

"Elle? Elle!" he roared.

"What the fuck is wrong?" Merrick demanded.

Without answering, Cade executed a sharp U-turn and floored the accelerator as he headed back in the direction of the office.

"Goddamn it, Cade! What the fuck is going on?"

"Elle," Cade croaked out.

He thrust the phone at Merrick so he could focus on driving.

"See if she's still on. Something happened at the office. She screamed, and I heard breaking glass."

Merrick grabbed the phone, nearly dropping it in his haste to get it to his ear.

"Elle? Elle? Goddamn it, baby, answer me. Are you all right? We're on our way."

"Anything?" Cade demanded.

Merrick pulled the phone away and then swore. "The call's not active anymore."

"Call her back!"

Cade ran through a series of stoplights, nearly rammed an oncoming car and barely kept control when he turned left onto the street where their office was.

The drive was an eternity when in reality it only took a few minutes. His heart was hammering in his ears, and his hands and forehead were clammy with sweat.

His heart plummeted as they drew closer and he saw black smoke billowing upward.

"Elle," he whispered.

He hit the last block going a hundred miles an hour. He spun into the small parking lot, spewing up gravel and fishtailing into the dumpster.

The entire office was on fire, smoke pouring from the ceiling and windows. Flames licked from the busted windows, and Cade saw no sign of Elle.

Oh God, was she still inside?

He and Merrick hit the ground running. They threw open the door and recoiled from the blast of heat and smoke that hit them.

"Elle!" Merrick shouted. "Elle! Where the hell are you?"

They charged inside, coughing as smoke filled their lungs.

"Here!"

Cade damn near hit the floor in relief when he heard her call.

"Keep talking," Cade hollered. "Can't see shit in here."

"I'm here," she yelled back. "By my desk. I tried to crawl out, but I can't see anything."

Cade and Merrick dropped down, lowering themselves as close to the floor as possible as they scrambled in the direction of her desk. Merrick mowed right over her, and when he realized that he had her, he hauled her up over his shoulder and then hustled toward the door, leaving Cade to follow him.

The three burst from the building just as the fire trucks rolled into the parking lot, sirens screaming.

Merrick collapsed to his knees at the bottom of the steps still holding Elle tightly against him. He tipped over, her landing on the ground with Merrick over her. Merrick coughed and choked, his body heaving as he pressed Elle to the ground.

Cade sank down beside them and hastily pushed Merrick off of Elle.

As soon as he managed to pry Elle free, he yanked her into his arms and ran his hands over her body, trying to determine if she'd been injured.

And then the paramedics surrounded them, and he was separated from Elle as he was pulled in a different direction from both Elle and Merrick.

"Damn it, I'm fine!" Cade snarled. "Let me see Elle. She was the one trapped in the building."

"Have a seat and let me put this oxygen mask on you," the paramedic tending Cade said in a firm voice. "If all goes well, you can get back to her soon, but for now, I need to assess your condition."

Only wanting to facilitate the process, Cade bit his lip and let the medic slip the mask over his face. He took in several deep breaths, his throat raw from smoke inhalation. The entire time the medic poked at him and took his vitals, Cade's gaze was directed across the way where two paramedics already had Elle on a stretcher. She was fighting tooth and nail and calling for Merrick and Cade.

He yanked the mask from his face and took off at a run. He shoved by one of the medics trying to restrain Elle and leaned over the stretcher to pull her into his arms.

"Thank God," she whispered in his ear. "Don't let them take me, Cade. Someone will find out about me."

"Honey, you need to go to a hospital. This is serious. We need to make sure you're okay."

Fear leapt into her eyes, and she shook her head adamantly. "Take me to see Dallas."

"Miss, you really need to be taken to the emergency room," one of the medics advised.

Again she shook her head. "I'm fine."

Her voice cracked and was hoarse from the smoke.

Christ. Where was Merrick?

Still holding Elle, Cade turned to look over his shoulder and rapidly scanned the area for Merrick. His gaze lighted on his friend sitting on the ground several yards away, an oxygen mask covering his face while a medic took his vitals.

Shit but this was the last thing Merrick needed when he was so close to his championship fight.

"I'll take her in," Cade said when he looked back at the medics. He needed to get on with it fast so Merrick could be checked out too. Dakota was going to shit a brick over this.

The medics frowned and shook their heads in disbelief.

"I need her to sign no transport papers," one of them said.

"I'll sign," Elle said in a firm voice.

The other medic sighed and turned to walk to the ambulance. He pulled out a clipboard and returned, thrusting a pen at Elle. He handed over the clipboard, showed her where to sign and then waited as she scribbled her name on the line.

As soon as she was done, she tried to get down, but Cade caught her against him and lifted her from the stretcher. He carried her to the SUV that now sported a dent in the side from the collision with the dumpster.

After settling her into the front seat, he buckled her in and then touched her face to get her attention.

"I'll be right back, okay? I need to check on Merrick and see what's up. Then I'll get you to Dallas."

She nodded and laid her head back against the rest.

Cade strode in Merrick's direction only to see Merrick push himself to his feet, strip off the oxygen mask and hand it to the medic standing next to him. He started in Cade's direction, meeting him there halfway.

"How's Elle?" Merrick demanded.

"I'm taking her to see Dallas now. What about you?"

"I'm good. Going with you. We'll take care of this later."

Cade nodded and hurried back to the SUV. There would be a shit ton of stuff to do later. Reports to file. Statements to give. Insurance to see to.

Just then, his dad roared into the parking lot and braked hard, kicking up dirt and gravel as he stopped just in front of Merrick and Cade.

Charlie jumped out, his brows drawn together in concern.

"What the hell happened?" his dad demanded.

Cade shook his head. "No time to explain now, Dad. Do you mind sticking around to take care of stuff here? We need to get Elle to see Dallas. She was trapped in the office when it went up in flames."

"Christ," Charlie muttered. "Go on. Take her in and see to her needs. I'll take care of things here."

"Thanks, Dad."

Before Cade could hurry away, his dad pulled him into a huge hug.

"Glad you and Merrick are okay, son."

## chapter twenty-four

CADE CARRIED HER INTO DALLAS'S clinic, and when the receptionist saw them, she immediately stood and motioned them through the door to one of the exam rooms.

Just a moment after Cade laid her down on the table, Dallas hurried in, a frown creasing his face. Then he got a look at Merrick.

"What the hell happened?" Dallas demanded.

"Fire," Cade said grimly.

"Bullets too," Elle blurted.

Merrick's face grew stormy. "What the *fuck*?"

Cade shook his head in confusion. "Back up. You said *bullets*?"

Elle nodded as Dallas put his stethoscope to her chest and asked her to breathe deeply. He was eyeing Merrick with concern even as he examined her.

"Someone fired bullets into the office. I dove under the desk, and that's when they torched the place. I saw the bottles hit the floor and explode with flames."

"Son of a bitch," Merrick swore. "She could have been killed!"

"Why would someone do this?" she asked, her eyes wide.

"Could be any number of people," Cade said. "Not like we don't have enemies."

Elle had gone pale, and she shook visibly. "You don't think it has anything to do with me, do you? Do you think...*he*...found me? Or that he knows I'm not dead?"

Dallas shot Cade and Merrick a look, quirking up his eyebrow as if to ask them if there was any credence to Elle's fear.

Cade pushed closer to Elle's bedside and rubbed his hand up and down her back. Merrick stifled a deep cough and went to Elle's other side. She reached for him blindly, tangling her hand with his.

"It probably has more to do with the asshole we caught trying to steal a car from Bo's dealership last night," Merrick said. "He was spouting threats. Most of the time, it's just talk, but it's worth looking into."

"Is he not still in jail?" Elle asked.

Cade shrugged. "I don't know. We don't typically follow up. Could be out on bail. But even if he's still locked up, he could have had others torch the office in retaliation. It probably has nothing to do with you one way or another, honey. You were just in the wrong place at the wrong time."

"So it was you and Merrick they were targeting then," she said, an unhappy twist to her mouth. "They were trying to kill you."

"We don't know that, baby," Merrick soothed. "It could have been a random act of violence."

Even as he said it, they all knew how unlikely it was. Their office wasn't in a residential section, and it wasn't in a part of town where drive-by shootings were a common occurrence.

It was personal.

"You should both get looked at," Dallas said to Cade and Merrick. "I need to do some blood work on Elle and put her on oxygen for a while. She needs to stay here so I can monitor her condition."

"I'm okay," Elle said softly. "See to them. I wasn't in there for too long."

Dallas put a gentle hand on her shoulder. "You were exposed to the fire and smoke longer than they were. I need to make sure you don't have any injuries that were overlooked in the excitement of the moment."

She reluctantly nodded her agreement.

Dallas called in his nurse practitioner and sent Cade and Merrick to the next room to be checked out.

Cade was reluctant to leave Elle but knew she was in good hands with Dallas. He went into the next room and waited impatiently as the nurse practitioner did a thorough examination of both him and Merrick.

When she left the two men alone in the room, Merrick turned to Cade. "She could have been killed. We can't leave her alone like that again even if it's just for a few minutes. Hell, we sent your dad to go stay with her. What if he'd been there when all this went down? We could have lost them *both*."

"I know," Cade said in a low voice. "What do you think? Retaliation? It's not like our information isn't all over the place at Bo's or any other place we do security for. Our advertisement of security monitoring and the warnings are posted around the perimeter."

"I think it's our best bet right now," Merrick said. "Doesn't make sense why we'd be targeted as some random business to torch. And I don't buy that whoever tried to kill Elle has figured out where she is and is trying to finish the job. Maybe that's naïve of me, but my gut tells me that whatever son of a bitch worked her over thought the job was done, and he's not even looking for whether her body ever turns up or not. If he dumped her in the river, he's probably betting on her *never* turning up."

"Yeah, I agree," Cade said. "I don't think this has anything to do with Elle. But the fact that she was caught in the crossfire because of some asshole wanting revenge on us pisses me off."

"I'll make some phone calls. Find out if our boy is still in jail and if the cops have any leads on what happened today."

Cade nodded. "I need to call Dad. He'll be worried about us and Elle, and I need to find out what's going on with the fire."

Dallas stuck his head in the door and both men stood.

"How is Elle?" Merrick demanded.

Dallas came in and shut the door behind him. "I think she'll be fine. I'm waiting on the results of her blood gasses. I didn't find any serious injuries. Just a few cuts from the glass, and she had scrapes on her hands and knees from being on the floor. I just want to keep her here for a few hours before I let you take her home. I have her on oxygen, and I gave her something to help her relax."

"Thanks, man, we appreciate this," Cade said.

Dallas hesitated as if he was going to say something but thought better of it.

Then he sighed. "You know you can't keep on in denial of Elle's situation. And I'm saying this as your friend. I know she's afraid, and

I know she's put her past out of her mind, but it's situations like today that make it all the more important that she at least has an identity. Hell, even if you had to create one for her. If something serious happens to her, you can't keep her out of the hospital because it means someone finds out that she has no idea who she is or where she came from. Have you tried running her prints yet? You guys know enough people in the police department that you could get it done on the sly."

Merrick's expression darkened, but Cade cut him off before he could get worked up.

"The only way running her prints would work is if she's already in the system. It's a long shot, and frankly, we've held back because if she's had trouble with the law in the past, we don't want it to affect her future. With us. We know we can't turn a blind eye to her past forever."

Cade broke off and ran a hand through his hair. He was tired. Worried. The issue of Elle was ever present in his mind and had worn him down over the past months.

"Maybe a part of me is afraid—like Elle is—to find out what's in her past. I don't want to lose her."

Merrick nodded. "She's remembering more. I don't want to rush her and force the issue before she's ready to handle it. What if we go dig it all up and find out who she is and she cracks under the pressure? I know it's not right, but I don't care about what's right. I care about what's best for Elle, and I care about not hurting her."

"I understand," Dallas said. "My main concern is that you get into a situation where Elle can't get the care she needs because of your fears of discovery. I have a few contacts who could get her an identity. Driver's license. Social Security card. Birth certificate. Think about it. She'd likely feel a little more secure if she didn't fear discovery on a daily basis."

Dallas tucked the clipboard he was holding against his side. "Get back to me if you want me to get in touch with a guy I know. He owes me a favor."

"Thanks," Merrick said.

"Now tell me how you're feeling," Dallas said to Merrick.

Even as he spoke, he prodded Merrick into sitting on the exam table, and he listened to Merrick's lungs and checked the rest of his vitals.

"I'm fine," Merrick said, but his voice broke as he coughed.

Dallas frowned. "Son of a bitch. You've got to be careful, man. A whole hell of a lot is riding on you remaining healthy. This is your one shot. You may never get another. I'm telling you this as your friend and as your doctor."

"What was I supposed to do? Leave her in there to die?" Merrick demanded.

His hands were curled into beefy fists, and he looked like he wanted to put one of them through the wall.

"Chill, man," Cade said in a soft voice. "She's okay. We need to focus on you. You can't go down now."

"I don't want you working out this evening," Dallas said with a frown. "Take it easy tonight. Rest up, and if you're feeling up to it, you can train in the morning. But I want your ass here at the clinic as soon as the session is over."

Merrick nodded.

Dallas put his hand on Merrick's shoulder. "I'm going back to check on Elle. I'll be back to let you know when you can see her."

The two men watched as Dallas left the room, and then Cade turned his gaze on Merrick.

"He has a point," Cade said. "Elle needs an identity. It can't help to wake up every morning worried what the day will bring. She can't even go to the grocery store without fear because she doesn't have a driver's license or any sort of identification."

"So, what, we get her a fake ID?" Merrick asked slowly.

"We could," Cade said. "But I was thinking along the lines of something a little different."

Merrick lifted one eyebrow. "What do you have in mind?"

Cade blew out his breath in a controlled manner as he figured out just the right way to say what he was thinking. It was something he should have thought of a lot earlier, but he wouldn't have wanted to pressure Elle too soon. Hell, maybe it was still too soon to be thinking along these lines.

"If we're going to invent an identity for her, then why not go with one that affords her the most protection?"

"I'm with you," Merrick said.

"We give her ours," Cade said in a low tone. "We make her Elle Walker-Sullivan."

# chapter twenty-five

MERRICK WAS SILENT FOR a long moment as he stared at his friend. "You mean, like marriage?"

Cade nodded. "Yes and no. I mean, there's no way to have an official ceremony where she marries us both. Look, I may be jumping the gun here. I'm only speaking for myself. I have no idea if you're ready for that kind of commitment or not—"

Merrick held up his hand to cut Cade off. "I've already committed to her, and I didn't do it lightly. I'm in this for the long haul, and marriage is a logical step. But as you said, there's no way to work that kind of thing out when more than two people are involved."

"Well, if we're going to create an identity for her, then we give her one of our names and then we go through the process of having a legally binding ceremony wherein she marries whoever's name she didn't originally take. She can keep her original name and hyphenate it so that she carries both our last names."

"So she'd only marry one of us," Merrick said grimly.

Merrick's heart thumped like a jackhammer against his chest. Sure, he knew what kind of relationship he'd signed on for. He'd never have Elle fully to himself, and he was okay with that on most days. He'd be a liar if he said he *never* struggled with it.

But for her to marry Cade? He wasn't sure he could live with that. Marriage *meant* something to him. Call him old-fashioned, but marriage was something to hold sacred, and he'd always imagined that he'd find the right woman, settle down and get married and grow old together.

He just never thought finding the person he wanted that kind of commitment from would mean sharing her with his best friend.

Cade slowly nodded. "Yeah. I don't see a way around that."

Merrick nodded, his lips pursed. "Okay, so who marries her?"

He watched Cade intently, searching for any signs that this was going to cause serious issues between them. Dread was tight in his chest as he waited for the answer. Could he be the bigger person here and act like it didn't matter when it did? He caught himself before shaking his head because no. Hell no. He wasn't going to pretend. This was too important.

Cade leaned against the exam table and shoved his hands into his pockets.

"As long as the agreement is made that nothing changes between the three of us, I don't really care who marries her on paper. That's all it'll be is a piece of paper binding her to one of us. It also gives her the legal protection of being able to be listed as a dependent and beneficiary. But she belongs to both of us, and we know that. You know it. I know it. And she knows it."

Merrick nodded.

"We can't even decide this kind of thing until we talk to her about it anyway," Cade said. "I'm jumping the gun here."

"But it's a good solution," Merrick said. "I like the idea. I like it a lot. I want Elle to feel like she belongs, and I want her to know that we're serious about her. This would go a long way in proving that to her."

"Yeah, it would," Cade said in a quiet tone.

"I want to be the one who marries her," Merrick said bluntly. "I won't lie to you or pretend it doesn't matter. If you're okay with it, I'd rather give her your name and then marry her so the paperwork lists her as my wife."

For a minute, Merrick thought Cade might argue. He didn't even realize he'd been holding his breath until Cade silently nodded his agreement.

"If it's that important to you, I can deal," Cade said.

"We'll talk to Elle when the right opportunity presents itself. If she agrees, then we can get with Dallas on getting her documents lined out."

Cade nodded again.

"She's yours too," Merrick said softly.

Cade lifted his gaze to Merrick, determination etched in stone and reflected in his eyes.

"Hell yes, she's mine," Cade said. "I'm making a huge leap of faith here, Merrick. Don't make me regret it."

In any other situation, the implied threat in Cade's voice would have pissed Merrick off, but he also knew how huge it was for Cade to bend on this. He didn't blame his friend for making certain that they were understood on all points.

"She's ours," Merrick amended. "And we're keeping her."

Cade held up his fist, and Merrick bumped it with his.

The door burst open, and Dakota strode in, followed closely by Catherine and J.T., one of the fighters who'd signed on to Merrick's camp to train with him.

"What the ever-loving fuck happened?" Dakota demanded. "Are you all right, Merrick? Where the hell is Dallas? Why are you here and not in the goddamn hospital?"

Merrick held up his hand to silence Dakota. "I'm fine."

Catherine's brow creased with worry, and she pushed in next to Merrick, her hand resting on Merrick's muscled arm. "What happened, Merrick?"

Merrick cleared his throat and coughed hoarsely. Dakota looked like he was going to combust at any moment.

"There was a fire at the office. Elle was trapped. Cade and I had to go in after her."

Catherine paled. "Oh my God. Is she all right?"

"How the fuck did a fire happen?" Dakota demanded.

"Let's calm down, guys," Cade said. "I'll explain everything. We only have a few minutes. Dallas is coming back for us so we can get back to Elle."

J.T. glanced up at Merrick. "You okay, man?"

Merrick nodded. "I'm out for today, but I'll be at the gym in the morning. Dallas wants to see me after the morning session so he can okay me for the afternoon."

Dakota swore. "We can't afford to lose any days this close to the match. Are you just trying to give me gray hair? Running into a burning building? Have you lost your goddamn mind?"

Merrick's lip twitched, and he glared at Dakota. Dakota who meant well. Dakota who always had his back. But Dakota was only focused on Merrick and his health. What he didn't realize was that if something had happened to Elle, Merrick wouldn't be worth a damn for this fight or any fight.

"Dakota, shut up," Catherine said in a firm voice as she edged away from Merrick.

"Someone shot up the place," Cade said. "Elle was inside, and after they shot it up, they torched it. With her trapped underneath her desk. I was on the phone with her when it happened, thank God, so we were able to get to her quickly."

"Christ," Dakota bit out. "You two got enemies? What the hell is going on? Merrick, we need to consider moving you to a different location for the rest of your training. Apart from the physical risks, the last thing you need is this kind of distraction. You have to be focused if you're going to win."

"Not now, Dakota," Merrick snapped. "Just let it go and back off."

"I won't back off," Dakota said, his temper simmering.

He was pale, and Merrick knew he sounded like a dick because he was worried. That was how Dakota always reacted when something stressed him out.

"Don't you think it's time Elle moved on? She can't stay with you two forever, and she's a huge distraction at a time when you can't afford the smallest lapse. I'll put Catherine on it. She can make some calls. We'll figure out a solution and make sure Elle is taken care of."

Merrick was on his feet before he could call back his own temper. He grabbed Dakota by the shirt and slammed him against the door.

"Don't you ever, *ever* say anything like that again," Merrick snarled. "Elle is with me. Period. She's not going anywhere. She's with me and Cade both. Deal with it."

Dakota blinked in surprise, his mouth dropping open in shock. "Think about what you're saying, man. Do you really want to throw the championship away over a woman?"

"You're being an asshole, Dakota," Catherine snapped. "Shut the fuck up before he beats your ass. Right now, I'm tempted to have him hold you down so *I* can knock the shit out of you."

Merrick slammed Dakota into the door again, hauling him upward until they were eye to eye.

"Let me tell you something," Merrick said in a dangerously low voice. "If it ever comes down to a choice between the IMMAO and Elle, I won't have to think hard about it at all. She comes first. You need to understand that and support it, or you won't have a place on my team any longer."

"Both of you stop before you say things you'll later regret," Catherine said quietly. "You've been friends for too long, and you're both reacting in fear. You scared us today, Merrick. We both love you, and when we heard what happened, our first thought wasn't oh shit, what if he can't fight? Our first thought was, he has to be all right."

Dakota blew out his breath and sagged in Merrick's grasp. "She's right, man. I keep imagining you in that building and it going up. I'm sorry for what I said about Elle."

Merrick slowly let him go and backed away. He turned to Catherine and then pulled her into a hug.

"Thank you," he said.

"Someone's got to be the voice of reason around here," she said pertly. "I'm surrounded by dumbasses."

"Hey!" Cade protested.

"I think she just insulted us all," J.T. muttered.

Merrick smiled, some of the tension escaping. Dakota looked warily at him and took a step closer, offering a bent arm with his hand upright.

"We good?" Dakota asked.

Merrick took his hand, their forearms pressed together, and he held on to it for a long moment as he stared at his longtime friend.

"I meant what I said," Merrick said in a serious tone. "Elle comes first. I need you to understand that, or there's going to be problems down the road."

Dakota nodded. "I get it. Cathy comes first with me."

Catherine snorted.

Dakota grinned. "Okay, maybe she comes second to fighting."

The door opened, and Dallas stuck his head in. "You guys can come see Elle now. She's relaxed from the meds I gave her, but she's comfortable. I want to keep her for a little longer, but you can sit with her while you wait."

Merrick turned to Dakota. "I'll make it in the morning. I'm fine."

Dakota bumped his fist to Merrick's. "I'm going to work your ass extra hard, so come prepared."

## chapter twenty-six

OTHER THAN A NAGGING COUGH and rawness in her throat, Elle felt fine. She was a little jittery after so much fear and adrenaline, but more than anything, she was ready to go back to the house she considered home.

Dallas kept her into the evening, and after he closed the clinic to the rest of his patients, he sent her home with Cade and Merrick with strict instructions for them all to rest.

Charlie was waiting for them at the house, and Elle realized that in many ways, it was just beginning. The danger to them all was over, but Cade and Merrick's business had been destroyed.

There were police reports and insurance claims to file, and they faced the arduous task of rebuilding their client records. Fortunately, one of the first things Elle had done when she'd taken over the clerical work was to back up all the office computer files onto a laptop that they kept at home.

But worse than that was the interruption to Merrick's preparation for his upcoming match.

Charlie met them at the door and pulled Elle into his arms for a quick hug and a kiss on the cheek.

"You okay, sweetheart?"

She smiled and hugged him back. "I'm fine."

"What about you boys?" Charlie asked.

"We're good, Dad," Cade said as he dropped his keys on the table. "If you'll hang out and give us all a chance to shower and get cleaned up, we'll talk about it."

"Take your time," Charlie said. "I'll put on a pot of coffee while y'all shower."

Fifteen minutes later, Elle, Cade and Merrick returned after a quick shower. Elle unwound the towel from her head and sat at the kitchen table, running a comb through the snarls, while Charlie set out cups of coffee for them.

"Was it a complete loss?" Merrick asked Cade's dad.

Charlie grimaced. "Yeah. Not much left by the time they put out the fire. All that's left is one big charred mess."

"Elle said that someone shot up the place before they fire bombed it," Cade said.

"The detective on the scene said he'd be by in the morning to talk to Elle and the both of you," Charlie said. "Not sure how you want to handle that with Elle's situation and all."

"We have a solution in mind," Merrick said in a quiet voice. "It'll just take a little time."

Elle's brows furrowed, and she glanced between Cade and Merrick, trying to decipher what they meant. But neither man offered anything further.

What solution did they mean?

Her pulse sped up, and her stomach balled into a big knot. Were they rethinking their situation? Had they decided that she was more trouble than she was worth?

Her mouth went dry, and panic seized her by the throat. She put aside the comb, her hands shaking as she ran her fingers through the still-damp ends of her hair.

She barely listened as Charlie said his good-byes and voiced his promise to help out the following day. She was frozen solid with fear.

As soon as Cade showed his father out, he returned, and he and Merrick faced Elle.

"We'd like to talk to you in the living room," Cade said. "We can take our coffee in there to finish."

She shook her head, her cup sitting unattended on the table. She hadn't taken a sip, too afraid her stomach would rebel. "I'm fine. Just say whatever it is you want to say."

Merrick's brows drew together at her tone, and he exchanged a quick look with Cade.

"What the hell do you think it is we want to say?" he demanded.

She swallowed nervously, her gaze skittering from side to side.

Cade's eyes narrowed, and he cocked his head to the side as he stared at her every bit as hard as Merrick was.

"I don't know," she said in a low voice.

"But you're worried," Merrick persisted. "I can see it all over your face. You think we're dumping you?"

She hesitated too long, and Cade swore. Then without another word, he pulled her from her chair and turned her toward the living room as he herded her out of the kitchen.

"Sit," he told her when they got to the couch.

She perched on the edge, her palms slick and her stomach churning precariously.

Merrick sat in the armchair diagonal to the couch, his elbows planted on his knees.

"Look at me, baby," he said in a soft voice that vibrated with intensity.

Cade slid onto the couch next to her. She lifted her gaze to meet Merrick's, unconsciously holding her breath as she waited for what he had to say.

"Cade and I want to talk to you about our relationship and taking steps to make it more permanent."

Her breath came out in a dizzying rush. They didn't want to get rid of her. They were talking about making things permanent.

She was so light-headed that she had to lean over.

Cade's hand slid over her shoulder. "Are you okay, Elle?"

She bobbed her head, sucking in deep breaths through her nose.

Merrick bit out a curse. "Baby, I don't even want to know what was going through your head. But whatever it is you're thinking, stop. Cade and I aren't going anywhere. *You* aren't going anywhere."

"What did you mean by taking steps to make things more permanent?" she stuttered out.

"Dallas knows someone who can create an identity for you. Social Security card. Birth certificate. Paperwork so you can get a driver's license," Cade interjected. "As Merrick and I were discussing it, we thought that if we gave you one of our last names, then the other could marry you so you would bear both our names legally."

Her eyes widened, and she stared between the two men in disbelief.

"Was that a *proposal*?"

Merrick grimaced. "Not a very well done one I'm afraid."

Her heart leapt into her throat as she waited for an explanation.

"No, it wasn't very well done of me," Cade admitted. "I'm sorry, honey. I made a mess of this. But it doesn't change what we want. We'd like for you to have both our last names and be legally bound to one of us. Marriage would give you protection and benefits."

She glanced between them both, weighing their reactions and trying to decipher the motive behind the proposal. Were they just protecting her as they'd done for the last several months? Or was this something altogether different and…emotional?

"Is that the only reason you want to do this?" she asked.

"Hell no," Merrick ground out. "I want you forever. I want you as my wife."

Cade cleared his throat. "Merrick and I talked, and we agreed that, if you're willing, we'll give you my name first, and then you'll marry Merrick in a legally binding ceremony. We like the sound of Elle Walker-Sullivan."

"I do too," she whispered.

Merrick pushed up from the chair and walked the few steps to where she sat. He went to one knee in front of her, closing his hands over hers in a tender gesture.

"I love you, Elle. I'd like nothing more than for you to marry me. But I want you to be sure this is what you want, and I don't want us to put any pressure on you."

She leaned forward until their foreheads touched. "I love you too. I was so scared. I thought for a minute that maybe you'd changed your minds…about me. About *us*."

Merrick pressed his lips to hers in a gentle kiss. "Not going to happen, baby. We're in this for the long haul."

"Yes, I'll marry you," she said. "I don't care about the past, and I'm tired of letting it control me. I'm ready to move forward. And if I never remember, that's okay too. As long as my future is with you and Cade."

Cade's hand slid down her arm and came to rest over her wrist. She turned, leaning into his chest as she fitted her mouth to his. She kissed him and then snuggled into his embrace, resting her head on his shoulder.

He palmed the back of her head, holding her solidly against him as he stroked her hair.

"I love you," she said against his neck.

"I love you too, sweetheart."

"Are you okay with this? Me marrying Merrick?"

Cade pulled her away, a warm smile on his face. "Yeah, I'm okay with it. I trust Merrick. I trust you. And I trust that you love the both of us and that there's room enough in your heart for us both."

"You can't imagine what this feels like," she said. "To have hope and the promise of a future when I've been without either for so long."

Cade pressed another kiss to her forehead. "Your future is with us, honey. Always. No matter what life throws at us, we'll always be here with you."

She glanced shyly back at Merrick. "When do you want to get married?"

"As soon as damn possible," Merrick said. "We'll call Dallas in the morning and get him started on the paperwork, and as soon as we can get that together and get you a driver's license, then we'll get married, and you'll be Elle Walker-Sullivan."

"I like the sound of it," she said.

"So do we," Cade said.

She inhaled sharply, gathering her courage tightly around her. There was no way for her to know if she could ever pull this off. They hadn't even come close to deeper intimacy. Cade and Merrick had been very careful not to push her.

But it was time to see just where she stood in her recovery. No, seven months wasn't a long time, but in her favor was the fact that she couldn't remember her attack. If those memories would stay buried, maybe she would be okay.

She *wanted* to be okay.

She wanted to be touched and held. Loved. She wanted to be made love to. And she wanted to make love to them.

"What is it, baby?" Merrick asked in a husky tone.

"Will you… Will you and Cade make love to me?"

# chapter twenty-seven

MERRICK'S NOSTRILS FLARED, AND CADE'S eyes ignited with quick fire. The two men stared intently at her, silent and assessing. They practically vibrated with anticipation. If she'd had any doubts about whether they wanted her in a physical capacity, she certainly didn't now. In fact, they looked very much like they were straining to keep a tight leash on their response.

"Elle, are you sure, honey?" Cade asked.

"We don't want to rush this," Merrick said in a steady voice rich with patience. And love. "We have all the time in the world."

"I want to try," she said huskily. "I want it very badly. I've dreamed of having the two of you kiss me and touch me."

"I've dreamed about it too," Merrick admitted.

"Then make both our dreams come true," she said.

Without saying anything further, Cade stood and held out his hand to her. Without hesitation, she slid her fingers over his palm and laced them with his, allowing him to pull her to her feet.

Merrick put his hand to her back and walked with her and Cade toward the bedroom.

The closer they got, the more nervous she became. It wasn't that she was afraid. Or maybe she was. Just a little. What she feared most was not being able to go through with it.

They stopped just in front of the bed, and she simply stood there, uncertain of what to do next. If only she was bolder, more confident.

She needn't have worried, because Cade and Merrick took the reins. Merrick pressed in close behind her, kissing her neck as his hands slid down her body to unfasten her jeans. Cade angled his head down to capture her lips, and he worked in opposition to Merrick, pulling up her shirt while Merrick divested her of her pants.

In a few seconds' time, she was standing in only her bra and panties. The men's hands were on her skin, their lips branding her flesh. Shivers of delight and anticipation licked over her body. She craved this. Craved them. She hadn't realized just how much she'd wanted and needed this until now, when she was on the very brink of discovery.

She wanted to touch them. Wanted to please them. The instinct was deep and pressing, an overwhelming urge to bring them the ultimate pleasure.

Before she even realized what it was she was doing, she slid to her knees in front of them, her head slightly bowed. When she lifted her gaze once more, wanting to see them undress, she saw confusion in their eyes.

Merrick reached for her, gently pulling her upward once more.

"No way, baby. You don't kneel in front of us. Ever. Come here."

He tugged her into his arms and kissed her deeply, passionately. Before he'd always been so careful, always restraining himself, as if he always feared unleashing the full force of his desire on her.

Not so now.

She moaned softly under the bruising force of his kiss. She loved the power emanating from him. Needed it like a drug.

Cade's hands coasted down her body, catching at her underwear and then pulling downward with a firm tug. And then his knuckles brushed her back as he unclasped her bra.

Merrick let her go long enough for Cade to pull her flush against his chest. Then Merrick reached forward to take the straps over her shoulders and down her arms until the bra fell away and she was finally naked in front of them.

She was molded tightly to Cade's chest, her behind cradled in his groin. His erection bulged against her, and instinctively, she rubbed, enjoying the friction against her skin.

"You're beautiful," Cade whispered in her ear. "Do you have any idea how beautiful?"

She tilted her head back, allowing him access to her neck. His mouth slid warmly from her ear to her shoulder, his teeth grazing the sensitive skin in between.

"I want to see you and Merrick undress," she murmured.

"That can be arranged," Cade said as he pulled his mouth away.

He guided her toward the bed, turned her around and eased her down on the edge. Then he backed away and began to undress.

Her gaze was riveted to the sight of the two men stripping out of their pants and shirts.

Merrick reached down and pulled his shirt up and over his head, baring his lean midriff. The muscles in his chest rippled and bulged as he tossed the shirt aside, and then he went for his pants, and she forgot to breathe.

Cade was quicker and more impatient. Neither man spared the other a single glance as they undressed. Their gazes were focused on her and only her.

When they got down to just their underwear, they slowed. They both looked at her, almost as if making certain she was still on board. Merrick wore plain boxers while Cade wore boxer briefs. But the two men could make even the plainest underwear damn sexy.

Seemingly satisfied that she wasn't going to bolt from the room the moment she saw their erections, they got rid of the underwear, and for the first time, she got an uninhibited feast for the eyes.

"Lay back, honey," Cade said, his voice gruff. "Get comfortable, because we're going to make you feel very, very good."

She swallowed hard and slowly reclined, allowing her back to push into the mattress. Her legs still dangled over the side, and she slid her heels onto the metal frame lip.

The action spread her thighs, baring her to their avid gazes. And suddenly they both loomed over her, one on either side as they got onto the bed with her.

Merrick lowered his head, his lips closing warmly over her nipple as he sucked it between his teeth. She arched into him, her back bowing as she strained to get closer. She wanted more. God, she needed more.

Her breath escaped in a ragged puff, and Cade swallowed it up as he claimed her mouth in a primal, possessive kiss that had her blood surging hotly through her veins.

It was getting harder and harder to breathe.

The palm of Cade's hand glided over her belly and lower to the juncture of her thighs and then lower still, until his fingers slid through the delicate folds of her pussy and over her clitoris.

She nearly disintegrated on the spot.

Merrick's mouth on her breast. Cade's fingers caressing her most sensitive spots. It was simply too much.

She let out a cry as her orgasm crashed through her in a split second, hurtling her over the edge and into the unknown. She was falling, falling, and then she slowed, floating and drifting like a leaf in autumn.

Merrick claimed her mouth the moment Cade pulled away. She could feel his smile against her lips.

"That was fast," he murmured.

She groaned. "Too fast. I didn't want it to be over so quickly."

"Oh, it's not over," Cade said. "We're only just beginning, honey."

She let out a sigh as Merrick continued to caress and pet her flesh. Cade dropped down her body, turning his attention to her breasts. As soon as his mouth made contact with her nipple, pleasure seeped through her body, flowing to every nerve ending.

"We want this to be perfect," Merrick said. "As perfect for you as it is for us."

"How does this work?" she breathed. "I mean, with both of you…"

"How do you want it to work?" Cade murmured against her breast. "Tell us what you want."

Erotic images flashed in her mind. She closed her eyes, chasing those pictures. Merrick behind her. Cade in front of her. Both inside her. Her on top of Cade. Merrick on top of her. Was it even possible the things she imagined?

"I want you…both," she said. "I want you touching me. I want you both inside me."

"Hell yeah," Merrick growled against her mouth as he took possession once more.

"Are you sure you're ready for this?" Cade asked, his tone cautious. "We can take this nice and slow and easy. We'll only do what you're ready for."

Deciding the best way to convince them was just to show them what she wanted, she pushed upward. For a moment, concern darkened their eyes until she positioned herself on her hands and knees, her knees at the very edge of the bed, and she looked up at Merrick, an unspoken invitation for him to claim her mouth.

"Oh hell," Merrick breathed.

Cade pressed a kiss to the cheek of her ass. "Let me get a condom, sweetheart."

She shivered from head to toe, chill bumps dotting and then racing across her skin. Her nipples puckered and grew hard. She was one huge ball of anticipation.

Merrick got up on his knees and threaded his fingers through her hair, guiding her down to his cock. He was firm but gentle, and yet she craved more…power? She wanted him to assert his dominance. It was an odd thought, but at the same time, it felt so incredibly…right.

He slid into her mouth, and she sighed softly at the satisfaction of his taste. The feel of him on her tongue. The idea that she was bringing him the same pleasure he'd already given her.

He retreated slowly, dragging his length over her swollen lips. Then he pushed forward again, feeding her, inch by inch, his rigid erection.

Her pulse bounded when Cade's firm hands grasped her hips. He smoothed his palms over her behind, spreading the cheeks in preparation for his entry.

She was tingling from head to toe, waiting, wanting. As soon as the head of his cock touched the mouth of her opening, she tensed and held her breath around Merrick's dick.

Then Cade pushed inward, testing the snugness of her passageway as she stretched around him.

She moaned, vibrating against Merrick's cock, causing him to groan in reaction.

"Feel good, sweetheart?" Cade asked.

She didn't have to answer. Her body answered for her.

Cade pushed harder, and she could feel herself opening for him as he pressed deeper. His fingers dug into her ass. She loved the sensation of his hands on her, knew she'd wear the marks for hours after.

"God, she's so tight," Cade said, his voice strangled.

"Her mouth is heaven," Merrick said.

Her skin prickled, and pleasure washed through her at the approval and satisfaction in both men's voices.

And yet she wanted more. Less restraint. She wanted them to let go. The ghosts didn't own her tonight. Her past was but a shadow in the corner of her mind. She wanted this more than she'd ever wanted anything else.

She pushed back against Cade, taking him deeper. The action sent her farther away from Merrick, and he pursued her, palming her head and reclaiming her mouth in a forceful rush that left her panting with excitement.

How could she want them to be so...powerful? Wouldn't it frighten her? *Shouldn't* it frighten her?

Nothing made sense to her. The mere thought of violence and assault, the very things that had happened to her, made her ill, and yet she wanted to feel the strength of these two men.

Not in a violent way. Even as she had the misgivings, she knew the answer. Their strength soothed her. Made her feel safe and cherished. Protected and loved. She reveled in the raw power they exuded.

They would never hurt her, and she knew it.

And that was the key to it all.

Faith.

Trust.

Love.

Merrick framed her face in his hands, cupping her lovingly as he thrust into her mouth. Cade's hands were splayed over her ass, holding her firmly in place as he thrust rhythmically.

The gentle slap of flesh on flesh rose and flowed erotically over her ears. So soon after one bone-melting orgasm, she was already fast riding the wave of another.

Cade's mouth pressed against her spine, eliciting another shiver. So very tender and loving. Her chest ached over it.

"I'm close, baby," Merrick said. And then he began to withdraw.

Her protest was immediate. She tried to guide him back to her mouth, but he gripped his erection and began to work it up and down with his fist.

"Not this time," he said quietly. "I'm on edge, and it's been a long time. I'm going to come a lot."

A hot burst landed on her shoulder. He held the tip close to her skin, and more jetted onto her flesh. Cade began to move faster and faster, and she threw back her head, closing her eyes, no longer focused on what Merrick was doing.

She cried out and then again. She called both their names. She was close. So very close.

Merrick's hands coaxed over her shoulders and then underneath to her breasts. He cupped the mounds and toyed with the nipples, pulling gently and exerting steady pressure as Cade thrust forcefully against her ass.

She put her hand down, sliding it over her belly and below to her clitoris. She needed that extra edge. Just a little more…

As soon as her fingers made a tight circle around her clit, she burst into flames. Cade stopped momentarily, his hands stroking her back as he held himself deeply inside her. He seemed to be giving her time to gain her bearings before he continued on.

She was so overwhelmed that she could barely hold herself up, and it must have been evident because Cade withdrew, and she found herself being turned so she was once more on her back.

Merrick had her recline on a towel he placed underneath her shoulders and then he carefully wiped the stickiness from her skin.

When Merrick was done, Cade slid his arms underneath her legs and pulled her toward him until her behind rested on the very edge of the bed. Then he was back inside her with one powerful stroke.

She closed her eyes, but Cade's voice commanded her, and she was powerless to resist the pull of his words.

"Look at me, Elle."

Her eyelids fluttered open, and she stared into his glittering eyes as he claimed her over and over.

"Mine," he said softly. "Mine and Merrick's. Ours."

"Yes," she whispered. "Yours."

Cade closed his eyes, his jaw tight and bulging. He leaned forward, his body pressing into hers, and then he went rigid, all his breath escaping in one forceful exhale.

He lowered his body to hers, until they were flush against each other, his weight anchoring her to the bed. He was warm and hard over her. She wrapped her arms around his body, holding him tightly to her as she reveled in his scent and the feel of him molded so tightly to her.

# chapter twenty-eight

THE NEXT FEW DAYS WERE a whirlwind of endless activity. They guys met with every one of their clients to reassure them that losing the office in no way diminished the services they were able to offer, and fortunately, since their client list was small but intensely loyal, only one opted to go with another company.

Cade's dad had pounded the pavement to find them office space to lease, and the men had worked around the clock to get the business back up and running. Elle restored their computer systems after the new equipment had been delivered to the house, and she soon had everything back in working order.

Merrick's workouts had suffered as a result. Though he'd gone the morning after the fire, he'd skipped several after in order to help Cade. When Elle cautiously brought up the fact that his fight was bearing down on them, Merrick had grimaced and muttered that shit happens and he had to do what he had to do.

Still, she hated that she couldn't do more to bear the load for Cade and Merrick. She put in long hours of clerical work. She took over all phone calls, whether it was making calls to reassure clients or taking calls from clients with concerns or needs.

She was a part of this. She *felt* a part of it. For the first time in so many months, she had a purpose, and she was part of something much bigger than herself. She had a family. Men who loved her.

After a week of no sleep for any of them, Elle drifted off at the desk of her makeshift office in their house. There were stacks of paperwork surrounding her, and she'd just completed doing manual updates from the back-up file to the brand-new computer the guys had bought to replace what had been lost in the fire.

And that was how Cade and Merrick found her. Cheek down on a stack of printouts, hair over her face, slumped over the desk, about to fall out of her chair.

"Hell," Merrick muttered. "We've been working her way too hard. She's exhausted."

"We're all exhausted," Cade said. "It's been a tough week getting back on our feet and keeping our clients. She's been a big part of that. We couldn't have done it without her and Dad."

"She's been nagging me about getting down to the gym," Merrick said grimly.

"Someone needs to," Cade said as he walked quietly toward the desk where Elle was sleeping so soundly.

Merrick's brows drew together. "Don't you start too. I couldn't leave this on you, man."

Cade looked up, pausing, his hand in midair as he'd reached for Elle. "This fight is important. You can't lose an entire week of training and expect to win. Dad and Elle have been invaluable in helping. We'll get back on our feet. But it makes no sense for the fire to take not only our office and part of our business, but your career as well."

"I'll get back," Merrick said in a determined voice. "I just needed to make sure we were going to be okay."

"We're going to be fine." He glanced back down at Elle, who hadn't stirred the entire time the two men had been talking. "Right now, what we need to do is get her to bed and make sure she stays there for about twelve hours. None of us have slept worth a damn in the last week, and we're all suffering for it."

"Amen to that," Merrick muttered. "Let's take her to bed and tomorrow… Tomorrow I'll head into the gym to start catching up. But I don't want Elle picking up my slack with the business. She's at the end of her rope."

Cade went to his knees by Elle's chair and pulled her gently into his arms so her head rested in the curve of his neck. He looped one arm underneath her knees and then pushed himself upward.

It was a testament to her fatigue that she never even stirred. She lay limply in Cade's arms as he carried her out of the office and toward the bedroom.

Despite the stresses of the past week. The fear of losing Elle in the fire. The utter devastation to their office. The missed workouts and the shift in focus from his upcoming fight to the preservation of their security business. Despite it all, Merrick was calm and centered, and he felt a bone-deep contentment.

Dallas was working on the paperwork for Elle, and it should be ready in the next couple of days. All that was left was for her to then marry Merrick and keep Cade's name as well as Merrick's on all her legal documents.

They'd already decided to circumvent any complicated, time-consuming steps and make a weekend trip to Las Vegas to tie the knot there. In Vegas, no one was going to blink an eye if Cade stood in the marriage ceremony and took an actual part.

Yeah, the legalities would be between Merrick and Elle, but Cade would be a part. She'd say vows to both men and they in turn would give them back to her.

It was the final step in not only giving her back an identity and a fresh start, a new lease on life, but also binding her irrevocably to them. And if Merrick was honest, the latter was what concerned him more. He wanted that knowledge, that *reassurance* that she was his. Not just as some private agreement between the three of them, but to the rest of the world as well.

He wasn't going to breathe easy until the "I dos" were said and their signatures were on the dotted line of a marriage certificate.

Cade eased Elle down onto the bed, and then both men worked to get her out of her jeans and shirt so she'd be more comfortable. Merrick unhooked her bra and left her in her panties before he lifted her and moved her to the center of the bed.

She still hadn't even so much as flinched, and it stirred the guilt inside him that she'd worked so tirelessly over the last week. He was going to make it up to her. A good night's rest. Breakfast in bed tomorrow. And then she was going to take it easy for the entire damn day.

"I'm going to grab a shower, and then I'll be to bed," Cade said in a low voice so he didn't wake Elle.

Merrick stripped down to his boxers and climbed into bed next to Elle, pulling her into his arms. She gave one of those contented, breathy sighs that he loved so much, and she snuggled into his body like a kitten seeking warmth.

He loved that about her. How affectionate she was and how she sought out his touch even in her sleep. Though he and Cade hadn't pressed the issue of sex since that first night they'd finally consummated their relationship and taken things to a whole new level, Elle had still slept between them every single night.

And with the fire and the fallout afterward, they were simply too damn tired at night to focus on the physical aspects of their relationship.

Merrick wasn't wholeheartedly convinced that Elle was ready to take on a normal, healthy physical relationship with one man yet, let alone two. The first time had been just fine. But who was to say that she wouldn't have issues the second or third time?

It was something he was already mentally preparing for because he knew Elle still had a long way to go in order to completely heal from her ordeal.

But she was his. And soon he'd have all the loose ends tied into a neat bow. Her past would no longer be a worry. Who she was no longer mattered. Because who and what she was…was his and Cade's. Their wife. Their woman.

She mumbled something in her sleep and then threw her leg over his. He smiled in the darkness and then tucked her leg between his so that he covered the lower half of her body.

He pressed a kiss to her forehead and barely whispered, "I love you, baby."

———

Merrick forced himself out of bed at five a.m. He didn't bother with a shower yet. He'd save that for after his run. He needed to get in at least five miles and hope to hell he wasn't sucking serious wind after having worked out so sporadically over the last several days.

He was dressing quietly in the dark and reaching for his cross-trainers when he saw Elle rise from the bed.

Cursing under his breath that he'd awakened her when he'd wanted her to sleep in this morning, he started to move toward her when she walked toward the door.

It was an eerie glide, as if she had no care of stumbling in the dark. It wasn't the careful walk of someone finding her way in a dark room. She walked boldly forward, out the door and into the hall.

Son of a bitch. It was happening again.

"Cade, get up!" Merrick called out as he made a run for Elle.

He heard Cade's feet hit the floor as he sped down the hall. This time he caught up to Elle before she left the living room. She was standing in the middle of the floor, her expression completely blank as she stared into nothingness.

Then her forehead wrinkled as though she were in pain, and her lips tightened.

"Elle. Elle!" he said louder as he approached. "Baby, it's me, Merrick. You're sleepwalking again, baby. Wake up for me."

"I trusted you," she said in an accusing tone.

"Huh? What was that, baby? Come on. Wake up for me. Let's go back to bed so you can rest some more."

His hands closed over her shoulders, and as soon as he touched her, she jerked to awareness. The cloudiness left her eyes, and she blinked rapidly, and then she lifted her gaze to Merrick.

Then she crumpled on the spot, as if all her composure fled. She sagged precariously, and Merrick caught her against him before she fell. Cade stalked forward, flanking her other side.

"Let's get her back to bed," Cade said grimly.

"It happened again, didn't it?" Elle asked in a small voice.

Merrick sighed. "Yes, baby, it did."

She closed her eyes as Cade led her gently back toward the bedroom. A moment later, she was sitting on the edge of the bed while Cade rubbed warmth into her hands. She was visibly upset and shaken by the events. And whatever she had dreamed.

"Who did you trust, honey?" Cade asked. "Who betrayed you?"

She raised startled eyes to Cade.

"In the living room, while you were still out of it, you said, 'I trusted you.'"

Her brow wrinkled, and for a moment, she seemed to fade out again. Then she simply said, "Him."

"The man who attacked you?" Cade asked gently.

"I think so. I don't know. Maybe?"

The frustration in her voice ate at Merrick. He hated that this caused her so much pain and heartache.

Merrick eased down on the bed beside her and pulled her into his arms, rocking her carefully back and forth.

"It'll come, baby. Don't rush. When you're ready, it'll come. When you're able to cope with the knowledge of what happened to you, then you'll remember. Until then, your mind is protecting you from what it believes you aren't ready to deal with."

She nodded mechanically and then buried her face in his chest. He pressed his mouth to her hair, inhaling her scent. Closing his eyes, he took in a deep breath and tried to still her quivering body.

He wanted to absorb the fear and darkness that invaded her soul. Take it from her so she never suffered again.

Damn it, but every time it seemed they were making progress, her past reared its ugly head. It wasn't that he and Cade had discounted her past. Or that they were stupid enough to think it would never matter.

But the selfish part of him wanted to make damn sure she was tied to him and Cade, emotionally and legally, before they dealt with whatever ghosts haunted Elle.

It made him sound like a manipulative asshole. No better than the bastard who'd abused her trust and hurt her physically and emotionally.

He curled his hand into a fist. Fuck that. He loved her. He wanted only the best for her. He knew damn well that Cade felt the exact same way. They wanted to be there for her every step of the way. Even if it meant the end result was having to give her up.

It sure as hell wouldn't be without a fight. But there was a small part of him, his deepest, most dreaded fear, that she could already belong to someone else. That one morning she'd wake up, remember her old life and realize she was in love with someone else. That she'd leave him and Cade and return to the life she'd once lived.

But he also knew that part of loving her was wanting her to be happy. It would gut him to have to let her go, but could he honestly ever try to manipulate her emotionally in order to make her stay?

Hell no.

Someone in her past had hurt her. Had betrayed her trust and made her the wounded, fragile woman they'd discovered in the gun shop so many months ago.

If Merrick had his way, that man would never have another chance to hurt Elle. He hoped like hell that Elle hadn't been in love with the bastard who'd raped and then tried to kill her.

All evidence pointed to a dirty cop, which meant that they couldn't just barge ahead and do a wide-open search for her identity or her past.

"Merrick, ease up, man," Cade said in a low voice.

Merrick looked down, realizing how tightly he was holding Elle and how fierce his expression must be. Rage had clouded his mind. And gut-wrenching fear of losing Elle.

"Go for your run," Cade said. "I'll take care of Elle. Go clear your head. You've got to get back into your routine."

Elle stirred in his arms and pulled her dark head away, her eyes finally reflecting calm…and determination that had been lacking moments earlier. It was as if she'd pulled out of the fog of sleep and was now fully aware and in the present.

"Go," she said softly. "I'm okay. You've got to do this, Merrick. It's too important to let go of. You—we—can't let what happened ruin this opportunity. You're at the top of your game. This may be the only title shot you get. You've worked too long and too hard to let it slip through your fingers at this stage."

He stared between Cade and Elle for a long moment as he carefully considered his words. It was a matter he'd given a lot of consideration to over the last few days.

"Sometimes goals and ambitions change," he said. "Sometimes what you want in one stage of your life isn't what you want—or need—in the next stage. And sometimes your heart lies in other areas."

Cade frowned. Elle's lips pursed, and her eyes narrowed in puzzlement.

"You're not saying that this is no longer what you want, are you?" Cade demanded. "You'd honestly give up before you ever take a shot at the title?"

Merrick didn't respond right away. In no way did he want it thought that he was rendering snap judgments.

"I'm not saying anything other than things change," Merrick said calmly.

Elle slid to her knees in front of him. She took his hands in hers and cradled them to her chest. Her gaze found his, and her eyes burned with sincerity. And worry.

"Please don't do this because of me," she choked out. "I know how much you want this, Merrick. You've eaten, slept and lived this ever since I came here. I've watched you train tirelessly. I've seen you spar with some of the best. I've witnessed a remarkable change in you as you've become more centered and focused. Everyone in your camp believes that this is your time. That this is the fight where you take it all. *I* believe this is your time," she added softly.

He slipped his hand over her jaw, cupping her cheek and caressing the silky lines of her face.

"What I care most about is you. Not a title. Not validation or recognition. I love you, and I want what's best for us. Not me. *Us*."

Her eyes filled with tears. "You can have us both, Merrick. I'm here. I'm not going anywhere. Cade and I stand behind you, and we believe in you."

She glanced up at Cade and then returned her gaze to Merrick. He sensed her hesitation, and then her chin jutted out, and she pressed her lips together in a firm, determined line as if she'd grasped the courage to say what she wanted.

"If Cade and I took over most of the office stuff, it would leave you free to train. Exclusively, I mean."

Merrick frowned, and she reached her finger up to hush him by placing it over his lips.

"I know this is yours and Cade's business. But you have a great opportunity ahead of you. And if you win? You aren't going to be out monitoring clients' businesses. You'll be training. You'll have endorsements. Your life is going to change."

His frown deepened, and he glanced at his best friend and the woman they both loved.

"Maybe I don't want things to change," he said quietly.

# chapter twenty-nine

"CAN WE TALK?"

Merrick turned from the window where he'd been standing and after a brief hesitation gave a short nod. "Where's Elle?"

"She's in the shower, so let's make this quick."

Cade shoved his hands into his pockets and exhaled deeply. "Look, I get it. The thing with the fight and training. And Elle. I do. But I think you're making a mistake, and I'd hate to see you make a decision you later regret."

Merrick's lips twisted, and he remained silent and brooding. Typical Merrick. Especially when he had something on his mind.

For a long moment, neither man spoke, and Cade was content to let Merrick stew until he finally broke and talked about it.

"I'm too old for a career in mixed martial arts, and we both know it," Merrick finally said.

Cade lifted one brow. "That was the last thing I expected you to come up with. Is that the best you can do?"

Merrick glared at him, his jaw twitching as he grew more pissed off. Hell, the way this conversation was going, they'd likely end up on the floor.

"You can't quit now," Cade said mildly. "I can think of a lot of reasons why you shouldn't, but I'll give you the most important one. Elle."

"She's precisely *why* I'd consider hanging it up," Merrick said, frustration edging his voice. "She's the *only* reason I'd give it up."

"And how do you think it'll make her feel to know you gave up a title fight for the heavyweight championship? For her. Think about what this does to our relationship. And then think about how sensitive she is about being a burden. Of intruding on our lives. Of our lives changing too much because of her. She worries that she's too much trouble all the damn time. And you're sending her confirmation of that paranoia by being a dumbass and giving up something you've worked your ass off for over the last few years."

Merrick frowned. He started to open his mouth and then snapped it shut.

"Hell," he finally muttered.

"Elle wants to contribute," Cade said, pushing his point when he knew he'd just scored a major hit. "She wants to feel like she's part of everything we do. So let her be involved in your training. Hell, she's watched you in the gym for months. She nags you about eating right. She wants to take over more of the business so you can train. And for the eventuality of you winning. She believes you're going to win, and she knows that when you do, things will change for you."

Merrick's brow furrowed, and he stared hard at Cade. "You don't think she worries that I'll dump her or lose my shit and become a different person if I win the title, do you?"

"No, I don't believe she thinks that at all. I'm not saying that worry won't come later, but I think all she's focused on is you getting to the top and making sure she doesn't interfere in your path to success."

"Goddamn it."

The heartfelt expletive blew out forcefully, and he curled his hands into tight fists.

"She's changed me, man. She's made me see what's important. She's not interfering with anything. What she's doing is showing me that what I have right now in front of me is pretty damn good and that I don't need to be off chasing a dream to be happy."

Cade nodded. "I understand. But what happens if you give it all up and you're left with a whole pile of what-ifs? What if you'd taken your shot and what if you'd won? What if you became a world champion in your thirties? It's not as if there haven't been a lot of other great fighters who mixed it up well into their thirties. Chuck Lidell and Randy Couture to name a few."

"I guess I'm just scared," Merrick admitted. "I don't want to lose her. You and I both know the closer we get to this fight, the more focused on it I'll become. To the exclusion of all else. I'll be training hard, and my focus will change. I don't want her to ever think that she's not the most important thing to me."

"I think you have to give her more credit than that," Cade said. "You have to trust her."

Merrick blinked as if the idea was ridiculous. "Of course I trust her."

"Then show her. Go hard at this. We'll work it out between the three of us. You know I'll be with her the entire time you're training, and you also know that I'm not going to be making a move to push you out of the picture. She won't be alone, and she won't be unprotected. And when you need her, she'll be right there waiting."

Finally Merrick nodded his head. He sucked in a deep breath and leveled a stare at Cade. "You're right. I need to go hard at this. I won't get another shot. I need to see where this is going to take me. I've worked too hard to climb up the ranks to be next in line for a title fight to quit now."

Cade held up his fist. "Then what do you say we shut the fuck up and get to work?"

Merrick bumped his fist to Cade's and cracked a grin. "I'm always in need of a sparring partner."

"Fuck you," Cade said rudely. "I'm not going to be your punching bag. That's what those other dumbasses are for."

Merrick grinned. "I'll make the call to Dakota and let him know I'm back in and we're going to go hard to make up for lost time."

# chapter thirty

"GO HARD AT HIM!" DAKOTA shouted from the corner. "Come on, Merrick, you aren't concentrating."

Elle watched from the far side of the room, her brow furrowing as Dakota slapped his towel down onto the mat. She knew Dakota loved Merrick. They'd been friends for a long time. Nearly as long as Cade and Merrick. But he always got so worked up. It made her cringe because everything was always an emergency, and nothing Merrick ever did seemed to be good enough.

Maybe that was the way of it in the fighting world, but Elle hated it.

"If this was a real fight, he would have wiped the mat with you, and he's in a different weight class, for Christ's sake," Dakota said in disgust.

Merrick turned his head just enough that he could look at her. Their gazes connected and held, and she held up her thumb in a ridiculously silly manner, but it was all she could think to do to let him know she believed in him.

His lips quirked up into a smile just about the time his sparring partner hit him. She flinched as Merrick reeled back and then focused his attention back in the ring.

Dakota's face drew into a scowl, and he looked directly at Elle, shaking his head. Then he walked around the ring and took position in front of Elle so Merrick couldn't see her and she couldn't see Merrick.

For a moment, Elle sat in stunned silence. Dakota was blaming her for whatever he perceived as Merrick's problem today? She'd been going to his training sessions since the very start. Merrick had missed several days after the fire. What did Dakota expect on his first day back? Perfection?

But then, really, would anything ever be good enough for Dakota?

When two of the other fighters who were standing ringside also turned to look at her, her cheeks burned, and she fidgeted self-consciously in her chair.

Was she a distraction? Should she have stayed at home? She just wanted Merrick to know he had her support.

A few minutes later, Merrick left the ring to go into the locker room, and Dakota immediately stalked in her direction. He tossed Merrick's keys onto her lap, startling her as she scrambled to catch them before they fell off and hit the floor.

Dakota looked pissed off—and determined.

"Look, why don't you head home for the day. I'll bring Merrick home when we're done. His concentration is shot to hell, and I need his head in the game before he gets himself hurt. With a month left before this fight, an injury could be devastating."

She stared at him and then glanced down at the keys in her hand. The hostility in Dakota's voice made her uncomfortable. What was she supposed to do? The last thing she wanted was to make a scene and wreck Merrick's training session.

Without saying a word or giving Dakota the satisfaction of seeing how nervous he made her, she simply got up and walked away, her fingers curled tightly around those keys.

The sunlight nearly blinded her as she came from the much darker gym. She blinked, thinking she saw someone close to Merrick's Hummer, but when her eyes adjusted, she didn't see anything.

She climbed into the vehicle and turned the key in the ignition. It was another beautiful day with a crispness to the air that was welcome. She punched the button to open the sunroof and then contemplated her options.

Cade was in a meeting with clients, and Charlie was meeting with the insurance adjuster to get the check for the damage to the office building.

She could either go sit in the newly appropriated, cramped office space, or she could go home to an empty house.

Either place she'd be alone, so she figured it was more welcome to just head home. She'd make lunch and wait for Merrick to finish and get home. And hopefully Dakota would just drop Merrick off and not stay.

Dakota had become testier and testier as it drew closer to the fight. Catherine had confided in Elle that Dakota was intense and that he didn't mean anything by it but he took his role very seriously, and she admitted that he became unbearable even to her when it got down to the last weeks before a major fight.

Catherine, at least, had remained as sweet and supportive as she always had. But lately, Elle had felt like an intruder when she went to Merrick's sessions with him. Even the other fighters looked at her like she didn't belong.

Maybe she was being overly sensitive, but she hated the way she'd been made to feel today. She was embarrassed to have been kicked out of the gym like an unwanted nuisance.

She pulled into the drive of the house and sat there a moment before turning off the engine. She left the path into the garage open because the Hummer didn't fit and it was where Cade parked his slightly smaller SUV.

She got out, fiddling with the keys to find the right one for the door and walked through the open garage toward the kitchen door.

Just as she started to insert the key into the lock, an arm slid around her neck and yanked her back against a hard chest. The grip on her neck was so firm she couldn't breathe, and before she could scream, a hand clamped down hard over her mouth.

She began to kick wildly as she was dragged backward against the wall. Pain shocked her into silence when her attacker punched her in the side.

"Shut the fuck up and listen to me," the man hissed in her ear. "I have a message for your boys, and I want you to deliver it word for word. You got me?"

She nodded, her head spinning from lack of oxygen and the pain in her side. His hand slid intimately up her body, lingering over her belly and then moving underneath her breast.

She began to struggle again, refusing to allow this son of a bitch to molest her in her own garage.

Her head flew back when he grabbed a handful of her hair and yanked. Tears sprang to her eyes as her neck craned at an impossible angle. With his free hand, he punched her again, and she nearly blacked out.

Dragging her limp body back up his, he forced his mouth close to her ear.

"You tell your boys that they fucked with the wrong person. If they don't drop the charges, I'll be back, and I'll fuck you up so they can't even recognize you. You understand?"

"Y-yes," she gasped out.

He jerked her around and then backhanded her, snapping her head back. She tasted blood, and this time when she staggered, he let her go down.

She fell in a heap on the garage floor, trying desperately to squeeze air into her lungs. Her side was hurting so badly that she worried he'd broken her ribs.

The one word that echoed over and over in her mind was no. No! This couldn't happen to her again.

Images flashed in her mind. The memory of being pushed roughly to the ground. Her face pressed into the dirt. The shock and…betrayal.

Betrayal.

She'd known her attacker.

It was someone she'd *trusted*.

She curled into a tight ball, hoping to protect the most vulnerable parts of her body. Pain lanced through her ribs once more as he kicked her.

Oh God, what could she do? She was helpless.

Rage exploded inside her. She was not going to be some helpless victim who couldn't even fight back.

She rolled quickly, hoping to catch her attacker off guard. And apparently she did. Ignoring the pain in her ribcage, she righted herself and lunged for the crowbar mere feet away on the floor.

She grabbed it and came up swinging.

He howled in pain when she connected with his face. His head snapped back, and blood spattered onto the concrete below them.

Not giving him a chance to break away, she nailed him again, this time in the ribs.

He doubled over, holding his midsection as blood dripped from his mouth.

"How's it feel, you son of a bitch?" she raged.

She hit him again, and he dropped like a stone onto the garage floor. For a long moment, she stared down at him, still holding the crowbar over her head.

Then it slid from her grasp and clattered loudly at her feet. Her knees buckled, and she went down. The material of her pants ripped where her knees scraped the concrete, and then she pitched to the side, every breath she took excruciating.

For a long moment, she simply lay there, trying to gain control over the pain that wracked her body. Then she became aware of the fact that she had a body lying in her garage. She may have killed a man.

She reached out, groping blindly for the purse that had gone flying when the man had grabbed her. Her fingers scraped across it, and she fumbled for it, dragging it close enough that she could dig her cell phone out of it.

Every breath was agony, and her hands shook so violently that it took her three attempts just to punch in 911.

Finally she put the phone to her ear, and when the dispatcher came over the line, she simply croaked, "Help me, please. I think I just killed a man."

# chapter thirty-one

CADE TURNED ON THEIR STREET and accelerated before slowing for the one stop sign before the house. He frowned when he saw a myriad of cop cars with flashing lights and two ambulances parked in what looked like *his* yard.

What the fuck?

He automatically checked his phone, wondering if he'd missed anything, but there were no missed calls or texts. He floored the accelerator and raced down the street, his pulse pounding in his ears.

He'd assumed when he'd gotten to the office and no one was there that Merrick and Elle had just gone home after his training session. He'd driven straight to the house thinking they could have a late lunch together.

As he pulled up, he saw Merrick's Hummer parked to the side, and to further his what-the-fuck reaction, two paramedics were loading a strange guy into the back of the ambulance. Even from a distance, Cade could see the blood on the man's face.

He slammed on the brakes and slid out, engine still running. As soon as he got to the edge of the driveway, he was held up by two cops.

"I live here," Cade bit out. "What the fuck is going on?"

One of them looked relieved. "Thank God. Maybe you can help us with her."

Cade froze at the mention of *her*.

"We can't get near her. She's out of it. She called 911 saying she'd killed a guy."

The cop jerked his thumb over his shoulder toward the ambulance the stranger had been loaded onto.

"That guy over there. When we got here, she was barely conscious and lying next to the guy on the floor of the garage. She took a crowbar to him. But as soon as we tried to touch her, she went ballistic. No one can get near her. Right now, someone's trying to get close enough to sedate her so we can take her to the hospital. She's pretty banged up. Looks like the guy worked her over before she got ahold of him with the crowbar."

"Where the fuck is Merrick?" Cade exploded.

The policeman's brow wrinkled. "There's no one here but her and the dude she beat the shit out of."

Not waiting to hear anything more, Cade broke and ran for the garage. What he saw made his stomach bottom out.

Elle was hunched in a protective posture, her legs drawn up as close to her body as she could get them. Her arms were wrapped tightly around her legs, and her head was buried between her knees.

A female police officer and one of the paramedics were a short distance away trying to talk her down. The police officer reached out to touch her arm, and Elle reacted violently, jerking away and sliding back in panic.

Cade pushed his way through and dropped to his knees beside her. He gathered her tightly in his arms, ignoring the way she went tense from head to toe.

"Elle, it's me, Cade. It's me, honey. I've got you."

For a long moment, he thought he hadn't been able to penetrate her consciousness, but then she went utterly limp and wrapped herself around his much bigger body so there wasn't a breath between them.

He kissed her head, his mind a whirl of confusion. What the hell had happened?

"Make them go away," she whispered. "Please, Cade, just make them all go away."

Cade stared at the sea of police officers and medical personnel. His heart sank. He knew how terrified she was of policemen, but he couldn't make them go away. Not even for her. "I can't do that, honey, I'm sorry."

She buried her face in his neck and clung like a burr to him. He shifted his weight so he could push up from the hard concrete. It couldn't be comfortable for her to be on the ground, and he needed to see the extent of her injuries.

"Talk to me, Elle," he gently coaxed. "How bad is it? Can you stand? Where are you hurt? Hold on to me, honey. I won't let you fall."

He rose, taking her with him before he allowed her to put her feet down. His arm stayed firmly around her because she was wobbly as a newborn colt, and he worried if he let go, she'd face plant right in front of him.

He was about to motion to the paramedic to bring the damn stretcher because she wasn't going to make it, when Merrick and Dakota shoved their way into the garage, their brows drawn in confusion and concern.

Dakota paled and rubbed his hands uneasily down his pants when he got a look at Elle.

Merrick promptly lost his mind. "What the fuck happened here? What the hell happened to Elle?" There was rage and fear in the big man's eyes. His hands were curled into tight fists at his sides, but Cade knew that look. Merrick was about to kick some serious ass, and if Cade didn't get a handle on this quickly, they'd all end up in jail.

Cade held up his free hand to stop the flow of Merrick's tirade.

"I don't know yet, man. I just got here. I don't know what the hell is going on. I'm hoping the police will fill me in, but first I need to make sure Elle is taken care of."

"Why the hell did you leave the gym?" Merrick demanded. "You should have never left on your own. We've been over this, Elle!"

Cade could hear the worry in Merrick's voice and knew he was reacting to the same gut-wrenching fear that had gripped Cade when he'd first arrived. But Elle went stiff next to him and then pushed away from his body. Her eyes filled with tears as she stared at Merrick and Dakota with so much hurt in her gaze that it took Cade's breath away. What the ever-loving fuck was going on here? Then she simply turned and slowly and painfully walked away, pushing into the house and slamming the door behind her.

He turned on Merrick. "Have you lost your goddamn mind? What the hell were you yelling at her for?"

Merrick was pale, and his fists still curled tight at his sides. "I didn't mean to yell at her, for God's sake. She scared the piss out of me. I just don't understand why she left the gym and came here alone. She's never supposed to go *anywhere* alone!"

Dakota looked like he was going to puke, but Cade didn't have time to figure out what the hell his problem was.

Two of the police officers stepped forward, and one spoke up. "We're going to need a statement from her, and she really needs to be looked at. When we arrived on scene, there was a lot of blood on her, and she was having a hard time breathing."

"Just give me a minute," Cade said holding out his hand. "I'll go in after her."

The officer put his hand out over Cade's. "With all due respect, sir, this is a crime scene. I'll be coming with you inside."

Cade looked at him like he was crazy. "You don't think she's committed a crime. Are you insane? Did you see her?"

The officer sighed. "I have to take her statement, and I'd like to do it as soon as possible. If she's well enough not to be transported to the hospital, then we can do it here. Otherwise we'll swing by the ER and talk to her there."

Cade blew out his breath, called back the torrent of curses and then stalked toward the door, determined to get to Elle and sort out this nightmare.

Merrick was on his heels, and the two burst through the kitchen and into the living room. Finding it empty, Cade headed to the bedroom they shared only to find it empty as well. He walked down the hall to the room Elle had first stayed in, and when he opened the door, he couldn't control his reaction to the sight before him.

Elle was sitting on the bed, her shirt pulled up to bare her ribcage which was already purple with bruising. One hand was pressed to her side and it was obvious she was struggling for breaths. Tears ran unchecked down her cheeks, mixing with the blood from her nose and mouth.

"Dear God," Merrick said in a horrified voice.

Her gaze yanked upward, hurt crowding her eyes once more as she looked at the two men. She pulled her shirt down and immediately covered herself protectively as he and Merrick surged forward.

Cade dropped to his knees in front of her, his hands immediately going to her shirt so he could pull it back up.

"What the hell happened, Elle?"

"He punched me," she said in a choked voice. "Twice. And then he kicked me. It hurts to breathe."

"She needs to get to the hospital," the police officer said in a terse voice. He'd followed Cade and Merrick inside, and his expression was grim as he took in the bruising on Elle's side and abdomen.

"Fuck yeah," Merrick growled.

Merrick strode forward, his intention clear as he reached for Elle. To Cade's surprise, she turned into him, huddling into his arms. She turned her face away from Merrick, and hot tears slid onto Cade's collarbone.

Merrick took a step back, shock and confusion etched in his expression. For now, Cade had to ignore whatever the hell was going on because Elle needed immediate care, and this time Dallas's clinic wasn't going to cover it.

With infinite care, he stood, cradling Elle in his arms, and then he walked out of the bedroom, leaving the cop and Merrick to follow.

When he got outside, he saw that a stretcher had been pulled into the garage, and he carefully lowered Elle onto it. Dakota pushed off the wall of the garage, his face ashen.

"Is she okay?" Dakota asked.

"We don't know yet," Cade said grimly.

Elle slid her hand into his, her grip so tight that his fingers were bloodless.

"Don't leave me," she whispered. "I don't want to go alone."

He leaned down and kissed her forehead as the paramedic began to push her toward the waiting ambulance.

"I'm not going anywhere, honey. I'll be right by your side the entire time."

# chapter thirty-two

MERRICK PACED THE WAITING ROOM of the ER about to go insane waiting for someone to come out and let them know how Elle was.

They'd given her name as Elle Walker and listed their address. When prompted for other identifying information, they'd simply said in the confusion and the rush to get her to the hospital that they hadn't gotten her wallet.

Until Dallas came through with her Social Security number and birth certificate, she was still...*nobody*.

God, he just wanted to hurry up and be able to see her so he could apologize for being such an asshole. He had no excuse. He'd seen her there, bloody and clothing torn, and he'd reacted emotionally in his terror.

Cade was in no better shape. He stood across the room staring out the window, his hands shoved into his pockets. But his foot tapped anxiously against the floor, and tension rolled off him in waves.

What surprised Merrick was how strung out Dakota looked. The man looked ill. His face was ashen and he sat in a chair away from Cade and Merrick with his head down, hands clasped over his nape.

"Son of a bitch, what's taking so long?" Cade burst out.

"I wish to hell I knew," Merrick said tightly. "I was a complete dick to her. She was attacked and injured, and I yelled at her for leaving the gym.

God, I'm an asshole."

Dakota lurched to his feet and looked like he'd vomit.

"Merrick," he began in an uneasy voice. "I have to tell you what I did. I can't let you think... Jesus..." He broke off and ran his hand wearily through his hair. "God, I'm sorry, man."

Merrick's stomach coiled into a knot as he stared at his longtime friend and trainer. At the guilt brimming in his eyes. "What the fuck did you *do*?" he asked in a low, menacing voice.

"Dakota?" Catherine asked in a worried tone from the doorway to the waiting room.

Dakota glanced in his wife's direction, shame dulling his features.

Merrick advanced. "What. Did. You. *Do*?"

"I told her to leave," Dakota choked out. "I was pissed because the sparring session wasn't going well and your concentration was shot to shit and you kept looking over at her and I knew you were distracted. So when you went to the locker room, I tossed her the keys and told her to split."

"You did *what*?" Cade yelled.

Merrick couldn't even respond. He was too dumfounded. Too rattled by the fact that someone he trusted so implicitly had placed Elle in a dangerous situation. She could have been killed. As it was, some asshole had beaten the hell out of her, and she'd had to defend herself with a crowbar. And now she was carrying the weight of nearly killing another man. And hell, he may die yet. He was in critical condition with a brain bleed. They were taking him to surgery right now.

"I never imagined something like this would happen," Dakota said, closing his eyes. His entire posture was defeated, his shoulders sagging. "I just thought it would be a good idea if she went home so you could get your head back into the game. We have four weeks until this fight, and I want you at the top of your game."

"So you sent the woman I love into a dangerous situation—a situation you were well aware of, Dakota. Hell, she just got caught in an office building after being shot at and the building torched. You knew we weren't sending her anywhere without one of us at all times. Why the fuck would you take it upon yourself to send her home behind my back?"

"I was doing what I thought was best for you," Dakota said in a frustrated voice. "You don't see it, Merrick, but the rest of us do. Your edge is slipping. You aren't as sharp as you were even a month ago. You're going to fuck up the *one* shot you have at the big time. If you won't think about yourself, then at least think of the rest of us who've spent years supporting you and building you up and making sacrifices because we believed in you."

A garbled sound of rage bubbled from Cade's throat, but Merrick held up his hand. He had this.

"You placed a woman in a position of danger and vulnerability. How exactly did you expect she'd defend herself if something like this happened? You didn't tell me what you'd done. You could have picked up the phone and called Cade to let him know. You could have called Dallas. Cade's dad. There's a hell of a lot you could have done, and you didn't do shit. This is on you, Dakota, and I'm not going to forget it. You're fired."

Catherine made a sound of pain, and when he looked at her, her eyes were wounded.

"I'm sorry, Cathy," Merrick said quietly.

Catherine walked forward, tentatively touching Merrick on the arm. "Think about it, Merrick. Don't make any hasty decisions. Dakota was a dickhead, but he's a dickhead who loves you and is loyal to a fault. Maybe too loyal. He's not used to having to share you with others, but he'll learn. Sleep on it please, and we can talk when emotions aren't so high."

Merrick kissed her cheek. "I can't guarantee anything, Cathy. He betrayed my trust. He betrayed Elle."

"I'm sorry, man," Dakota said, sadness so deep in his eyes that it made Merrick's gut clench. "I fucked up. I hope you can find it in your heart to forgive me. I don't want to throw away the years we have together over this."

"*You* did this," Merrick pointed out.

"Yeah, I know," Dakota said quietly. He turned to his wife. "Come on, Cathy. Let's leave them to see to Elle."

With an unhappy frown and one last look in Merrick's direction, Catherine followed her husband out of the waiting room.

"Son of a bitch, I fucked up," Merrick swore when Dakota and Catherine had gone. "I was such a bastard to her. And fuck it all, I'll never forget that look in her eyes when I yelled at her about leaving when Dakota was the one who kicked her out. I can only imagine how she felt and how embarrassing it was for her when Dakota acted like a dickhead and tossed her out of the gym. And then I blame her for what happened to her. Jesus, but when I fuck up, I fuck up big."

"We still don't even know what happened," Cade said wearily. "It's all very bizarre. It's pissing me off that they kicked us out of her room and won't let us be in there with her."

"That's bullshit," Merrick fumed. "They can't keep us away from her, and you know what? I'm tired of this crap. I'm going in to see her, and they're going to have to arrest me to keep me out."

Cade grinned. "Sounds like a plan to me."

Merrick pushed through the door leading to the exam rooms, Cade on his heels, and he went down the hall, peeking into every single one until finally he came to where Elle was.

His heart squeezed nearly out of his chest when he saw her lying in the hospital bed curled into a small ball. A police officer sat next to the bed, and it appeared that he was questioning her in a gentle voice. But Elle was terrified, her face so ashen that she looked close to passing out.

"What the fuck is going on here?" Cade demanded, his voice cracking like a whip through the room.

The officer jerked around, his brows drawn into angry slashes. "I'm questioning Miss Walker. Get the hell out."

Cade advanced menacingly. "I was very explicit that no one, and I mean *no one*, was to be in this room unless Merrick or I were with her. She's scared shitless, and you're going to intimidate her into answering your questions?"

"I wasn't intimidating her," the officer snapped. "I was trying to get her side of the story. There's a man in ICU, and she looks like a bus ran over her. And there's blood all over her garage floor. I'm just doing my job, so chill out."

"You don't say *jack* to her without us present," Merrick snarled. "And only if she consents. Did you even ask her if she felt well enough to talk to you?"

The officer remained silent.

"I didn't think so," Cade bit out.

Cade plopped into the chair on the opposite side of the bed, staring challengingly at the police officer. "We aren't leaving."

The police officer turned to Elle. "If you'd prefer they not be here, I'll make sure they're escorted out."

One part of Merrick appreciated that the cop was looking out for Elle. The other part wanted to ask him and what *army* would be escorting them out?

"They can stay. I want them to stay. They need to hear what happened. The threat was to them," she said, her voice still shaking.

She fingered the sheet covering her nervously, the tips white from her grip. She was obviously terrified of the cop and trying valiantly to hold it together.

Cade leaned forward, his frown dark. "I'm more concerned with whether you've been taken care of first. Have they treated you? Are you in any pain? Your statement can damn well wait until after you're more comfortable."

She smiled faintly. "They did x-rays already, and they gave me a shot of pain medicine." She lifted her wrist where the IV was inserted to show him. "Just waiting on the doctor to come back with the report."

"She was nearly hysterical. She *was* hysterical," the cop said grimly. "They had to give her something to calm her before she hurt herself."

"Ever occur to you that you could be part of the problem?" Cade said rudely. "No one should have so much as looked at her until we were allowed to see her. She's been brutalized by some creep, and then she was surrounded by strangers."

The officer nodded. "I understand. I apologize, Miss Walker, if I frightened you in any way. I only want to help you, and in order to do that, I have to get to the bottom of this."

She nodded hesitantly, but the fear was still there in her eyes.

Merrick sat on the end of the bed, anxious to be rid of the cop so he could make things right with Elle. It was killing him not to touch her or hold her in his arms.

The officer cleared his throat. "If I can get back to the matter at hand. Can you tell me exactly what occurred when you arrived at your home?"

Elle swallowed and grew paler. It was automatic for Merrick to place his hand over her sheet-covered leg. Just so she'd know that he was there and that things were okay now.

"Will I…" She drew in a big breath and then grimaced and put her hand to her ribcage, flinching in pain caused by the deep inhalation. "Will I be arrested for what I did?" she asked in a small voice.

"What the fuck?" Cade exploded. "Over my dead body! Is that what they've been telling you, Elle?"

The officer held his hand up. "No one has said anything of the sort. Preliminary evidence shows this to be a matter of self-defense. The sooner

I can get her statement, the sooner we can be done with this. I don't see any reason that any action will be taken against her unless we find evidence that contradicts her statement."

Merrick's lips twisted as he tried to control his anger.

"Now, if you can start from the beginning," the officer said patiently.

He shot Cade and Merrick a quelling look before directing his attention back to Elle.

"I got out of the truck and went through the garage to the kitchen door. Before I could unlock it, he grabbed me from behind. He wrapped his hand around my neck and squeezed so hard I couldn't breathe."

As she spoke, her hand fluttered to her throat where bruises had already appeared. It pissed Merrick off all the more that she'd been there alone and unprotected when she damn well should have been with him at the gym. He was going to take Dakota apart over this.

"He yanked me backwards, and when I tried to fight, he punched me in the side."

Cade balled both hands into fists, and his entire body vibrated with rage.

"I don't remember a whole lot more," she confessed. "He told me that he had a message for 'my boys' and that if they didn't drop the charges, he would come back and 'fuck me up.'"

The officer was steadily jotting down her every word, and he frowned as she said the last. Then he turned in Cade and Merrick's direction.

"Drop what charges?"

Cade sighed. "I can't be one hundred percent sure, but I'm at least ninety-nine that this is retaliation for the guy we had arrested a while back for trying to steal a car from a client's car lot. Our office was shot up and torched the very next day and now this."

Merrick shook his head, sick at heart that Elle was being targeted because of him and Cade.

To Cade and Merrick he said, "I'll need to know more about what happened after I've spoken to Miss Walker." Then the officer turned back to Elle. "So what happened after that?"

"He punched me again in the side and then he turned me and hit me in the face. He let me fall, and I remember lying on the floor of the garage thinking that I couldn't allow it to happen again."

The police officer frowned. "Again? What do you mean by that?"

Elle immediately went silent. Her gaze skittered toward Cade, fear making her eyes large against her pale face.

"Someone hurt her before," Cade said shortly.

Before the officer could pursue the matter, Elle stammered on, trying to cover what she'd let slip.

"I just knew I had to get away. I didn't know what he planned to d-do to m-me. I thought that he wouldn't expect me to do anything but lie there, so I lunged for a crowbar that was a short distance away and…I hit him," she finished quietly.

"Good for you," Merrick said fiercely.

Even the cop looked approving.

"I hit him more than once," she said in an almost apologetic tone. "I was so scared. I thought he would kill me."

The officer put his hand over Elle's and squeezed soothingly. "You did fine, Miss Walker. I don't think there's any doubt you acted in self-defense. Hell, if you had killed him, I don't think anyone would hold it against you."

Elle went quiet, eyeing the officer's hand, but she was still. Oddly so. Whatever panic she was feeling, she controlled it well.

"Son of a bitch needs killing," Cade growled. "He has a beef with us so he roughs up a woman?"

The officer muttered his agreement.

Elle carefully extricated her hand from the officer's grasp before continuing on. "After he went down, I fell and then I called 911. I don't remember anything else. Just so many people showing up and all the noise and questions."

Merrick slid his hand up her leg and squeezed her knee. "You did great, baby. You were fierce."

She smiled faintly, but her smile looked sad. "I don't feel great. It made me remember things."

She bit her lip and looked away as if realizing once again she'd spoken out when she shouldn't have.

"Is that all you need?" Cade asked brusquely, looking pointedly at the cop. "She needs to rest. She's been through hell."

The officer rose. "I appreciate you talking to me, Miss Walker. I know it wasn't easy for you and that you're in a lot of pain. If I need anything else, I'll be in touch. I don't anticipate any problems. Obviously we're waiting to see what the condition of your attacker is. He'll most certainly be charged with assault and attempted murder, but between you and me, it'll save a lot of trouble if the asshole just dies."

Elle's eyes widened in surprise, but Merrick wholeheartedly agreed with the officer's assessment.

Merrick rose and extended his hand to the cop who shook it.

"If you need to talk to Elle again, you'll need to go through me or Cade," Merrick said firmly.

The officer nodded and then jotted down both their cell numbers. After telling them he'd be in touch to get the details on the arrest at the car lot and their office being burned, he excused himself from the room.

With more than a little dread, Merrick turned to face Elle, prepared to grovel on his *knees* if necessary for the hurt he'd caused her when she'd already suffered so much pain.

# chapter thirty-three

ELLE LAY BACK AGAINST THE pitiful excuse for a pillow and closed her eyes wearily as the door closed behind the police officer. If she didn't have so many drugs in her, she'd be a shaking, sobbing mess. As it was, she was just incredibly weary, and all she wanted was to go to sleep and escape her reality for a few precious hours.

"Elle?"

Merrick's gentle voice crept into her consciousness. His hand smoothed over her brow and then caressed a line down to her jaw.

With effort, she managed to open her eyes and focus her bleary gaze on him.

"I won't keep you awake long, baby. But I need to say this, okay? I can't let you think this any longer."

He eased onto the bed at her side and angled his body so he was sitting right next to her, his head just over hers.

"It's okay," she said, her words slurred. She just wanted the whole mess to be over.

He took her hand, warming it between his much larger ones. "No, it's not okay. It's not okay at all. Dakota had no right to tell you to leave the gym, and I had no right to jump down your throat. God, I was so scared when I saw you, baby. And I was angry because you should have been with me where you were safe. I fired Dakota. It won't happen again."

She gave him a stricken look, flabbergasted that he'd fired his trainer, someone he'd been with since the very start.

"Why would you fire him?" she asked, appalled.

Merrick gave her a perplexed, bewildered look that clearly said he hadn't expected her response.

"Because he put you in danger. He presumed to tell you what to do and where to be." His voice rose as he grew angrier. "He had no right to tell you anything at *all*."

"He was only looking out for your best interests," she said wearily, so tired that her ache was bone deep. "You *were* distracted, Merrick. Even I could see it."

"Do you honest to God think that you were the reason I wasn't focused?" He studied her a moment and then shook his head. "Don't answer that. It's clear that's exactly what you think."

"Merrick," Cade interjected carefully. "Now isn't the time, man. She's about to fall over."

Frustration ate at Merrick. He couldn't let her go on thinking what she was thinking. He leaned down close, cupping his hand over her forehead and smoothing her hair back as he stared into her eyes.

"Listen to me, Elle. I admit I was distracted. But it had nothing to do with you. If you want to know why I kept looking over at you, it was because it felt good to know you were there. When I felt myself losing focus, I'd look at you and it would reinvigorate me. It would remind me of what I was fighting for. I like you being there. I've become dependent on you being there. I don't want to think about you not being around when I'm training. You're like my security blanket.

"We fighters are a superstitious lot, and for me, you've become my talisman. I need you there. I *want* you there. And Dakota had no goddamn right to tell you to go home. From now on, I want you to have the confidence to stand up and say no. Because there's never going to be a time when I don't want you around, baby. Do you understand that?"

She nodded slowly, her eyes dull with fatigue and the cloud of the medication.

He leaned down to kiss her forehead, leaving his lips there a long moment.

"I love you and I'm so damn sorry for yelling at you. I was scared to death, and I was pissed because I wasn't able to protect you. I was pissed that some son of a bitch put his hands on you. You'll never know how it felt for me to see you there with blood on your face and your body so bruised."

She smiled sluggishly. "You're forgiven. I love you too, Merrick. But don't fire Dakota. You'll regret it."

Merrick worked to keep the frown from his face. He didn't want to upset her, not when she needed rest.

"We'll see," was all he was willing to concede.

At this juncture, Dakota would be lucky if Merrick didn't kick his fucking ass.

"Get some rest, baby," Merrick said gently. "Cade and I will be right here with you."

She sighed and closed her eyes and was out in mere seconds. For a long moment, Merrick watched the steady rise and fall of her chest and how her eyelashes rested delicately on her cheeks.

His thoughts were in turmoil. Something had to be done. They couldn't continue on this way. Things were too chaotic. Out of control. Elle wasn't safe. None of them were.

The door quietly opened behind them, and Merrick swung around to see Dallas stick his head in. Merrick motioned him inside, and Dallas came in, a concerned look on his face.

"What the hell happened?" Dallas asked in a hushed tone.

Merrick relayed the events, and Dallas's face darkened into a fierce scowl.

"Son of a bitch. This is getting ridiculous."

"Tell me about it," Cade muttered.

"Has the doctor been by?" Dallas asked.

Merrick shook his head.

"I'll go see what I can find out since I'm her general practitioner."

"Thanks, man. We appreciate that," Merrick said.

Dallas left and returned just a few minutes later with the ER physician in tow.

After the doctor introduced himself, he cleared his throat. "Miss Walker has two broken ribs and severe bruising around her ribcage. She's going to need to take it easy for the next little while. We'll bind her ribs before she leaves so she doesn't incur further injury. I'd prefer to keep her overnight, but Doctor Carrington has assured me that he'll be looking in on her so I'm agreeable to letting her go so long as she is on complete bed rest for the next twenty-four hours and that she takes it easy for the next two weeks."

Cade and Merrick both nodded, and Merrick sent Dallas a grateful look for stepping in.

"I'll let her sleep off the pain meds, and when she comes around, the nurse will bind her ribs and give her the discharge instructions," the doctor said.

"Thank you," Cade and Merrick both said at the same time.

Now that the formalities were taken care of, Merrick was tired of sitting back when all he really wanted was Elle in his arms. He climbed gingerly onto the bed next to her and carefully positioned himself on his side so he could pull her up against him. He fussed with the blanket and her pillow so she'd be comfortable, and then he went still so she wouldn't be disturbed.

Cade and Dallas stood on the other side of the bed, and after Cade related all that had happened between Dakota and Merrick, Dallas blew out his breath.

"Damn," he murmured. "That's tough, Merrick. You know Dakota is a focused son of a bitch and he can be a selfish bastard when it comes to training. But he's good, and he's been loyal to you and has been with you since day one. Are you really going to fire him?"

"I can't believe you're even questioning that," Merrick said darkly. "He tossed Elle out of the gym and sent her home where she was attacked by some asshole with a grudge. That would have never happened if he'd just kept his mouth shut or, even better, come to me and talked it out before acting on his own and being a complete dickhead."

"I agree there. He fucked up," Dallas said bluntly. "But did he cross a line that he can never go back from? That's the question you have to ask yourself. He has a lot to make up to Elle. No doubt there. But don't you think he should be given the chance to do it?"

Merrick clenched his teeth so he didn't bite the head off of his best friend. He knew Dallas's heart was in the right place, and he knew he was making sense. But *damn it*.

"Look," he finally said. "Right now I'm too pissed off to deal with Dakota. All I'm worried about at the moment is Elle. I want to get her someplace safe. I want to make damn sure she's okay. I'll deal with Dakota when I've calmed down some."

Elle murmured something in her sleep and nuzzled her face closer into his chest. He automatically put his hand to her hair and stroked the dark strands.

"It's okay, baby," he murmured close to her ear. "Rest now."

"I've got to run back to the clinic. I left a few patients waiting when I heard what happened," Dallas said.

Cade's brow furrowed. "How *did* you know what happened?"

"Cathy called me."

Merrick sighed. The whole thing sucked. No, he didn't want to lose longtime friends. But neither could he keep a person around who was purposely trying to drive a wedge between him and Elle. Over his dead body would he ever let anyone come between them.

"I'll check in on Elle tonight if that's okay," Dallas said as he turned toward the door.

"We'd appreciate that, man," Cade said. "Thanks."

Dallas held up his hand in a wave and then disappeared out the door.

Merrick sighed and closed his eyes, suddenly as weary as Elle had looked. Damn but the entire day had sucked.

"What are we going to do about this, Merrick?" Cade asked in a grim voice.

Merrick didn't pretend not to know what Cade was talking about.

"I don't know," Merrick said honestly. "One thing's for sure. They've declared war, and they've made it obvious that they aren't above stooping to the level of attacking an innocent woman to get their point across."

# chapter thirty-four

MERRICK AND CADE HAD TAKEN Elle and checked into a hotel for the night. Their house was a police crime scene, but even if it wasn't riddled with police tape, there was no way in hell they'd take her back to a place where her attacker had already boldly waltzed in.

After the way the office had been shot up and torched, the next logical conclusion was for there to be a similar attack on their home.

Elle had still been groggy even after sleeping off the pain medication, and as soon as she'd become aware enough to get up and go to the bathroom, Cade had given her another dose of pain killers and tucked her promptly back into bed.

Cade and Merrick took turns checking in on her until they were certain she was down for the count. Still, they stayed close by her door in case she woke up in pain or just scared.

Dallas showed up at nine p.m. with Chinese takeout. They sprawled in the sitting area of the suite far enough away from the bedroom so Elle wouldn't be disturbed but close enough that they could get to her fast.

"So what are you going to do, man?" Dallas said bluntly. "You've got a fight in four weeks, and you just fired your trainer."

"I don't know yet," Merrick ground out. "I need some time to think."

I've been a little worried about Elle at the moment. She's more important than some damn fight."

"I get it," Dallas said calmly. "But I don't want you to fuck around and let this go. You'll regret it later, Merrick. I know you. I've known you too many years."

Merrick scraped his fork against the takeout box and shoved another bite into his mouth. Too many carbs. But tonight he didn't give a shit. Dakota would have his ass over eating this crap.

He leaned back in his chair and then looked at his two best friends.

"What's on your mind, Merrick?" Cade asked calmly.

Yeah, Cade would know something was bothering him. Other than the obvious.

He battled with whether to bring it up so close on the heels of what had happened. It would seem reactionary and like he was too quick to jump the gun. But the longer he pondered the solution, the more at peace he felt about it.

"I've been doing a lot of thinking. This will sound crazy, like I haven't thought it through, but I've thought of nothing else since seeing Elle bloodied and bruised in our garage. Elle, who was forced to defend herself with a fucking crowbar because some asshole wants revenge because we had his ass arrested. Fuck that."

Dallas and Cade exchanged curious glances.

"You both want me to go hard at this title."

Cade and Dallas both nodded.

"You want me to focus. You want me to move past the distractions. Well, I can't do that until I know Elle is safe."

"I get that," Cade said.

Merrick leaned forward, putting his carton of Chinese food down so he could rest his forearms on his knees.

"I think we should hang up the business for now," he said bluntly.

Cade's head reared back. "Have you lost your goddamn mind? You know how hard I worked to get that off the ground."

Merrick nodded. "I do."

"Then what the fuck, man?"

Wisely, Dallas remained a quiet observer to the tense exchange.

"Elle said it best," Merrick said. "When she was talking about wanting to take over the office with you. She said if I won the title, my life would change and I wouldn't be working in our business. She's right. Things will change. The thing is, I don't want to be the only one who changes while you two are left behind holding the bag."

Cade started to open his mouth, but Merrick shut him down with a look.

"Let me finish. There are so many reasons to do this, and I'll start with the most important. Elle's in danger because of us and our business. Because we crossed the wrong person and he wants revenge. The motherfucker isn't going to stop just because Elle beat the shit out of his flunky. Hell, I don't even want to take her back to that house. I'd rather us sell it and move someplace that fits the three of us better."

Cade's eyes narrowed, but he kept silent.

"The other thing is, if I win—and I *want* to win… I know none of you believe that. You think I'm fucking away the opportunity of a lifetime. I'm going to win. And when I do, I want you and Elle both right there with me. You've always been there, Cade. You don't call what you do for me a job, but it is. You're part of the camp, the team. I'll need you more than ever if I win this thing. I can't do it alone, and I want people I trust around me. I'll need you and Elle to keep me grounded. None of us will have time for the business.

"If we're going to make this work with Elle, we can't be in two separate places," Merrick added softly. "We want her with us. You want me to win. We can't have both if you're here and I'm somewhere else."

"So you want me to just quit and ride your star like some fucking charity case?" Cade bit out.

"Oh, fuck you," Merrick said rudely. "You've got goddamn money saved. You've been saving since you were a damn teenager. You hoard cash like Scrooge. You'd be paid a salary, and you'd damn well earn it. There's no charity case, dumbass. If we're going to make this work with Elle, then we need to figure out a way to be together and to work together where we aren't worried every day that some asshole with a grudge is going to retaliate by assaulting the woman we love."

"I hate to be the voice of reason here, because I'm always the voice of reason," Dallas said dryly, "but Merrick has some very good points, as much as it pains me to agree with his ornery ass."

"Thanks a lot," Cade snapped.

"Think about *Elle*," Merrick said. "Think about the fact that it would be much easier to keep her with us when we're not split up all the time.

And really, the timing is perfect. We can walk away from the business or sell it to someone else. Our building was destroyed. We're renting shitty office space until we rebuild. So, what if we don't?"

Cade blew out his breath. "Jesus, man. What a time to hit me with this."

"It's the best time to hit you with it. If we wait, it could be too late. I won't risk Elle again. We've got to take this threat seriously, and we've got to become better at making sure one of us is with her at all times."

Cade rubbed his hands over his face. "I can't even believe I'm considering this."

"I'm not asking for a split-second decision," Merrick said in a quiet voice. "I know how hard you worked for this. Sleep on it. We can talk about it again."

"Where the hell would we live?" Cade asked.

Merrick knew he'd scored a major victory by getting Cade to consider details like where they would live. It meant he was already looking at the possibilities and weighing them in his mind.

"Dakota's been talking about moving our gym to Denver. If I win, we get increased exposure and a bigger city to draw in new fighters. We buy a house there and take the necessary precautions to safeguard Elle."

Both Dallas and Cade lifted their eyebrows.

"Does this mean you *aren't* firing Dakota?" Cade asked.

"Fuck," Merrick said, the curse exploding out of his mouth. "I want to kick his goddamn ass."

Dallas nodded. "Understandable. He certainly owes Elle an apology, and he probably *needs* his ass kicked."

"And after you kick it, you can rehire him," Cade pointed out.

Well, at least there was that. And he had to admit, he looked forward to flattening Dakota a few times before he played nice again.

"If I rehire Dakota, will you at least consider my suggestion?" Merrick asked Cade.

Cade expelled a long breath, his shoulders heaving with the effort. Then he looked at Merrick, his lips tight.

"Yeah. I'll consider it."

Then Merrick turned to Dallas, his chest tight because he knew what it would mean if he and Cade moved to another city.

"I want you there, man. Every damn time."

"And I'll be there," Dallas said, his voice serious. "You know I will. When I can't be at the clinic, my nurse practitioner does a crack job of keeping things flowing. It won't be the same without you guys here where we can eat dinner together or shoot the shit at the house whenever we want. But I'll never be further than a phone call away."

Merrick held up his hand, and Dallas bumped his fist to Merrick's.

"I want what's best for you," Dallas said sincerely. "I may not be able to fully wrap my head around this relationship you and Cade have with Elle, but I want the three of you to be happy, and I want you to succeed. You're the best, man, and this is your time to shine."

Merrick sighed. "If I haven't fucked it up already."

Dallas shrugged. "Just work harder. You've got four weeks. Get your shit together and then focus. If anyone can do this, you can."

Cade leaned forward. "This isn't just about you, Merrick. A lot of people have put a hell of a lot of time into your training. Dakota's an asshole, but he and Cathy both have banked everything on you. Don't let everyone down."

A sense of purpose gripped Merrick by the throat. "Yeah, I get it."

"Just remember that the most important person you do this for is yourself," Dallas added.

Merrick nodded. "I'll talk to Dakota in the morning. Tonight… Tonight I'm going to watch over Elle and try not to torture myself with all that could have happened and all that *did*."

# chapter thirty-five

WHEN MERRICK AND CADE WALKED back into the bedroom after Dallas left for the night, Cade was surprised to see Elle awake and lying on her uninjured side.

Her face was nestled into the pillow, but her gaze was distant, and she didn't react to their entry, which told him wherever she was, it wasn't here.

He settled down on the edge of the bed and trailed his finger down the silky skin of her arm.

"Elle? Are you hurting, honey? Do you need something else for pain?"

For a moment, she didn't respond. It wasn't until Merrick crawled onto the bed behind her and sat up against the headboard so her body was flush against his that she stirred and directed her unfocused stare on Cade.

"I hurt," she said simply. "It hurts to breathe."

Merrick made a sound behind Elle that could be rage, or it could be grief. Then he carefully lifted the hem of her loose pajama top they'd put on her so that he and Cade could see the extent of her bruising. The ER nurse had wrapped her ribs, but Elle hadn't been able to bear the discomfort of the tight encasing, so they'd reluctantly allowed her to remove it.

Merrick sucked in his breath when the now-blackened flesh came into view. Cade had to swallow back the growl that boiled in his throat.

With a shaking hand, Cade reached out to carefully touch the injured skin. Merrick leaned his head down and pressed a gentle kiss to her ribcage.

"Let me get you some medicine, honey," Cade said in a low voice.

"Want to talk to you," she murmured.

He kissed her on the forehead as he rose to get the prescription bottle. "We'll talk when you're more comfortable, okay?"

She nodded, and he went to the dresser and shook out a pill and then reached into the minibar to get a bottle of water. When he returned, he frowned to see Elle struggling to sit up while Merrick was doing his best to keep her down.

"Let me sit up please," she pleaded. "I'm so tired of lying on my side, and I can't lie on the other side because it hurts. If I could just sit up and prop some pillows behind me, I think it would be heaven."

"Just be careful," Merrick cautioned. He glanced up at Cade. "Pick her up, and I'll arrange the pillows."

Cade put the pill and water on the nightstand and then reached for Elle, pulling her into his arms and up against his chest. After Merrick propped a mound of pillows against the headboard, Cade eased her down until she settled on the mattress and leaned back against the pillows.

When he was convinced she was comfortable enough, he turned and took the pill and the water to hand to her. She swallowed it down and chugged thirstily at the liquid before handing it back to Cade. Then she sagged against the pillows and briefly closed her eyes.

He moved, and her eyes flew open. "Don't go," she blurted. "I wanted—needed—to talk to you and Merrick."

Cade settled on the bed, pulling up one knee so he could angle toward her. "I'm not going anywhere, honey. I was just getting comfortable."

She glanced at the bedside clock and frowned. "It's late. Aren't you coming to bed?"

Cade glanced down and then over to Merrick. They'd already showered and changed, but they were still dressed in jeans and T-shirts.

"Tell you what. Give me two seconds to get undressed, and I'll crawl in with you and then we'll talk about whatever you want."

Merrick was already getting out of bed and shedding his jeans and shirt. Cade did the same, and then he and Merrick got onto the bed, pulling the covers back so they could get up next to Elle.

Cade shouldered up against the pillows and rested his hand down the length of her leg. Merrick pulled the covers up and then propped his head up in the palm of his hand.

"What's on your mind, baby?" Merrick asked.

She licked her lips nervously and then closed her eyes, her features drawing until she looked sad and...defeated.

"Today, when this happened... When he grabbed me, I was so terrified. It was a shock. You know, like I wasn't expecting it. I mean, who expects to be grabbed when they're trying to walk into their house?"

"Understandable," Cade murmured.

"But it made me realize the difference from before. When I was attacked before."

Tears filled her eyes and leaked down her cheeks. Cade pressed his lips to her shoulder, his heart aching for all the hurt she'd endured.

"What was different?" Merrick asked gently.

"I *knew* the man who attacked me before. I *trusted* him," she choked out. "It was a different kind of shock. It was...*betrayal*."

Cade slid his hand up her leg to lace his fingers with hers. "I suspected as much," he murmured.

Merrick nodded his agreement.

"Everything you've remembered so far adds up to it being someone you knew and him being a police officer or having something to do with law enforcement."

Her entire body trembled, and she pulled the covers farther up her body in a protective gesture.

"A cop did this to me," she whispered. "But did I trust him because he was a cop, or did I trust him because he was someone I knew?"

The undertone was there. The question that wasn't voiced. Had it been someone she'd been intimate with? A boyfriend. Lover. *Husband*?

The thought sickened Cade to the point of discomfort.

"Whatever the case, he can't hurt you anymore, baby."

Merrick's quiet vow echoed through the room and vibrated over Cade in its intensity.

Merrick very carefully nudged her chin toward him, and then he caressed her cheek with his big hand. Such gentleness was in total contradiction to his size and strength. He looked like he was just as easily capable of crushing her with that one hand.

"Listen to me," he said in a husky voice. "What happened today is not going to happen again. You'll be with either Cade or me every minute of every day. I don't care what anyone else says. If someone tells you differently, then you tell them to fuck off and you find one of us."

Merrick glanced at Cade for a long moment, question in his eyes. Cade knew what he was asking. Knew what he wanted to share with Elle.

In his heart, Cade knew it was the right thing to do even if it wasn't the easiest.

Slowly he nodded, silently agreeing to what Merrick had suggested earlier. Satisfaction and relief shone in Merrick's eyes.

Elle was starting to nod off again, though, the effects of the pain medication taking hold, and she was already exhausted enough.

Cade glanced at Merrick and shook his head. "Tomorrow."

Merrick nodded and then gently eased Elle lower in the bed, arranging the pillows so she'd be comfortable. She moaned once when the movement caused her pain, and Merrick flinched, his face a wreath of regret.

But then she nestled into the pillow, gave a soft sigh and went utterly still. Her soft breathing filled the space between them, and Cade simply watched the rise and fall of her chest.

What was it about her that had captivated him from the very beginning? He couldn't explain it. He didn't even really care about why or how. She was it for him. Some things just were, and this was one of them. Hell if he was going to fight it. Not when he was perfectly content to be right where he was.

Change was inevitable. But then they'd been barreling toward change for some time now. It was naïve to think their lives wouldn't be altered when Merrick won the championship.

Merrick had thought out the possible roadblocks and come up with a solution, something Cade had failed to do. There was no way they could both maintain a relationship with Elle if Cade was in Grand Junction and Merrick was off fulfilling his obligations as the champion. And they sure as hell weren't going to pass Elle back and forth like a child custody case in a divorce.

Cade had been rooted in denial, not wanting to think of the changes that were most certainly coming.

"We could have lost her," Merrick whispered painfully.

"I know. The more I think about it, the more it pisses me off that Dakota took it upon himself to toss her out of the gym."

Merrick's gaze narrowed. "You think I should stick to my guns?"

Cade sighed. "Goddamn. Part of me wants to kick his fucking ass and then tell him to hit the road. What he did was unforgivable. He could have gotten her killed. The other part knows deep down that he never meant her harm. He's a dick, yes, but he's a dick who loves you and is fiercely loyal, and I honest to God think he's sick at heart over what happened."

"Yeah," Merrick muttered.

"I think he's got some making up to do where Elle is concerned. He made her feel unwanted. Like we didn't want her. That I won't forgive."

"I hear you," Merrick said through his teeth. "We'll talk to Elle in the morning, and then I'm going to have a come to Jesus meeting with him to clear the air."

# chapter thirty-six

WHEN ELLE WOKE THE NEXT morning, she was alone in bed and the sun was streaming through the window. She blinked and then flinched away from the brightness before turning her head away.

Her body screamed in pain. It was like nothing she'd ever felt before. Every breath hurt. The nurse in the ER had bound Elle's ribs, but Elle hadn't been able to tolerate the wrapping. Now she wondered if she wouldn't have been better off.

Her face and jaw were swollen, and it hurt like hell to even move her lips. Moving anything was an ordeal. She felt like she was a hundred years old.

And the problem was, she had to pee really bad.

"Cade? Merrick?"

Their names came out a mere croak. Her throat was bruised and swollen from where her assailant had choked her.

She waited a moment, but with each passing second, the need became more pressing.

Gritting her teeth, she inched her way toward the edge of the bed, tears of pain pricking her eyelids. By the time she had one leg over the side, she was gasping and tears slid freely down her cheeks.

When she finally managed to get both feet on the floor, she straightened and immediately regretted it. Her cry of pain blistered her lips, and she bent over, agony wracking her body.

"Elle, what the hell?"

Cade's demand blew over her, and then he was there, easing her to sit back on the bed. She couldn't even breathe around the quiet sobs and the gasps of pain.

Merrick stood in front of her, his face a mask of worry. Just beyond him, Dallas stood, concern bright in his eyes.

"What on earth were you doing?" Merrick asked.

"Bathroom," she managed to get past stiff, swollen lips.

"Aww, honey."

Cade slid his arms underneath her and lifted her up. She couldn't call back the near shriek as her body was jolted. Cade swore and then stalked toward the bathroom. He set her down in front of the toilet and then unceremoniously yanked down her underwear before easing her back onto the commode.

"Oh God, this is humiliating," she moaned.

"Shut up," he said in an almost polite voice. "I don't want to hear it. Get over it because right now you can't move without causing yourself considerable pain."

"I can do the rest," she gritted out. "Turn around or something. This is embarrassing."

He sighed but did as she asked. And God, but it was the most difficult thing she'd ever done to complete the task of using the bathroom. By the time she was finished, sweat had broken out over her body and she was nauseous.

Cade steered her around and then glanced into her eyes. "It hurt you when I carried you in here. Do you think it would be better if you walked?"

She thought for a minute, and the memory of the jolt of him picking her up was enough to persuade her that she would rather risk walking.

Like an old woman, she trudged into the bedroom where Merrick and Dallas stood by the bed, both frowning.

"Elle, sweetheart, don't take this the wrong way, but I need you to show me your pretty ass," Dallas said.

Her eyes widened, and she halted.

He held up a syringe. "I'm going to give you an injection. You're in considerable pain, and to be honest, at this stage, those pills aren't going to help you much. This will work much faster."

She nodded, not even offering argument. She'd bare any part of her body if it meant getting faster relief.

She crawled onto the bed and face planted in the pillow, rolling slightly onto her uninjured side so no weight was on the injured one.

Merrick reached to carefully pull the band of her panties far enough that Dallas could swab the skin where he was going to inject her. Then the prick of a needle and the burn of medication as it pushed into her hip.

Mere moments later, she melted into the bed as the edge lessened on the pain. The discomfort became more tolerable, and she sighed in relief.

"Better?" Dallas asked.

"Better," she mumbled against the pillow. "Can I sit up now?"

"Just take it easy and let Cade and Merrick help you," Dallas cautioned.

As soon as she started to push upward, Cade and Merrick were there. They lifted her, careful not to touch any of the bruised areas. Then they turned her so she could sit up in bed.

The medicine made her swimmy, but she welcomed it because she wasn't in pain. *Finally* not in pain.

"Thank you, Dallas," she said, slurring her esses.

He smiled. "You're welcome, sweetheart. I had to come check on you this morning. I had a feeling you were going to hurt like a son of a bitch when you woke up."

She grimaced and nodded. "You were right."

"You too out of it to talk, baby?" Merrick asked.

She shook her head. "I'm okay. Just a little slower."

"I'm going to leave you three," Dallas said. "I'll be back tonight after the clinic closes. If you need anything, though, call me. I'll be right over."

He reached down to squeeze Elle's hand, and she smiled at him. "Thanks, Dallas."

Cade and Merrick walked him to the door, and a moment later, they were back. They both sat on the bed on either side of her, and she glanced more closely at Merrick. His hair was damp with perspiration, and he had sweat spots on his T-shirt.

"You worked out," she said.

Merrick looked uncertain for a moment. "Does that upset you? Cade stayed here with you the entire time. You were out like a light when I got up."

She was temporarily dumfounded. "Why on earth would that upset me? You have four weeks until your fight. You can't slack off now."

Cade grinned. "Little slave driver's right."

Merrick relaxed. "We need to talk about Dakota."

Elle sighed. Talk about a mood dampener.

"Don't look like that," Merrick said, his voice pleading.

"I may not want you to fire him, and I may think you need him, but it doesn't mean I want to think about him or deal with him," Elle said.

Merrick touched her hand, running his finger up and down her palm. "Dakota and I are going to have an understanding today concerning you. I'm not going to fire him. Yet. He only gets one shot at this, though. He fucks up, he's out. He has to understand your position in my life. A position I want you to be in very much."

She nodded.

"The second thing we need to talk about is Dallas brought by your paperwork," Cade said. "Birth certificate. Social security card. Everything we need to establish your identity."

She blinked and then swallowed. This is what she wanted. She was sure of it. And yet now that it was happening, she felt a moment's panic. It was as if it were the final step in erasing her past completely. Dissolving who she'd been and creating a whole new person.

There was a tinge of sadness, and for what, she couldn't even place. A fleeting moment of grief for someone she couldn't remember.

"Elle?"

"Who knows if that's even my real name," she said in a cracked voice.

Cade cupped her chin and then quickly pulled his hand away so he wouldn't touch the bruised, swollen part of her face.

"You're Elle to us," he said gently. "You're Elle Walker soon to be Sullivan, and that's all that matters."

"I don't think we should get married yet," she blurted.

Merrick's face immediately went dark, and Cade frowned.

"Why the hell not?" Merrick demanded.

Cade shot him a warning glance, and Merrick snapped his mouth shut.

"Why not, honey?" Cade asked in a quieter tone.

"Distraction," she said honestly.

She turned her gaze to Merrick, determination edging her words. "You have four weeks to get ready for this fight. And you know what? I want a honeymoon. There's no way getting married now helps you get ready for this fight. It's time away from your training."

Merrick puffed up, his face reddening, and she knew he was about to start arguing.

"After the fight," she said firmly. "After you *win*, we get married. We go to Vegas. Get married and then we go somewhere where it's just the three of us and there's no crazy asshole trying to get revenge. No Dakota. No nothing except us."

"That's a pretty persuasive argument," Cade admitted.

Merrick swore. "I want you to be mine."

She smiled then. Crookedly. Around the pain in her mouth and swollen jaw. "Don't you know, Merrick? I'm already yours."

Merrick leaned forward, pressing his forehead to hers. He seemed emotional. His eyes were closed as he murmured, "Okay, baby. Just... okay."

She reached for Cade even as Merrick kept his forehead to hers. The three of them touching, connecting.

Some of the earlier melancholy lifted away, leaving lightness that danced its way into her heart. It was senseless to dwell on her past when she had Cade and Merrick as her future.

"There's something else we need to discuss," Cade said.

She looked hesitantly at him as he and Merrick exchanged looks.

"We want to move," Merrick said bluntly. "For a whole host of reasons. Namely your safety."

When she started to protest, Cade cut her off. "We're selling the business. If Merrick wins—and he's going to—we aren't going to need it. We won't have time for it. We're thinking of moving to Denver to start a new training camp there. Bring on some up-and-coming fighters to train under Merrick and Dakota and our team. We won't stay here where some asshole has a vendetta because our business had him arrested and he took it out on you."

"But," she began only to be silenced by Merrick this time.

"You said it, Elle. If I win this, my life is going to change in ways we don't even perceive yet. And I don't want us going in opposite directions. I don't want you and Cade here, struggling to keep the business afloat while I'm off traveling and making appearances and doing publicity shit. I want you both there with me. By my side. I'm a selfish bastard, but I don't want to split my time with you between me and Cade. I want you with me all the time. Cade has money saved up. The miserly bastard has the first dollar he ever made in a savings account. Plus he'll draw a salary as my manager. Dakota's going to only focus on the training aspect. Cade's going to handle the business, and that's something you can help him with."

She blew out a deep breath. "Are you sure this is what the two of you want?"

"Hell yeah," Merrick growled. "We want you. Safe. With us. In our arms. In our lives. That's all that counts in the end."

She smiled. "I think I can live with that."

# chapter thirty-seven

THE ARENA WAS BUZZING WITH excitement. The night had been rife with upset victories, and speculation was high that the main event could well be another upset where the champion would be dethroned.

Elle could barely contain herself in the locker room. She'd already been out to view the raucous crowd three times, and she couldn't sit still as she paced the confines.

She'd stayed well away from Merrick, not wanting to in any way compromise his focus. For the last two days, he'd gone quiet and intensely brooding, almost as if he'd turned inward for the incentive necessary for the task ahead.

An arm slid around her shoulders, and she turned hastily to see Dallas standing beside her.

"How you holding up, sweetheart?"

She smiled. "Nervous as hell. Oh my God, I don't know how you've stood this for so long."

"I puked my first couple of fights," he admitted. "Too much adrenaline. I was so amped up that I was in overload."

She laughed. "Yeah, I can totally relate." Her laughter died, and she went quiet for a moment. Then in a fierce, low voice she said, "He's going to win."

She said it as a statement, but she still couldn't quell the need for reassurance. Dallas kissed her temple. "Yeah, he's going to win. No doubt."

Dakota walked out of the dressing room and made a beeline for Elle. His expression brooding and intense. A look she'd fast come to associate with Dakota when he was in fight mode.

"He wants to see you."

Elle frowned. "Do you think that's a good idea? I've tried to stay out of his way all day. I don't want to mess up his concentration now."

Dakota smiled. The two had reached a truce while she'd still been laid up in a hotel room recovering from her attack. He'd been appalled and horrified that his actions had led to such a horrific event.

He'd been utterly sincere in his apology—and just as sincere about his love and loyalty for Merrick. In the end, she couldn't hold that loyalty against him. She knew she'd do anything to protect Merrick, so she couldn't fault Dakota for trying to do the same. Even if he'd gone about it all wrong.

"I think he needs to see you, babe. You'll center him. He needs to be grounded right now. He needs to see what he's fighting for. You'll remind him of that."

Elle's heart melted. "Okay. I'll come."

She followed behind Dakota into the locker room, where Merrick's shoulders and arms were being massaged and rubbed down. He had on a satin jacket with the hood up, and he looked…formidable. Not at all like the loving, gentle giant she knew him to be.

But then he looked up and found her gaze, and he softened all over, losing the brooding intensity that could easily scare a grown man.

"Elle," he whispered.

The room cleared in about three seconds, and then they were alone. Just her, Merrick and Cade, who stood to the side. But he came in closer as Elle approached Merrick.

Cade sat on the bench next to Elle where she'd taken a seat directly across from Merrick. Their knees touched, and Merrick reached for her hands, clumsy with the gloves on.

He extended his fist to Cade so they bumped knuckles, and they held them there while Cade reached for Elle's free hand.

"This is it," Cade said simply. "Don't leave anything in the ring, Merrick. Go hard. No regrets."

"No regrets," Merrick echoed.

"You can do this," Elle said softly. "I believe in you, Merrick. I love you."

He put his gloved hands clumsily to her face and pulled her into a deep kiss. "I love you too. This. *All* of this. Is for you. For *us*."

Dakota burst into the room followed closely by Cathy.

"It's time, Merrick. I'm going to have Cathy take Elle to her seat, and she's going to stay with her for the fight. Front row. She'll be close. Cade and Dallas are going to stay in the corner with me."

Merrick nodded and then leaned forward again to claim Elle's mouth in a lusty, possessive kiss that left her breathless.

"Win," she whispered. "Do it for *you*, Merrick. Nobody else."

---

Elle and Catherine were escorted ringside by two security guards. Catherine latched onto her hand and pulled her up close while the two guards moved only a short distance away, flanking the women.

"I've never been so oh-my-God nervous in my life!" Catherine yelled in Elle's ear. "This is it, Elle. This is what he's worked for over so many years."

"He's going to win," Elle said with calm she didn't feel.

All she could think was what if he didn't win? Every plan, every action over the last month had been made with the assumption that Merrick would win the title.

The three had picked out a home in Denver. Dakota and Catherine had begun negotiations on a training facility. Their house in Grand Junction had been put up for sale, and Cade had sold his business.

Even Charlie was making the move to Denver and would be a part of Merrick's training team.

The only dim spot in the last weeks was the fallout from Elle's attack, and she'd worried endlessly that it would prove to be a huge distraction for Merrick and split his concentration at a time it had to be completely focused.

Her attacker had survived, but fortunately for Elle, he confessed everything. He pled guilty to assault, and he testified against the man Cade and Merrick had captured stealing the car. Other than statements provided by all three of them, nothing further was to be done, and they'd been able to push the incident from their minds.

The flurry of activity surrounding the move and Cade selling their home and business had helped to distract Elle so she didn't spend much time dwelling on the terror of what had happened to her.

But only in the last week, three weeks after the attack, had the bruising finally faded, and she could move without pain or discomfort.

Thank God she'd healed before the fight because it was a madhouse, and if Merrick won? There was going to be mad hugging and even madder celebration.

Tonight, because Merrick was the contender, he'd enter the ring first. When the lights dimmed and the first strains of Merrick's entry song began, goose bumps chased up Elle's arms. She yanked her gaze up the aisle, straining to get a glimpse of Merrick when he appeared.

His nickname still made her giggle. Merrick "The Hit Man" Sullivan. It sounded so…mafia. But he'd gained the nickname because it was said he had lead fists and, with one well-placed punch, could drop a much larger guy like a stone.

Merrick began his jaunt down to the ring, surrounded by Dakota, Cade, Dallas and Charlie along with several security guards. He looked loose, but more important, he looked focused and calm. Confident.

He walked by Elle without a glance, something she didn't take offense to. His gaze was riveted to the ring, and she doubted he even saw her. This was one time she *wanted* to be invisible. She wanted nothing to distract him from his goal.

The crowd roared when Merrick was introduced, and Merrick raised his gloved hands in the air, rotating in a 360, inciting the crowd to yell even louder.

Her heart surged with pride. This was *her* man.

Her gaze slid to Cade a short distance from Merrick, at the confidence in his eyes. Confidence radiated from every member of Merrick's camp. Then, to her surprise, Cade found her in the crowd, and he winked at her.

Not caring who saw or what they made of it, she blew Cade a kiss. To her utter shock, Merrick turned, touched two fingers to his lips and then extended his arm toward her.

Her heart felt like it was going to explode right out of her chest. Automatically she blew him a kiss in return, and he made a show of catching it and pressing it to his chest.

It was so deeply romantic and *public* that her knees threatened to turn to jelly.

Once again the lights went down, dousing the arena in darkness. The spotlight swung to where Lash was making his appearance, and the crowd erupted just as the first strains of his music began blaring.

Her stomach twisted into nervous knots. Lash was *huge*. And mean-looking. He looked intensely focused and ready to tear Merrick apart.

The belt he wore around his waist shone in the spotlight. He took his time walking down the pathway to the ring and stopped for the referee to check his gloves. Then he stepped into the ring, and the announcer began the impressive introduction of the World's Heavyweight Champion.

Elle felt like she wanted to puke. She wasn't sure she could watch this.

When the two men met in the center of the ring, Elle blinked, her eyes widening as she realized that Merrick was every bit as big as Lash. The champion just looked so intimidating to her, but for the first time, she looked at Merrick the way most other people likely viewed him.

He was big, heavily muscled, and he looked like a complete badass.

Would she have ever given him a second glance if they hadn't met the way they had? If he hadn't been so kind and gentle with her?

"Here they go!" Catherine shouted next to her.

Elle blinked again, realizing the bell had rung and the two men were dancing around each other in the ring. Oh shit. It was here. The culmination of all Merrick's training. All his hard work. It came down to tonight. One night. One fight. Everything was on the line.

Lash landed the first punch, snapping Merrick's head back. Elle flinched and looked away but quickly yanked her gaze back to the ring to see Merrick follow up with a flurry of punches that drove Lash back against the cage.

Her own fist curled into a tight ball, and she found herself holding her breath.

"Lash will never beat him in a boxing match," Catherine yelled. "The only way he can win is to get Merrick on the ground. If Merrick can stay on his feet, he'll win this quickly."

Elle grabbed hold of Catherine's confidence and held tightly to it. She was so nervous and uptight that each second was an eternity. She'd never felt so miserable in her life. The anticipation was agony. The knowledge that one lucky punch could kill Merrick's dreams. One slip and Lash could get him in a hold, forcing him to tap.

Merrick drew blood with a forceful jab, opening up a cut on Lash's cheek. But then Lash landed a left hook that sent Merrick reeling back, and Elle saw blood above Merrick's left eye.

*Shit.*

Lash made several attempts to take Merrick down, but each time, Merrick sprawled, making it impossible for the other man to take him to the mat. It was obvious that Lash was getting frustrated, and Elle saw it as a positive sign that Merrick was still focused and calm.

At thirty seconds left in the first round, Merrick went for the kill shot, and Lash dodged and lunged forward, slamming Merrick onto the mat. Elle's throat hurt, and she realized she'd yelled at the top of her lungs the moment Merrick went down.

"He's okay. He's okay," Catherine hollered next to her ear. "Lash doesn't have his back. He doesn't have position."

The two men scrambled and rolled, a flurry of bodies as they grappled, twisted and turned. Merrick suffered a series of blows to the head and side that had Elle wincing.

She turned anxiously to the clock, counting down the seconds until the end of the round.

*Hold on. Hold on.*

The chant echoed through her mind as she watched, unable to look away as Merrick's blood smeared onto the mat.

Finally the bell sounded, and the referee pulled Lash off Merrick. Merrick rolled to his feet, quickly jumping up. Elle wasn't sure if he truly wasn't affected by the pounding he'd just taken or if he just wanted to get into Lash's head by making him think he wasn't.

She watched as Dakota got in front of him, talking earnestly and gesturing. Cade handed Merrick water, and Dallas watched closely as the ringside doctor assessed the cut over Merrick's eye and applied Vaseline to stop the bleeding.

"What is Dakota saying to him?" Elle asked anxiously.

"He's just pumping him up. Telling him to stay on his feet and not to let Lash take him down. Merrick keeps the advantage if he stays off the mat."

"Who won that round?"

Catherine's lips tightened. "I don't know. It was close. It might go to Lash because of that last thirty seconds. He landed a lot of punches, and he gets points for the takedown."

"Damn," Elle swore.

Catherine burst out laughing. "I do believe that's the first time I've ever heard you say a cuss word. Stick with us, kid. We'll have you swearing like a sailor before long."

All too soon, the bell rang, signaling the start of the second round. Lash came out with more determination, calmer, more focused. He seemed to have gotten his frustration under control, and he looked…cold and deadly.

Merrick appeared unruffled. But the cut above his eye bothered Elle. The fact that Lash had made him bleed. It didn't matter that there was as much of Lash's blood coating the mat as there was of Merrick's. She saw only Merrick's, and she flinched with every blow that Lash landed.

"I give that round to Merrick," Catherine said, edging close to Elle when the second round was over."

"I wish it was over," Elle said, her stomach in a vicious knot. "I wish he'd knock him out so this would be over!"

"You and me both!"

The third round, Merrick started to show wear. Up to then, he'd been fresh, almost robotically so. Untouchable. He moved slower, and Lash, sensing his opponent's change in strength, began pressing. Taking him to the mat more. Merrick bounced up. Lash took him down.

In the fourth round, Merrick showed a resurgence, and Lash began to fray. Elle was beside herself. She knew many fights went the full five rounds, but they were often brutal, bloody matches of endurance.

She sagged when the bell rang, ending the round, and the fighters returned to their corners. Both men looked worn, and fatigue was starting to show in their movements.

"Tied," Catherine said grimly. "This last round is it. Merrick's either got to have a dominating round or knock him out. He's likely to lose in a coin flip because the edge will go to the champion. And if Merrick did get the decision, there'll always be question regarding his title worthiness. Lash will say he was robbed."

Elle closed her eyes and sucked in a deep breath as the final round began. The two fighters touched gloves in a show of respect and then warily began circling each other.

Merrick drove Lash back against the wall of the cage, connecting with a series of punches that had Lash off balance. Lash wrapped Merrick up, defending himself against the blows and then, with a leg sweep, took Merrick down.

Elle lunged forward, screaming Merrick's name. "Get up! Get up! Don't let him have your back."

Oh God, it didn't look good. Lash had a choke hold, and the entire arena buzzed as they sensed a dramatic end to an epic battle between two of the best fighters in the world.

Merrick had his hand underneath Lash's arm, and he pried, gradually exerting enough pressure to loosen the hold. How Merrick had any strength left was beyond her. He had to be running on sheer grit and determination.

"Holy shit, he's getting out!" Catherine cried. "He's broken the hold! Lash isn't going to get the submission!"

Merrick rotated around, grasping Lash's wrist and twisting into an arm bar. He planted his foot on Lash's shoulder and anchored the hold, his face drawn in grim determination.

"Oh my God," Elle whispered. "He's going to tap. Merrick's going to make him tap!"

She held her breath and glanced up at the clock. Her heart sank. Only ten seconds left. Surely Lash could hold out that long. The *championship* was on the line.

Merrick's lips formed a tight line, and he exerted more pressure, his entire body straining. Lash's face was creased in agony, and his free hand balled into a tight fist, a seeming vow not to tap.

Five. Four...

Lash's fist loosened. His palm went flat on the mat.

Three...two...

He tapped three times in rapid succession, and the arena erupted as the referee threw himself between Merrick and Lash to end the fight.

Elle stood there, numb, as she stared at the crowd going crazy. Catherine hugged her and whirled her around, and still Elle stared dumbly at the ring, watching as Merrick raised his hands in victory while Lash's people rushed in to assess his injuries.

"Oh my God," she whispered. "He did it!"

"Hell yeah, he did!" Catherine shouted.

Cade and Dallas ran into the ring and picked Merrick up, swinging him around. Dakota was jumping around, slapping his towel over Merrick's shoulders.

Excitement invaded Elle's veins as realization sank in. Merrick was the World Heavyweight Champion! He'd done it!

And then Merrick tapped Cade on the shoulder and motioned for him and Dallas to put him down. Merrick walked to the edge of the ring directly in front of where Elle and Catherine sat, and then he pointed at Elle and crooked his finger to her.

Her eyes widened. "Me?" she mouthed.

Merrick smiled and nodded.

The two guards who'd escorted Elle to her seat and had remained close stepped forward to flank her, and then they walked her up to the cage and lifted her up so she could go inside.

As soon as she stumbled toward Merrick, he met her halfway and enfolded her in his arms. He picked her up and swung her round and round.

With the crowd roaring their approval, he let her slide down his sweaty, bloody body, and then he fused his mouth to hers in a long, breathless kiss. And God help her, but she kissed him right back there in front of a million viewers.

# chapter thirty-eight

THE DRESSING ROOM WAS INSANITY. Champagne was sprayed everywhere and on anyone in close proximity. As soon as the media had been allowed access, Cade herded Elle into one of the smaller changing rooms.

It was a bit like closing the barn door after the horse already got out. Merrick had just kissed her in plain view of not only those in the arena but the millions watching the fight on pay per view. But Cade was adamant that he and Merrick both didn't want her directly exposed to the media.

So she rolled her eyes and sat while the insanity went on outside the door. To her surprise, a mere twenty minutes later, the door burst open and Merrick came in, Cade close on his heels.

Without a word, Merrick stalked to where she sat in a chair across the room and hauled her up and into his arms. His mouth crushed down over hers with bruising force that left her gasping for breath.

His need was a tangible thing, thick in the air. It vibrated from him in waves.

"Need you," he growled against her mouth. "Right here. Right now. Jesus, baby. I need you."

Her heart pounded like a freight train, but she put her arms around him, holding him close, and she murmured next to his ear, "Okay, then. Okay. I'm here. Take me, Merrick. Take what you need."

He set her down only long enough to free himself from the trunks he wore and to reach underneath the filmy skirt she wore and yank away her underwear.

Then he lifted her again, hoisting her up his body.

"Wrap your legs around me," he said hoarsely.

She wrapped arms and legs around him, anchoring herself to him. He grasped her behind, lifting and then settling her down over his rigid erection. Then he walked her back until she bumped against the wall, and he thrust hard and deep.

The angle was impossible. She was too far forward, too smashed between him and the wall. She pushed at him, wanting him to get the hint without her interrupting the desperation that gripped them both.

Muttering a curse, he gripped her tighter and turned away from the wall.

"Hold her, Cade."

Heat prickled up her nape. Her nipples hardened, and her pussy clenched around Merrick's cock. The sheer eroticism of what Merrick suggested had her flushed with arousal.

Cade's chest met her back, his warmth invading her body as he slid his arms underneath hers, holding and supporting her weight while Merrick gripped her hips and plunged deeper.

"Lean back against me, honey," Cade whispered.

She let her head fall back against his shoulder, and Cade turned his mouth to nuzzle her jaw while Merrick fucked her with an intensity he'd never unleashed with her before.

There, held between the two men she loved, one holding her while the other drove into her over and over…it was more than she was able to withstand.

She came quickly. No build up. No prolonged, slow rise to completion. She hurtled over the edge like a plane falling from the sky. And still, Merrick plunged deeply into her body, as if he'd never get enough.

"Need you so much," Merrick panted.

She reached to touch the damp hair at his shoulders and then gently ran her hands over his jaw, framing his face.

"I need you too," she said softly.

"Table," Merrick gritted out.

He withdrew only long enough for Cade to carry her to the padded exam table against the far wall. Cade positioned her on her belly, her legs down, feet just touching the floor, and then Merrick was inside her again, thrusting into her from behind.

His hands caressed her back, running up and down her spine with gentleness that was contradictory to the way he was driving into her.

So much adrenaline. This was his outlet. She was the one person he wanted. Who he trusted. He'd come to her. He loved her.

The stirrings of another orgasm rose from deep within. The position he had her in forced him deeper, at a different angle. His cock touched different parts of her pussy, and she gasped as the familiar flood of pleasure began foaming through her body.

Then he tensed against her. And then he went hard. Fast. Rocking her forward, almost rough as he came in wave after wave.

And then finally he lowered his body over hers, lying flush against her back, his breath whispering harshly in her ear.

God, but she was so on edge. So close to another climax. Her entire body tingled, and she unconsciously bucked her ass upward, wanting, needing more.

Merrick lifted himself up and gently pulled out of her body. She moaned, wanting that fullness back. She needed it.

"Take care of her, Cade," Merrick said in a low voice. "She's close. She needs to finish."

She heard the rasp of a zipper, and her pulse shot up about twenty beats a minute. Warm gentle hands on her behind, spreading and caressing.

And then Cade was inside her. Just as hard. Just as thick. Only a bit slower and not as desperate as Merrick had been.

She closed her eyes and lay her cheek on the soft pad covering the table and gave herself over to the two men who loved her.

Cade leaned down and kissed between her shoulder blades, and then he picked up his pace, driving harder, as if he'd lost the ability to be patient. His need took over, and it drove her own relentlessly on.

"Take what you need, Elle," Cade commanded. "Come for me."

She twisted restlessly, unable to remain still under the delicious onslaught. She bucked upward, meeting every thrust.

Cade grasped her hips and pulled her back each time he drove forward.

Then his grasp tightened, his fingers digging into her flesh and she cried out as, for a second time, her orgasm flashed and swallowed her up in its fiery pleasure.

And then as Merrick had done, Cade blanketed her body, his hips still twitching against her ass while he lay, his breaths coming hard and long over her shoulder.

"Love you," he whispered.

As soon as Cade carefully pulled out of Elle's body, she was in Merrick's arms again, cradled in his hold.

"Jesus, baby," he murmured over and over again. "We did it. We goddamn did it."

She smiled and rested her head against his chest. "No, *you* did it, Merrick. You kicked his ass. You're the champion."

"Did I hurt you?" he asked, worry thick in his voice.

She smiled at that too. "Oh no, my love. If you do that after every fight, I might not be so reluctant for you to fight more often."

Merrick smiled, and then she looked up at his battered face in worry.

"How hurt are you? God, Merrick, you shouldn't have been having sex after you just got the hell beat out of you."

He arched one eyebrow. The one not cut and bleeding. "I thought you just said I kicked his ass."

"Yeah, well, he did some kicking of his own. You have to be in so much pain."

Merrick shook his head. "Not yet. Adrenaline still flowing. It's why I had to have you right here, right now. Later, I'll feel it. That's when Dallas will shove some meds down me and make me rest. I won't be worth killing in a few hours."

She turned and held her hand out to Cade, wanting him close. As close as she was to Merrick. Cade pushed in until she was sandwiched between the two men. It was a comfortable, familiar place to be in. Between them. Where she felt the safest. Where she was loved.

"I love the two of you. I hope you both know that."

Cade smiled. "Yeah, I think we do."

She glanced up at Merrick. "Hey, what's with kissing me in front of live television? I thought we were keeping me secret."

Merrick went quiet a moment and glanced Cade's way. "I'll admit, I wasn't thinking about it at the time. I only knew I wanted you to share in that moment with me and Cade. It wasn't complete without you. I wanted the whole damn world to know that I love you. And...if someone, somewhere sees you and recognizes you and even tries to contact you, then we'll deal with that when it comes up. At some point, we have to address the issue of your past. Maybe this will help us do just that."

She leaned her head over on Cade's shoulder while still remaining in Merrick's arms.

"And maybe no one will come at all," she said softly, hope for just that outcome brimming in her heart.

# chapter thirty-nine

THE THREE STAYED IN LOS Angeles for four days after the fight. Merrick had meetings with the president of the IMMAO as well as their publicity team, not to mention countless other media for post-fight interviews, videos and a radio appearance.

Elle didn't know how he did it. He was tired. Physically and mentally exhausted, and he was in considerable pain from the pounding he'd taken. Dallas stayed all four days, giving Merrick a thorough assessment each morning.

The fifth morning, the late nights and endless appointments had caught up with Elle, and she was sleeping soundly when Merrick slid out of bed to meet Dallas.

She stirred and automatically stuck her head up, bleary-eyed, ready to be with Merrick, but Cade slid his strong arm around her and pulled her back down next to him.

Merrick bent over the bed, smoothed her hair from her forehead and then kissed her. "Stay in bed, baby. I won't be long. Dallas is heading home this morning, and he wanted to check in on me one more time before his flight to Denver."

"Love you," she murmured.

The smile split his face and wrinkled his lean jaw. "Love you too."

She watched lazily as he dressed and then left the bedroom of the suite. Then she turned, seeking Cade's warmth and the comfort of his body. She snuggled tightly against him and sighed in utter contentment when he wrapped his body around hers and held her close.

His cock was rigid and straining at his boxer briefs, and without thought, she let her hand wander down his body to cup the bulge between his legs.

"Watch it," he murmured. "You have no idea how much I want to fuck you right now."

She kissed his neck, inhaling his scent as she nestled even closer, her fingers sliding delicately over the ridge in his underwear.

"And this would be a bad thing?" she whispered. "But you know, if you're going to, I'd suggest doing it now before Merrick gets back. He gets sort of demanding after Dallas gives him his checkups."

Cade chuckled. "Are we too much for you, sweetheart?"

Over the last three days, since the incident in the locker room after the fight, the two men had fucked her together, separately, in as many ways, positions and locations as possible. And every morning, without exception, the minute Dallas left their room, Merrick very possessively made love to her.

For so long, the men had treated her so very gently, as though they were afraid of pushing too hard and too fast, and then when they'd finally broken the ice and consummated their physical relationship, she'd been hurt so they hadn't made love to her for several weeks.

But now? It was as if the floodgates had been opened and they were making up for lost time. They couldn't seem to get enough of her, and she couldn't get enough of them.

She reveled in their possession. The tenderness with which they made love to her but also the rough edge of their possession where she could tell they were holding a tight rein on themselves because they didn't want to hurt her.

"Never too much," she said against his skin. "Never enough."

"Climb on top of me," Cade said in a husky voice. "I want you astride me."

While she pushed away the sheets, Cade quickly divested himself of his underwear, and then she swung her leg over his muscled thighs and tentatively reached down to run her fingers over his length.

"Put it inside you." Cade's eyes darkened with excitement, and he reached for her hips, his fingers digging into her skin. "Take me whole, honey. Hard and deep."

Breathless with excitement, she rose up on her knees and slid the head of his cock over her clit and through damp flesh to her opening.

He seemed so much bigger this way. He stretched her, filling her as she eased down his length. His eyes never left her face as she took more and more of him, but when she came to rest at the base of his cock, he closed his eyes and inhaled deeply, his entire body shuddering with pleasure.

When he reopened his eyes, they were glowing with arousal. There was a dark, primitive spark there that made her shiver.

His hands left her hips and skimmed up her arms, rubbing lightly over her skin and then to her breasts where he toyed with her nipples.

"Tell me something. Have you ever imagined taking me and Merrick at the same time? Like this, you on top of me, but him behind you?"

A delicate shiver began in her legs and worked its way up her belly and into her chest until the hairs at her nape stood out.

"Yes," she admitted. "I think about it, but I don't know how it would be possible. You and Merrick are so...big."

Cade chuckled. "You're good for my ego. Yeah, we're big and you're small. But you were made for us, honey. And we'd be careful with you. We'd never hurt you."

"I'd love to try," she said honestly.

"You might get your chance sooner than you think," Cade said wryly.

His gaze had moved beyond Elle, and Elle turned to see what he was looking at only to find Merrick standing in the doorway, his eyes hooded and hungry. His pants were already unzipped and shoved down past his hips.

"Do you want this, Elle?" Merrick asked in a strained voice. "Do you want me to take your ass while Cade's in your pussy?"

"I trust you," she said.

Without another word, Merrick went into the bathroom and returned a moment later with a tube of lubricant. He was also minus his pants. He dropped the tube on the bed and hastily finished undressing.

"I'm going to need to move you, honey," Cade said. "Just stay where you are. Let me do the moving. I like you just where you are."

With Elle atop him and his cock still buried in her body, he rotated around so he was cross-ways over the bed and his legs dangled over the edge, his feet planted on the floor. It put her at the very edge, accessible to Merrick.

"Lean forward, into me," Cade whispered. "And relax. If at any time you want us to stop, say so."

She nodded and leaned her body forward into Cade's hands. He stroked her breasts, tugging gently at her nipples. He caressed every inch of her belly and chest until she squirmed restlessly around his cock.

When Merrick's hand came down over her ass, it was instinctive to flinch. But then he kissed her on the cheek and murmured, "Relax, baby. I'm going to take my time here. I won't hurt you."

He fingered the opening of her ass, tracing a line around the tight ring. Then the cool glide of lubricant traveled the same path. With the blunt tip of his finger, he pushed inward, adding more lubricant to ease the passage.

Her breath skittered over her lips, and then she sharply inhaled when his finger slid deeper.

It was an utterly wicked sensation to have both openings breached. Raw hunger gripped her. She wanted this. Wanted both men inside her, possessing her, staking their claim.

She shuddered when he eased a second finger inside her opening. Her entire body went tight, and she sat rigidly atop Cade, holding her breath so she didn't orgasm this soon.

"Okay?" Cade asked, his eyes flashing with concern.

"Not yet," she said from behind clenched teeth. "I'm so close. Don't want it yet."

Merrick kissed her shoulder and then nipped playfully at her skin. "No, not yet, baby. I need you on edge when I put my dick inside you. If you've already come, it's not going to feel as good."

He kissed a path over her shoulder and down her spine. He held his fingers still inside her, waiting for her to come down from her impending release.

"Easy," Cade soothed.

She planted both palms over Cade's chest, loving the hardness of the muscles and the supple feel of his skin beneath her fingers. This was hers. He was hers.

They were hers.

Merrick ran his fingers up and down the cleft of her ass, spreading the lubricant liberally around her entrance. Then she felt both hands cup her cheeks and gently spread.

She went still, and Cade automatically lifted his hands to her waist, holding her and caressing up and down her sides in a soothing pattern.

"Relax for us, honey," Cade murmured.

It was hard to do when she was burning with anticipation. She let her breath escape raggedly and forced herself to go limp.

The tip of Merrick's cock pressed against her opening, and it took everything she had not to jerk in reaction. Her breathing sped up, and his grip tightened on her behind.

He pressed firmly, and she began to open around him. She closed her eyes against the burn and threw her head back.

Cade caressed his way to her breasts, cupping and mounding them with his palms. He caught her nipples between his thumb and forefinger and gently squeezed, sending an electric arc bolting through her body.

A soft moan fluttered past her lips when Merrick exerted more pressure and he pushed in farther.

"Halfway there, baby. Push against me. I want all the way inside you."

God, she wanted him to be all the way in. She wanted to know what it felt like to have two men deep inside her body.

One of Cade's hands left her breast and trailed down her belly to where their bodies were tightly joined. Carefully he slid his hand between them and fingered her clit just as Merrick's hips met her ass.

He was all the way in. She was stretched so tightly around both of them. She couldn't even process the bombardment of sensation. Her body shook and spasmed as each nerve ending twitched in utter delight.

"Oh hell yeah," Merrick breathed. "Ours, baby. If you only knew how often I've dreamed of having you this way. I'll never get enough. Never."

Cade arched his back, pushing upward, and she gasped at the fullness, the intensity of being so stretched. She was hypersensitive to every movement.

"You're so damn beautiful," Cade said in a strained voice. "I love the sight of you astride me, your hair down your shoulders and that drugged look on your face, the way your eyes glaze over. So fucking beautiful you make me ache. Let us have you now, honey. Trust us to give you what you need."

"Take me," she whispered. "I need you. I love you both so much."

Her words incited an instant response. Their hands tightened on her body. They began to move with greater urgency, foregoing the lazy pace they'd previously set.

Merrick began to thrust, withdrawing and then plunging deeply into her ass while Cade lifted her hips and then pulled her downward to meet his upward thrusts.

The ferocity of her orgasm frightened her. It was unlike anything she'd ever experienced. It was so powerful. So intense. Building… building…and building still. Every time she thought surely she would topple over, the tension kept rising and the pleasure intensified until she was nearly delirious.

Her body was no longer her own. It belonged to them. They commanded it. She writhed uncontrollably, her hands everywhere on Cade's body.

She panted breathlessly and squeezed her eyes tightly shut, her teeth clamped together to keep from screaming as her orgasm swelled, becoming an enormous ball of tightly leashed fury.

When she thought she couldn't stand it a moment longer, Cade flicked his finger over her clit, and she hurtled out of control.

She had to have blacked out momentarily, because the next thing she was aware of was being sprawled over Cade, her cheek pressed tightly to his chest. She couldn't suck in enough air to appease her burning lungs, and her entire body tingled, so sensitive that each of Merrick's thrusts sent aftershocks racing through her abdomen.

Cade stroked her back. Up and down. Slow, loving and achingly gentle. And then Merrick growled low in his throat and thrust into her so hard that it rocked her body upward. Cade anchored her to him and held her as Merrick slowly settled down over her back, sandwiching her firmly between the two men.

A sigh of utter bliss escaped her. She was numb. She couldn't feel parts of her body, and she couldn't care less. She'd never been so at peace in her life.

This was her life. Her future. Her past no longer mattered. Where she belonged was here. Between these two men. Men she loved with every bit of her heart and soul.

"Love you," she whispered. "So much."

"Love you too, baby."

"I *adore* you, honey," Cade said as he stroked her hair. "You're the best thing that's ever happened to me."

"Fuck the championship. You're definitely the best thing that's happened to me," Merrick said with complete sincerity. "I could hang it all up tomorrow as long as I have you."

Tears pricked her eyelids, and she bit her lip to prevent them from leaking down her cheeks.

She turned her mouth down to kiss Cade's chest, and she lay there, content to remain blanketed by so much delicious male flesh.

"Want to talk to you, baby," Merrick said, his words a little slurred.

"Mmmm," was all she could muster.

Merrick kissed her shoulder. "How about I order some breakfast, and we'll talk while we eat."

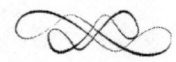

---

After the room service cart was wheeled into the sitting area of the suite, Merrick signed the check and then pushed it the rest of the way into the bedroom.

There was something supremely decadent about having breakfast in bed with two deliciously gorgeous alpha males.

Elle sat cross-legged in the middle, her back against a pillow, while Cade reclined on his side next to her. Merrick served up the plates and then crawled up on the other side of Elle and propped his back on the headboard.

"What did you want to talk about?" Elle asked as she cut into her omelet.

Merrick paused and glanced at Cade before lowering his fork. Cade pushed up to a sitting position that put him more at eye level with Merrick and Elle.

Then Merrick cleared his throat. "You said you wanted to wait until after the fight to get married. Okay, so the fight's over, and Cade and I would like to marry you if you're still willing."

Elle's hand shook, and she had to set her fork down to keep it from falling onto the plate. She'd been so happy and…content…over the last weeks that she hadn't given marriage any further thought. All her focus had been on Merrick and Cade and the impending fight.

"I want that more than anything," she said, her voice trembling as hard as her fingers.

The relief in Merrick's eyes was stark. Cade's eyes darkened, and he slid his hand over Elle's leg, gently squeezing her knee.

"Then I'm going to book an afternoon flight to Vegas," Merrick said. "We'll be there tonight. Tomorrow we'll take you shopping for a kick-ass dress and everything you need to look and feel your best. Whatever you want, you'll have."

Elle smiled, her heart fluttering wildly at the tenderness—and excitement—in Merrick's face. She reached down to put her hand over Cade's where it rested on her knee, and she squeezed, her own excitement overtaking her.

"After we go shopping, I'll book you into a spa where you'll be pampered. You can have your hair and nails done, and then Cade and I will pick you up and take you to the chapel in the hotel."

"You both spoil me so much," Elle said.

"Get used to it," Cade said in a gruff voice. "We plan to do a lot more of it."

Her face flushed with happiness, she threw her arms first around Cade, squeezing him fiercely. He laughed as he caught her and returned her affectionate hug. He kissed her temple, and then she pulled away and launched herself at Merrick.

She pulled up at the last second, remembering how sore and bruised he was. But he wouldn't let her get away with that. He hauled her up against him.

"Don't hold back with me," Merrick said. "I want all of you all the time. Stop worrying about hurting me. I'm fine."

But still, she carefully wrapped her arms around his neck, and though she hugged him, she didn't squeeze as fiercely as she'd done with Cade. Then she kissed the side of his neck and whispered next to his ear, "I love you so much."

"I love you too, baby. Always. Remember that. It's not going away. I'm not going away."

She sat back against the pillows and surveyed the gorgeous specimens in front of her. A feast of male flesh. Finely toned bodies. She could look her fill for hours. And touch. She loved touching them. Simply running her fingers over their skin, feeling the hardness of their muscles.

"How long do we have until the flight?" she asked.

"I haven't booked it yet," Merrick said. "Was going to call Cathy and have her do it."

Cade studied her curiously. "Why do you ask?"

She grinned slyly. "Because I wanted to know if there was enough time to show you and Merrick just how much I adore you both."

"Oh hell," Merrick breathed. "Let me call Cathy now. I'll make damn certain we have time for whatever it is you want to do."

# chapter forty

SHE'D NEVER HAVE IMAGINED CADE or Merrick dress shopping, or that they'd be so patient. They indulged her every whim, though, and encouraged her to find the perfect dress and not to settle.

In the fifth shop, she found perfection. It was a strapless silver dress that fell down her legs in a shimmery curtain. It conformed to her every curve and gathered gently at her ankles.

Next she bought a pair of three-inch Cinderella heels that sparkled and caught the light, reflecting it so they shimmered when she walked.

Afterward, Cade and Merrick carried the bags to the spa and handed them over to the receptionist with strict instructions to pamper and indulge Elle and then have her dressed for the ceremony.

If the woman thought it strange that two men would be so adamant about having her ready for a wedding, she didn't say anything. But when it came time for the two men to leave and they both kissed her long and hard, Elle could swear she saw a look of pure envy on the other woman's face.

For the next two hours, Elle was immersed in pleasure. She was massaged, her toes and fingers done, and then her hair was swept into an elegant knot and arranged so that several tendrils floated down her face.

Then it came time to put the dress on, and Elle's stomach was in knots as her excitement grew.

It was really happening. She was dressing for a dream wedding in Las Vegas, and Cade and Merrick would be here any moment to pick her up.

She slipped on the heels and surveyed her reflection in the mirror. She looked…radiant. Blissfully happy. Just like all women should on their wedding day.

As she stared back at herself, an image flashed in her mind. A fleeting memory, or maybe it was just a sensation.

*Will he ever ask me to marry him?*

It was a thought she knew she'd had before. More than once. There was lingering sadness—and worry—feelings she knew she'd experienced before.

Who was she thinking of?

The knot of anxiety grew in her belly. Was she doing the right thing? Was it really fair to Cade and Merrick to commit to them when she couldn't remember her past?

"Miss Walker, Mr. Sullivan and Mr. Walker are here for you."

Elle shook off the lingering uneasiness and turned to the woman standing in the door of the dressing room. Cade and Merrick were waiting. For her. They wanted to marry her and build a future together with her.

No matter what was in her past, they were her future.

At peace with her decision, she walked out the door and into the waiting room where Merrick and Cade stood. When they saw her, their faces lit up and there was approval in their eyes.

When she saw them, her heart pounded a little harder.

They were both wearing black suits. Expensive. Well tailored. They looked absolutely mouth-watering, and they were all hers.

"Elle, you look beautiful," Cade said as he came forward.

"You look fucking amazing," Merrick breathed.

Cade reached into his pocket and pulled out a jewelry box and handed it to her. With shaking fingers, she opened it to find a pair of glittering diamond earrings.

Merrick held up a necklace that matched and motioned for her to turn around so he could clasp it around her neck.

She felt like a fairy-tale princess.

They both reached for her hands after she'd attached the earrings to her ears, and they led her out of the spa to the waiting limousine.

Fifteen minutes later, they pulled up to a casino and were ushered out. The two men led her to the wedding chapel, where they were met by a couple who explained how the ceremony would be held.

Though the legalities concerned Merrick and Elle, there would be a special vow exchange between her and Cade at the beginning. At the end, instead of pronouncing Merrick and Elle husband and wife, the declaration would be made that Elle was given into the care of Merrick and Cade and that they would love and cherish her all the days of their life.

She was so jittery as they walked into the room where the ceremony would be held that she nearly stumbled. Cade caught her elbow, and then he pulled her in close to his side as they continued forward.

Positioned between the two men in front of the man performing the ceremony, she turned first to Cade as they exchanged vows.

His eyes were full of love as he held her hand, his thumb stroking over her knuckles. To her surprise, he produced a sparkling diamond solitaire and slid it onto her ring finger.

It was the most gorgeous ring she'd ever seen, and it fit her perfectly.

When their vows were said, Cade leaned in and kissed her long and deep, his hands framing her face.

"I love you," he whispered.

She smiled and kissed him again. "I love you too."

He gently let her go, and she turned to Merrick.

His eyes were fierce, and to her complete shock, they glittered wetly. He caught hold of her hands and held on so tightly her fingers were bloodless. It was almost as if he were afraid if he let her go, she'd disappear.

His voice was choked with emotion as he recited his vows, and when she in turn recited hers, he swallowed visibly.

Then, as Cade had done, he produced a ring. He slid her diamond off and pushed on the platinum band before sliding her solitaire back in place.

"On the inside is inscribed, Merrick, Elle and Cade forever," he said, his voice thick with emotion.

"I love it," she whispered. "It's perfect."

And then he kissed her. Sweet. Hot. Deep and aching.

"You're mine now," he said softly, fiercely, his voice ringing with possessiveness.

She slid her hands into his and leaned up to kiss him once more. Then she reached back for Cade, pulling him in close so she was flanked by both men.

She listened to the rich, beautiful words that bound her to Merrick and Cade for all time. Absorbed them and held them precious in her heart.

A year ago, she'd been no one. Desperate, cold, more dead than alive. Cade and Merrick had taken her in. Given her care and love and had been infinitely patient, allowing her time to recover both physically and emotionally.

Now she had a new life. She had focus. And she had a future.

She loved and was loved in return.

She gazed up at her husbands' faces, saw the joy and adoration in their eyes.

A year ago, she wouldn't have considered herself lucky or fortunate. But now, she realized that whoever had tried to kill her had in fact done her a huge favor.

"Come on, Mrs. Walker-Sullivan," Merrick said, pulling her toward the doorway. "I feel the distinct need to make love to you for the next forty-eight hours straight."

"Only forty-eight?" she teased.

"To start with," Cade said. "After that? Who knows. We have all the time in the world, and I plan to make love to you for the next forty-eight *years.*"

# chapter forty-one

ELLE WOKE SPRAWLED OVER CADE'S body, her legs tangled with Merrick's in the huge king-size bed in the posh resort where Merrick had booked their honeymoon.

Two whole weeks on the beach. A private beach where they wouldn't be disturbed by the outside world. A veritable paradise where their every whim would be catered to.

They could make love, they could never dress if they wanted. They could play in the ocean or swim in the private pool assigned to their villa.

But the outside world *had* crept in via her dreams.

Even now as the fog surrounding her mind began to lift, she was left with a heavy ache in her chest that threatened to suffocate her.

Bits and pieces came back. More vivid than in the past. They lingered where before they'd always faded as soon as she'd awakened.

An image flashed. A man. A strong, hard man with piercing eyes. Even as she thought of him, her breathing sped up, and she wasn't sure if it was fear or something quite different that made her react.

She shivered despite the fact she was sandwiched by two warm, male bodies.

She should be glowing in the aftermath of the tender lovemaking the two men had bestowed on her. They'd kissed and touched and caressed her for hours. Driving her to the brink of insanity with mindless pleasure. Only then had they let her achieve the ultimate satisfaction, and afterward, she'd lain in their arms, listening as they whispered their love for her.

And now, a shadow had intruded, and she hated it. Hated it for evaporating her earlier euphoria.

Knowing there was no way she was going back to sleep and wanting time to sort through the dream while it was still fresh in her mind, she carefully extricated herself from Cade's hold.

He muttered a protest, and she whispered, "Bathroom."

He let her go, and she slid down the length of the bed, careful not to disturb Merrick as she got up from the bed. She did go into the bathroom, but only to get one of the fluffy robes she'd thrown over the hook on the back of the bathroom door.

Cinching the belt tightly around her, she padded out of the bedroom and through the sitting area to the French doors leading onto a veranda overlooking the ocean.

As she slid open the doors, the sea breeze ruffled her hair and teased her nose. She inhaled deeply as she stepped outside, and instantly, the song of the ocean danced over her ears.

Overhead, the full moon shone brightly, surrounded by a crystal clear sky and a million stars that twinkled like fairy dust. The light from the moon reflected off the water and lit up the entire horizon like a splash of silver.

Taking a deep breath, she curled her fingers around the edge of the railing that circled the veranda, and she leaned forward, absorbing the serenity around her. She needed it because her thoughts were in turmoil.

Alabama. The ocean. Warm, sultry summer nights. Her feet in the sand. Warm Gulf water foaming around her ankles. And a warmer than usual October night where her life had been irrevocably changed.

She squeezed her eyes shut, wanting to still the images, the memories, but for once, they wouldn't stop coming. Random. Impossible to sort out. So fast and senseless that it left her head spinning.

Eden, Alabama.

A coastal town.

Maybe being here in Fiji with Merrick and Cade had prompted her to remember the place where…

She shook her head because she couldn't be certain it was where she'd lived at all. But she knew she had history there. She could feel it. She could remember vaguely. The name felt right. If she concentrated hard, she could conjure up images of the ocean and feel the hot sun beating down on her shoulders.

It was where she'd been betrayed.

"Elle?"

She turned to see Cade and Merrick stepping onto the veranda, the moon illuminating the area so she could easily see the concern on their faces.

"Is something wrong, baby?" Merrick asked.

The two men stopped on either side of her, both reaching to touch her in some way, whether it was to reassure her or them. She wasn't certain which.

She took a deep breath. "I'm remembering," she said in a soft voice.

Cade tensed. "What do you remember?"

She turned back to stare over the ocean, her hands curling tightly around the rail once more.

"Eden, Alabama."

There was a long pause.

"Is that where you lived?" Merrick asked, finally breaking the silence.

She lifted one shoulder in a shrug. "It's where I was raped."

Cade slid his hand over her shoulder to her nape, and he squeezed comfortingly.

"There's something there," she said baldly. "Something familiar. I can almost see places. It's so strange. They dance like images in my mind, but they're just out of reach. I can't touch them, but they're there, and it's so frustrating."

Merrick put his hand over hers, his warmth bleeding into her cold fingers.

Then she looked up at him, their gazes meeting.

"I need to go back," she said quietly. "I have to face my past and find out what happened to me. Who I am."

"There is no way in hell you're going alone," Cade said in a menacing voice.

Startled, she swung her gaze to him. "I hadn't even considered it."

"Good," Merrick said gruffly. "I don't like the idea of you going back at all, but I understand why you have to. I don't have to like it, though."

She slid her arm around his waist and then reached for Cade. They pushed in close until she was surrounded by them. Their touch. Their heat. Their love.

It emanated from them in a tangible wave that she could sense with every breath.

"No matter what my past is, you're my future," she said, her jaw firming with resolve.

She didn't want them to have doubts even for a minute.

"Damn straight," Cade growled.

Merrick's hold on her tightened, and he pressed his lips to her temple. "We're keeping you, baby. Always."

Some of the tension that had knotted her insides loosened and relinquished its stubborn hold. When she'd awakened, she'd been terrified. Afraid of what the future would hold. Afraid that somehow her past would threaten her present with the two men she called husband.

Now, standing between them, their quiet vows echoing in her ears, a perfect companion to the rush of the distant waves, peace enveloped her.

Her past couldn't hurt her. It couldn't control her. She'd survived whatever horrific thing had happened to her. Her future was with these two wonderful, amazing men, and no matter what, she'd never look back with regret.

"We have all the time in the world," she said. "No hurry. First I intend to have the best honeymoon a girl could ever ask for. And then we're going to go home and finish settling into our new house and celebrate Merrick's victory with family and friends. Then and only then will we worry about what's in Eden, Alabama."

Cade tugged at the belt of her robe, loosening it so Merrick could pull it away. As it came free, the moonlight splashed over her naked body, and both her lovers lowered their heads to press kisses to her flesh.

"Eden, Alabama can wait," Merrick said, his voice thick with desire. "Right now we're going to make love to you until the sun creeps over the horizon."

"I love you," she whispered. "I love you both so much."

Cade's mouth closed over one taut nipple. "I love you too, honey. Always."

Merrick claimed her mouth, and then he walked her backward to the plump couch just under the lanai at the edge of the veranda.

"Two whole weeks of you naked the entire time," he said, satisfaction etched in his voice. "I can't wait."

Stay tuned for the next book in the
TANGLED HEARTS TRILOGY,

# ALWAYS MINE

coming soon from Maya Banks!

When Elle disappeared without a trace, police officer Morgan Beckett was devastated. The two shared a relationship where she relinquished absolute power to him, and he knows he failed to protect her. When he sees her again outside a coffee shop they used to frequent, he's stunned. But then she runs—terrified of him—when he calls out to her, and he knows that things are not what they seem.

Upon tracing her back to the hotel where she's staying, he makes a discovery that threatens to tear him apart. Elle, the woman he loved, the woman he thought he'd lost forever, has not one, but two men in her life, and they're both fiercely protective of her. And worse, she has no memory of Morgan—or their life together before her disappearance.

Morgan only knows one thing. He's not letting her go without one hell of a fight. But there's also the question of why she disappeared and who tried to kill her. Now he and Elle's two lovers must combine forces to protect Elle from her dark past. And the man who'll stop at nothing to make sure he succeeds in killing her this time.

For up-to-date news on book releases, visit Maya's website or Facebook page.

www.mayabanks.com
www.facebook.com/authormayabanks

Printed in Great Britain
by Amazon.co.uk, Ltd.,
Marston Gate.